Operation Red Dawn and the Siege of Europe

Book Three of the World War III Series

By

James Rosone & Miranda Watson

Copyright Information

Table of Contents

Triumphant Landing

1 June 2041
Kodiak, Alaska

As General Jing Zhu stepped off of his boat and onto the shore near Kodiak, Alaska, he felt the breeze against his face; the texture of the stones beneath his feet, the metallic smell of the blood poured out from all the dead, and the rumbling sounds of machine gun fire in the distance all made him feel the thrill of being lucky to be alive. The Americans had not succeeded in stopping his men; he was filled with confidence and pride.

He was ushered into the temporary command center, which was nothing more than the ransacked remains of a blown out town hall. The setting was not quite as glorious as he had hoped, but he would not be deterred. Jing Zhu had waited for this day his whole life. As he entered the room, the others stood, bowing slightly as was their custom.

"Generals, Admiral," he began. "For the first time in modern history, a foreign army has invaded America. Today marks the end of America…and the rise of the People's Republic of China."

****

Once the ceremony of the moment was over, the work of making the building an acceptable site for the new headquarters began. Numerous communications and computer technicians began to rummage through the ruins, setting up various computer screens, holographic communications systems and what seemed like miles of wiring. Engineers started erecting a roof over the destroyed portions of the building, shoring up the various support beams to ensure the building would be a safe location for the management of the war effort, at least until the series of underground bunkers that were planned could be constructed. General Zhu walked over to Admiral Lang Xing, the overall PLAN naval infantry commander, and asked, "What is the status of our forces at the frontlines?" He was trying to get a feel for the current situation.

Over the past decade, Lang Xing had meticulously studied the United States Marines' amphibious program and their training exercises. He had modeled the PLAN naval infantry tactics around the Marines and drilled his forces relentlessly for years, weeding out those who could not hack it, and fine tuning his military force. When the plans for Operation Red Dragon were drawn up, it was clear the Chinese would need a large amphibious capability if they were to secure a beachhead for the PLA and their heavier equipment to get on shore. Admiral Xing had created an amphibious landing force of nearly 180,000 soldiers, the best soldiers of any branch. During the first four months of the war, his troops had gained experience fighting in Taiwan, Guam and the Philippines. Now they were leading the invasion of America.

"General Zhu, my naval infantry has dislodged the Americans on the beach and cut through their second line of defense three kilometers inland. They are currently engaging the Americans about ten kilometers inland at a much more substantial defensive position. Our light tanks are helping, but we now need the much thicker armor of the PLA's heavy tanks. We will require additional artillery and air support to break through their defensive works."

Pulling up some images on his tablet, Lang Xing continued, "As you can see, they also have heavy artillery that appear to be sliding in and out of hiding locations in the mountains."

General Zhu studied the maps, images and video for a few minutes, thinking to himself, *The Americans have been very busy preparing this position for our eventual arrival.*

Zhu responded aloud, "Admiral, the PLA is landing heavy tanks and artillery as we speak. I want your naval infantry to begin withdrawing as new PLA units move forward over the next twenty-four hours. I want your forces to reorganize and prepare for the next landings at Anchor Point, Homer and Seward and the drive towards Anchorage. The Americans are probably going to be defending these landing zones with many more soldiers. I will need your forces ready for the next landings," General Zhu directed.

"Yes, General. My men look forward to leading the way," the Admiral replied. He smiled to himself, knowing that his naval infantry had thus far performed to perfection.
******

Over the next three days, the PLA landed 190,000 soldiers on the Alaskan shores, and began to phase out the naval infantry so they could be used for the next critical seaborne landing. As additional heavy tanks and artillery were brought aground, the American positions came under increasing pressure from the PLA. They had held the line, despite numerous human wave and armored assaults, but that would only last for so long. American casualties continued to mount, with no means of evacuating them to the mainland.

The Americans had known for several months that the Chinese would try to capture Kodiak Island, and had built a series of heavy defensive networks about ten kilometers inland from the shore along the various ridges and low lining mountain ranges. Most of these defensive positions were independent of each other, but they were all built to provide each site with both direct and indirect fire support to help defend each other. With heavy railguns, artillery and mortars, the Americans could rain down indirect fire all across the approaches to their positions, making it incredibly difficult to attack without taking substantial casualties. Aside from the various trench positions, the engineers had built numerous reinforced bunker positions to allow the defenders to ride out enemy bombardments and quickly man their fighting positions when needed. Tunnels had been dug beneath most of the strongholds, allowing the defensive commanders to shift soldiers from one defensive firebase to another without the enemy knowing what was happening.

Major General Justin Daily and his 58,000 soldiers needed to hold Kodiak Island for as long as possible. As long as they remained on the island, the Chinese could not use it as a base of operations for their aircraft or supplies. American 155mm artillery pieces could hit nearly every position on the island. The PLAN and PLAAF had yet to identify all of their positions despite the relentless bombing and artillery barrages they hit the Americans with. As artillery scouts would identify a supply transport heading to the beach to offload their cargo, they would call in a couple of well-placed artillery rounds to destroy it and then quickly pull the artillery guns back under cover.

Walls and Trenches

4 June 2041

Kodiak, Alaska

Private First Class (PFC) Lenny Peters had joined the Army right after the war had been declared against the Islamic Republic. He had an older brother who had joined the Navy several years earlier and was one of the sailors who had died during the IRs surprise attack against the 5th Fleet in the Red Sea. Lenny had been working for the American First Corporation and had a good paying job; his parents were distraught over his decision to leave his position to join the Army. However, he felt he needed to do something to avenge the loss of his brother and get some payback.

After completing basic combat training, Lenny had been assigned to the 2nd battalion, 3rd brigade, 12th Infantry Division as part of an 81mm mortar team. They arrived on Kodiak Island in March of 2041, and immediately began construction of their defensive positions with the Army Corps of Engineers. Despite it being winter, the island had been spared from the extreme weather that much of Alaska had experienced; as of yet, Kodiak Island had not had a heavy blanketing of snow. This enabled a lot of work to still be done on the island. Lenny's platoon had been assigned to build a series of five-foot-deep trenches, bunkers, machine gun nests and mortar pits. As the winter turned to spring, they began to clear trees and identify pre-targeted positions for their mortar tubes. The plan was for them to fire several rounds from their first position and then rotate to their next position. This way they would not attract counter-battery fire, and if they did, they would be long gone from that position and firing from another one. Their sergeant had them build five mortar pits, thinking that should be enough. However, during the first three days of the invasion, three of the five had been destroyed. When they were not conducting fire missions, their sergeant had them rebuilding the demolished mortar pits. They were conducting dozens of fire missions a day, sending hundreds of mortars at the Chinese.

Over the past two days, the Chinese counter-battery fire was starting to become more effective, and they had lost nearly half of the soldiers in their platoon. They had also seen a difference in the forces they were facing. The first day it was clear they were fighting Chinese naval infantry; those soldiers were equipped with exoskeleton combat suits and fought more as individual teams rather than large clusters. During the second day of the fighting, they began to be swarmed by human wave attacks, overrun by just the extreme number of fighters. They reported their observations to higher headquarters. Their sergeant came back and told them, "The naval infantry is probably gearing up to invade the next set of islands, or maybe the mainland."

The fighting was gnarly and bloody, raging nearly non-stop since the Chinese had invaded. Slowly and steadily, the PLA had captured one firebase after another, despite the valiant efforts of the division to repulse them. The PLA's heavy use of artillery and human wave assaults were starting to take their toll. The American lines continued to shrink.

Battle at Anchor Point

4 June 2041

Anchor Point, Alaska

Staff Sergeant (SSG) Paul Allen was a twenty-one-year-old young man from Wisconsin. He had joined the Army after graduating high school during the American military build-up. His main objectives in volunteering were to get the $25,000 signing bonus and GI Bill to pursue a degree in mechanical engineering once his four-year commitment was done. SSG Allen had been transferred to the 32nd Infantry Division, XI Army Group, Second Army, Alaska after recovering from the wounds he received while fighting as part of the 1st Infantry Division in the battle over Jerusalem. He had managed to survive several bullet wounds to the chest, and after going through several surgeries and physical rehabilitation, he was ready to continue his service to his country. His wounds had afforded him a promotion to Staff Sergeant, a Bronze Star and a Purple Heart medal. Now his experience was being put to good use in helping form the NCO leadership of the new 32nd Infantry Division. Close to half of the NCOs and officers had been previously wounded in the Middle East or Europe--rather than returning to their old units, they were becoming part of the nucleus of the new infantry divisions being formed in the US.

Paul missed his friends from his old unit and tried to stay in touch with some of them as best he could. They had been together during the initial invasion of Mexico, and then through the war in Israel. He knew they were fighting the Russians now, and he was glad to see that several of them were still alive after the last major battle. A couple of them had not been so lucky…this saddened him greatly. He had lost so many good friends during these past eight months. It was a lot to take in for a twenty-one-year-old man. On top of the loss of his comrades in arms, SSG Allen was dealing with tragedy on the home front. Both of his parents had been killed in Baltimore while visiting his sister and her husband for Christmas. No one could have predicted that the IR would detonate a nuclear bomb in the city. Paul still had two brothers, both living in Madison, Wisconsin, where they were from, but the weight of the grief SSG Allen carried was beginning to wear like a heavy anchor around his soul.

Since arriving in Alaska six weeks ago, Paul had been assigned as the platoon sergeant until their new Sergeant First Class completed his advanced NCO career development course. The Army was trying to run as many of their NCOs through these advanced courses as they could when the soldiers were not actively in combat (they were doing their best to rebuild and expand their NCO cadre after so many losses and the massive expansion of the military). Paul's company had been assigned to Anchor Point, less than a few miles from Homer, Alaska. They had the unenviable task of defending the several mile-long beach front from the Chinese. It was anticipated that the Reds would land their troops all along the peninsula to secure it for their eventual assault on Anchorage and the rest of Alaska. It was up to the men of the 32nd Infantry Division to stop them.

An engineering battalion had assisted them in developing a series of integrated trenches, machine gun nests and bunkers to ride out the eventual Chinese bombardments. They knew the Chinese naval infantry would be using their new exoskeleton combat suits, so to slow them down they had designed a number of obstacles and mazes of concertina wire that would force them to have to navigate into carefully designed kill boxes. Thousands of landmines, claymore anti-personnel mines and other explosives had been woven all across the beaches and the first several hundred meters inland. They had also set up numerous anti-tank and anti-aircraft guns and missile systems in their defensive network. The 9th Armored Division deployed a battalion of Pershing main battle tanks, and the engineers dug a number of tank berms for them to hunker down in. A tank would usually fire a couple of shots from one berm, and then quickly move to the next one, rotating between locations to avoid shooting from the same position too many times and being easily identified.

When the construction of this well-laid trap was complete, SSG Allen had looked at their work, stretching back to see the entire landscape. He smiled confidently, thinking to himself, *"When the Chinese do eventually land their forces on Anchor Point, they will be in for a surprise."*

General Black had positioned nearly 60,000 soldiers on the Peninsula, along with 400 tanks. It was important to bog the Chinese down on the beaches for as long possible and to bleed them dry. The Reds could only bring a limited number of soldiers with them for the invasion. Preventing them from establishing a strong foothold was key to keeping them out of Alaska. That was why General Black had spent so many resources on turning Kodiak Island and Anchor Point into the fortresses they had become. It would take time for the Chinese to ferry troops from the mainland to Alaska, and the longer they could keep the Chinese from establishing a forward base of operations, airports and seaports, the better the chances were of eventually repulsing their invasion before the weather turned back to the Americans' favor with the arrival of winter.

Despite the best-laid plans, the past three days had been horrific for the soldiers of the 12th Infantry Division. The Chinese fleet had parked their ships offshore, and were launching volley after volley at the American coastline. Though most of the attacks were taking place on the Aleutian Peninsula and Kodiak Island, Anchor Point and Homer were starting to be bombarded on a regular basis. Since the Americans still did not have visual contact with the Chinese landing craft, most of the soldiers continued to ride out the bombardments in their various bunkers, turrets and machine gun bunkers, reading books, praying, writing letters to home or simply sleeping, waiting for the inevitable.

On the second day of the invasion, several Chinese ground attack aircraft and drones started to bombard the trench networks, only to be shot down quickly by the various air defense systems. The battle for the skies above Anchorage continued to rage as hundreds of drones and manned fighter aircraft continued to fight for dominance. This limited the volume of air strikes that could hit Anchor Point and Homer, but did little to dissuade the Chinese navy from using their naval guns.

It was not until the fifth day of the arrival of the Chinese invasion fleet that the soldiers of the 32nd Division started to see the first sign of a potential landing force. Several Chinese destroyers moved into the bay of Anchorage and sailed to within a mile of the shore to start providing more direct fire against some of the heavier fixed American defenses. The Reds started sending out a few smaller vessels ahead of the group as bait; as the Americans would fire on the ships, the Chinese were quickly identifying the camouflaged gun emplacements and counter-attacking those targets.

As the destroyers moved into position and began to open fire, several 155mm artillery guns that had been leveled to act as shore battery guns opened fire, engaging the destroyers. A handful of 20mm railguns also joined the fray, adding their own firepower to the short engagement. From a distance it looked like a laser show as the tracer rounds, missiles and explosions shook both the land and ships. The ships being shot at were quickly becoming riddled with holes and began to sink quickly as the railguns cut right through their armor igniting ammunition stores and fuel. In less than ten minutes, three of the five Chinese destroyers had been sunk in the shallow waters, while the other two destroyers limped back to deeper waters and the rest of the fleet. When the Chinese invasion fleet did make their move on Anchor Point, they were going to have to fight through a well-established fortress at the head of the bay of Anchorage.

By the end of the sixth day, the PLA had successfully landed and secured most of the Kachemak Bay State Park and began to set up hundreds of 152mm artillery pieces and a variety of rocket artillery. It was at this point the artillery duels began in full force, with the Chinese firing thousands of artillery and rockets at Homer and Anchor Point while the American artillery did their best to conduct counter-battery fire. The PLAAF had also established nine small airfields along the Aleutian Peninsula, ferrying in hundreds of fighter and bomber attack drones from Mainland China. With the defeat of a large portion of the American fighter and bomber drones at Eielson AFB in Fairbanks during the first day of the invasion, the Americans were slowly losing control of the skies over Homer and Anchor Point. With the air war starting to tilt in the Chinese favor, they began to conduct more precision bombing of Anchor Point, hitting a number of the artillery and heavy gun emplacements and some of the Pershing tanks. It would not be long now until the Chinese launched their landing force.

******

In the early morning hours of the seventh day of the invasion, the PLA, PLAAF and PLAN launched a massive artillery, missile, naval and air bombardment at the Anchor Point peninsula. The assault lasted for several hours; as dawn drew near, the PLA shifted their attacks to hit the peninsula with hundreds of smoke rounds, adding a heavy layer of dense visual cover to the moonscape defensive lines. The American commanders on the ground knew this was probably when the PLAN would launch their amphibious landing and begin to secure the peninsula for the eventual assault and capture of Anchorage. Despite the heavy smoke bombardment, the American commanders could see right through it; dozens of miniaturized surveillance drones were launched into the air, feeding the data collected by their thermal cameras to the displays in their helmets.

Using the cover of smoke and the bombardment, the PLAN had maneuvered dozens of cruisers, destroyers and frigates into the channel to provide cover fire. Now hundreds of landing craft and thousands of amphibious assault vehicles were swarming towards the beach. As the commanders saw the images of the sea vessels headed their way, they quickly grabbed their coms, "The Chinese are in full-out landing assault pattern. Be prepared to engage!"
****

As Paul sat inside of his command bunker eating an MRE (Meals, Ready to Eat), he couldn't help but admire the beauty in his surroundings. Despite the beach in front of his position being ringed with concertina wire and other obstacles, you could still see the mountains off in the distance across the bay. The waves were lapping against the gravel shore and the seagulls were squawking as they flew around the coastline. Soon this area would be turned into a cauldron of death, but for right now, it was peaceful.

As he munched on the jalapeno cheese sauce and crackers (his favorite part of the meal), his blissful reflection was interrupted. His HUD suddenly became a loud barrage of instructions being barked at him. He shoved the remainder of his crackers and cheese into his pocket (he wasn't about to waste those, he had traded for them in the first place), and sprang into action. His platoon was to man the two heavy machine gun nests and the one hundred meters of trench line that connected them both. After receiving his orders, he started handing out instructions of his own. "Listen up, platoon! The Chinese are headed our way. Time to man the battle stations! Stop whatever you are doing, grab your gear, leave the bunkers and get to your assigned position now!"

His platoon had four .50 M2 machine guns in each of the two bunkers and two M134 7.62mm Miniguns. Two of the M2s were aligned to the right of the bunker, providing a ninety-degree arc of covering fire along the beach and the second bunker his platoon manned. The other two machine guns covered the left side of the bunker with the same ninety-degree arc covering the other machine gun first platoon manned and part of their trench line. In between both M2s was the venerable M134 Minigun. The M134 was a belt fed, electrically operated rotating six-barrel machine gun that could be set to fire between 2,000 and 6,000 7.62mm rounds a minute. Both of these machine guns were old in comparison to the more advanced M5 AIR, but their rate of fire and ability to defend the beach were all that mattered. All of the bunkers had been designed to provide each other interlocking fields of cover, so as the landing craft got near the beach they could engage them. Then, as the enemy came ashore, they would rake the beach with heavy machine gun fire. In the rear of the bunkers were built several magazine holds for all of the ammunition for the heavy machine guns. There were 750,000 rounds for the M2 and nearly 2,500,000 rounds for the M134. Despite several days of heavy bombardment, the bunkers were still intact--damaged albeit, but still functional.

SSG Allen continued handing out orders, "Those of you manning the trench line—keep your heads down until the Chinese land the first wave of troops. There is no need to expose yourselves until absolutely necessary. The bunkers will draw most of the enemy fire until the soldiers in the trenches have to engage the troops coming ashore."

SSG Allen was standing in one of the bunkers, watching through a spotter scope as the wind blew most of the smoke away from their view of the water. Suddenly, he saw hundreds of landing crafts and vehicles heading towards the beach to his front. "Echo Five, this is Bunker 34. We have visual of *hoards* of Chinese landing crafts headed our way. Requesting immediate fire support, over."

"Bunker 34, this is Echo Five. We copy. Fire mission on its way."

Within minutes, artillery and mortar rounds started to hit numerous predetermined points in the water several hundred meters in front of the beach. Some of the landing crafts exploded as an artillery or mortar round scored a direct hit; others were sloshed around by near misses.

As the landing crafts neared the beach, SSG Allen ordered, "Soldiers with the .50s—time to open fire. Start taking them out."

"FGM-148 Javelins, start firing!" came the next call. The Javelins were fire-and-forget anti-tank missiles, with a longer range than the venerable AT6 rockets. They were guided missiles, which gave the soldiers the power to correct their flight path if needed.

A few moments later, several landing craft reached the beach, and then suddenly, as if appearing from thin air, there were hundreds of PLAN infantry in their exoskeleton combat suits rushing towards the American soldiers with superhuman speed and agility. SSG Allen felt his stomach drop through his knees. "Everyone, engage the Chinese on the beach! Kill them all!"

The M2s and M134s began to traverse back and forth across the beach, decimating the ranks of the PLAN. As the one-inch diameter rounds of the .50 hit their targets, they severed arms and legs, and absolutely shredded the Chinese body armor. Soldiers were literally being ripped apart. The miniguns were devastating the remaining Chinese soldiers rushing the beaches. The volume of fire was awe-inspiring for the defenders as they could see entire squads of Chinese soldiers simply cut apart by the two Miniguns working in tandem. The soldiers manning the trenches began engaging the enemy infantrymen as quickly as they identify a target.

Several of the sergeants manning the various claymore anti-personnel mines started to detonate them as small clusters or groups of enemy soldiers started to coordinate their attacks against the American positions.

Across the beach and trench line, there were airburst explosions from artillery and rockets throwing shrapnel everywhere. The cacophony of high explosives, machine guns, grenades, missiles and rockets was numbing.

SSG Allen tapped one of his heavy machine gunners on the shoulder and pointed towards a target. The gunner moved his gun towards a landing craft just as the front door dropped and opened fire. He quickly walked his stream of bullets through the entire landing craft as Chinese soldiers were desperately trying to crawl over the sides of the craft to get away from the slaughter. Within seconds, the machine gunner had killed nearly everyone in that landing craft before setting his sights on the next closest Chinese vehicle bringing more soldiers to the beach. While one soldier began to reload the M2, another soldier began to pour a bucket of water slowly across the red hot barrel. They did not have time to change the barrels, so they needed to cool the gun so it wouldn't melt and become unserviceable.

Dozens of Chinese soldiers were getting bogged down in the concertina wire and the various anti-personnel obstacles that the engineers had placed in their paths. Several PLAN soldiers were trying to cut a hole through the wire when an artillery round exploded ten feet above the ground, throwing shrapnel and body parts everywhere. Despite the enormous losses the Chinese were taking; SSG Allen could see the enemy was starting to get off of the sandy beach and move inland. He was starting to get a little nervous. The Chinese appeared like a plague of locusts, consuming and destroying everything in their path.

Trying to remain positive, Paul continued to relay calming words of encouragement to the men and women in his platoon. It had been nearly twenty-five minutes since the first Chinese soldiers landed on the beach, and it was a bloodbath.

SSG Allen could see on his HUD that eight soldiers of his fifty-two-man platoon had been killed; another eleven more were injured and currently being treated by the medics. A couple of the wounded were being moved back to the second line of defense, while the others were being treated and thrown back into the fight. Near Bunker 34 (the machine gun bunker SSG Allen was directing his platoon from) was a steel door that led to a tunnel that went to the second trench line 500 meters behind them. Every fifty meters, the tunnel made a short right or left turn, preventing the enemy from being able to fire down the entire tunnel or shoot a rocket down it. If it appeared that their position was going to be overrun, this would be the tunnel where the platoon would attempt to make their great escape. When the last soldier closed the door, there were several heavy bolts that would lock the door in place, and at the end of each tunnel section there was a charge that could be detonated, imploding that portion of the tunnel and preventing the enemy from being able to use it.

While SSG Allen was watching the medics move two wounded soldiers to the rear, he looked up and saw the third wave of landing craft heading towards their position. Paul contacted the company commander on his HUD, "Captain Shiller, this is SSG Allen; the Chinese are continuing to bring in additional landing craft. We need an air strike or additional artillery support to help take them out!"

"Copy that Allen. I will try to get some air support, but artillery will be our best option."

"I'm not sure we can hold up against a third wave, Sir," Paul responded. "We more or less stopped the first wave at the beach. The second wave has made it past the beach and is nearly at our current position. A third wave will likely overrun us…"

"A platoon of Pershing Main Battle Tanks (MBTs) and several armored personnel carriers are moving up to your position. Hold the line; support will be there soon!"
****

Sergeant John Porter moved his Pershing MBT right behind Bunker 34 as he was directed to and immediately began to engage the landing craft and amphibious vehicles heading towards the beach. Porter could not believe his eyes; the horizon was covered with landing craft. He took a deep breath, then turned to PFC Higgins, his tank operator. "It's time for us to start engaging targets; as I call them out, you begin to fire."

"Roger."

Porter keyed his sights in until he identified an amphibious assault craft. "Fire!" he commanded.

"Firing," Higgins responded.

In quick succession, Porter's tank began to engage one craft after another, destroying them swiftly. In just moments, they had taken out twelve landing craft before they could get to the beach.

Suddenly, a loud explosion rocked a nearby location, filling their chests with the reverberation of the sound vibrations. Once Porter had recovered from the shock, he grabbed his scope and saw that to their left, Sergeant Louis' Pershing had exploded from a direct hit.

Several more blasts rocked Porter's tank as Chinese destroyers began engaging his tank. Porter was about to give the order for them to reposition when the tank was impacted with a direct hit. In an instant, the cabin was on fire. Sergeant Porter just could not get the hatch open fast enough…the tank exploded.

****

SSG Allen's bunker shook as the battle tank near them exploded. Additional ship and artillery rounds began to hit their bunker, rattling everyone in it. He was amazed at how many landing vehicles and amphibious vehicles had been destroyed by the tanks within just a few minutes of their arrival; it was tragic that they were destroyed so quickly. Fortunately for SSG Allen and his team, none of the rounds from the naval guns were flying at a flat enough trajectory to hit the gun slits in the bunker. The PLAN infantry had also made several attempts to hit their position with RPGs, but they had not gotten lucky so far.

PFC Gomez turned from his scope to provide an update, "SSG Allen, the third wave is getting ready to land, it looks like our tanks took out a few dozen of the larger landing crafts before they were destroyed."

"Private Gomez, shift fire from the beach to those landing craft that are heading towards Bunker 33," SSG Allen ordered.

"On it, Sergeant!"

Gomez shifted the .50 back to the water and fired a stream of rounds into one of the amphibious vehicles that was closing in on the beach. After firing a few dozen rounds into the vehicle, it exploded, killing all of its occupants. Gomez redirected fire to the next landing craft as it started to exit the water, driving up on the beach. Just as the vehicle dropped the rear ramp, it exploded; several PLAN infantrymen came running out of the vehicle on fire. Gomez quickly gunned them down.

As the third wave of naval infantry hit the beach, they quickly began to join their brethren, who had hunkered down behind anything that would stop a bullet. Suddenly, a massive surge of infantry began to rush Bunker 33 and the trench near it. SSG Allen saw a rather brave Chinese soldier jump up with an RPG7 and fire it at Bunker 33. His shot was perfectly aimed, and it hit the gun slit, exploding into the bunker. Within seconds, there was a small explosion inside of the bunker and the guns went silent. At that moment, SSG Allen yelled at Gomez, "Shift fire! Lay into them before they reach the bunker and trench line."

The minigunner also redirected fire to the bunker. She cut down several dozen Chinese soldiers in the span of a couple of seconds. Unfortunately, a number of Chinese soldiers launched themselves into the trench line and began fighting the Americans in hand-to-hand combat before Gomez or the minigunner could mow them all down.

One Chinese soldier threw a satchel charge into the back entrance of Bunker 33. Seconds later, it exploded, blowing flame and smoke out through the gun slits. The bunker was thoroughly destroyed as additional naval infantry continued to rush the trench line.

With one bunker down, it meant that SSG Allen's bunker was now exposed. He looked down and saw the Chinese rushing his position. He quickly detonated the last of his claymore mines, wiping out dozens of enemy soldiers. Allen stepped out of his bunker and fired a green flare in the sky, letting the second line of defense know their lines had been penetrated and to signal to his own platoon it was time to bug out.

The remaining soldiers in SSG Allen's platoon began to run down the escape tunnel for safety. SSG Allen stayed behind longer to seal the bunker door just as the last soldier made it in, then he ran for the escape tunnel. He blew the charge in the bunker, destroying it behind them. After he reached the first turn, he detonated the second charge, destroying the first part of the tunnel to ensure no Chinese soldiers could follow behind them. As the remains of his platoon emerged from the tunnel, they were welcomed by defenders who praised them for their valiant effort at the beach. They had succeeded in slowing down the Chinese advance and effectively wiped out the first two waves of their assault.

Thoughts raced through Paul's mind. He felt lucky to have survived, and grateful that close to half of his platoon had made it out with him. The images of the battle raced through his head, overloading him with gruesome scenes. These pictures at the beach and in front of the bunker would haunt him for the rest of his life; thousands of PLAN infantrymen had been wiped out trying to secure his platoon's two bunkers and trench line.

****

Today was the day the PLAN was going to begin its final amphibious assault. They had handed over Kodiak Island to the PLA and reformed up at sea, ready for their last attack that would pave the way to Anchorage. Corporal Chang, like the other soldiers, was nervous about the coming assault. The Army, Navy and Air Force had been pounding Homer and Anchor Point peninsula for days. Rumor had it, several destroyers had been sunk when they got too close to the peninsula. A number of the soldiers in Chang's squad wondered how their lowly landing vehicles would get close enough to the beach if the shore guns had defeated a couple of destroyers.

Everyone's coms came to life at the same time, "Board the amphibious assault vehicles and landing crafts. Move quickly! Our time to invade has arrived."

Chang and his squad boarded the landing craft along with the rest of their platoon; his squad was towards the back of the craft which meant they would be the last off. He realized that this was not a good place to be if he wanted to get to cover quickly. Everyone performed their final checks on their exoskeleton combat suits and equipment as the landing craft moved away from the troop transport and started to form up with the other ships. Steadily, the group of landing crafts began to navigate around the channel until they could see Anchor Point in the distance.

Chang lifted himself slightly above the lip of the landing craft to sneak a peek at the beach. He saw hundreds of rockets and artillery rounds impacting all along the shore, sending geysers of sand, dirt and other materials into the sky. As his boat advanced towards the beach, he saw flashes of light from several well-hidden bunkers on the beach reach out and destroy several of the vessels around him. Red tracers (like lasers) could be seen crisscrossing the water, hitting several vehicles; some rounds bounced off harmlessly while others penetrated the lightly armored landing craft, causing some of them to explode.

As Chang's landing craft neared the beach, he readied himself and did a check on his exoskeleton suit. He reminded his squad mates of their objective, "Men, we are assigned to take out the machine gun bunker to the right of our landing craft once we hit the beach. You have your weapons—satchel charges and RPG7s. Our goal is to disable or destroy our target as quickly as possible to make way for the second and third waves to advance."

The soldiers had been told to expect the Americans to have heavy M2 .50 machine guns in the bunkers, but none of them were anticipating the two M134 miniguns as well. As their landing craft neared the beach, several machine gun rounds hit the front ramp and bounced off. Within seconds, the ramp dropped. Chang's platoon began to rush forward with the rest of the swarm, trying to advance quickly towards the beach. As they were running, one of the heavy machine gunners turned their sights towards his platoon. Within seconds, nearly a dozen men in his platoon had been mowed down by the heavy guns. Chang knew he had to get his squad to some cover quickly or that heavy machine gun was going to cut them apart. Suddenly, Chang heard a loud buzzing sound and saw what looked like a flickering laser reach out from the bunker in front of him and massacred an entire platoon to his left. He had never seen one of the American miniguns used at a beach invasion, and could not believe how fast the platoon had been wiped out. They desperately needed to take out those bunkers before they were all killed.

About 100 meters in from the shoreline was a bank where the sand ended and the grass began. As Chang looked up at the horizon to the small dips and rises in the ground past that point, he could see rows of torn and partially destroyed concertina wire and obstacles, spaced about ten meters apart. PLAN infantrymen were rushing these obstacles, doing their best to either destroy it or cut open wide holes for others to follow through. Several of the armored amphibious landing vehicles did their best to plow through as much of the defensive line as they could before they were destroyed by enemy railguns, mortars and artillery. Their sacrifice was heroic, and probably the only thing preventing the first wave of the assault from being completely wiped out.

Chang moved along with his squad through the various obstacles. They all did their best not to get cut down by enemy fire, and took advantage of as many opportunities to shoot back at the Americans as they could. They were managing to plow along at a fair clip, considering the immense amount of crossfire. In an instant, an explosion occurred near Chang that was so powerful, it picked up the soldier behind him and threw him at Chang's back. Chang fell flat on his face. He groaned; his nose was partially filled with sand, but the concussion from the blast had stunned him enough that he was powerless to move in that instant. For a brief moment, he lost consciousness. When he came to, he struggled to push the soldier off of his back. As he heard the thump of the man rolling off of him, Chang could see that he was clearly dead.

Looking back, he saw several members of his squad thrown around, some were moving slowly, recovering from the shock, and others were not moving at all. One of the soldiers had stepped on a landmine; it had nearly taken the entire squad out. He was reeling from the shock of it all.

Another loud explosion brought Chang back to reality. He quickly glanced to his left and saw that further down the beach, sand, dirt, and body parts were being blown into the air as several artillery rounds hit the beach. Seconds later, Chang was back on his feet. He yelled at his squad, "Continue to advance to the embankment for cover! And try to take that gun bunker out!"

Hundreds of other Chinese soldiers in their new exoskeleton combat suits were also moving quickly through the obstacles, rushing for the embankment and the sense of shelter. Chang was nearly to the embankment with his squad and the rest of his company when a series of explosions in front of the embankment went off. Several of the claymore anti-personnel mines had been triggered; the concussion was so strong that Chang was hurled backwards into several of his soldiers.

Each of the claymore mines had released 480 steel balls as it detonated, like a shotgun at very close range. As Chang recovered from the blast, he felt a twinge of pain in his left arm, and a throbbing in both of his legs. He looked down and saw that he had been hit by a couple of the steel balls in the arm; each of his legs had taken at least one round as well. He could not immediately get up, so he quickly crawled to the embankment, which was less than 50 meters in front of him. When he looked back, he saw that only three members of his squad remained from the ten men that had been with him when they left the landing craft. When his comrades realized that he was injured, they ran to him and dragged him by the shoulders to pull him further into the embankment. One of the soldiers began to work on his injuries with Chang's first aid package, while the other two engaged the American soldiers in the trenches. They were about 150 meters from the bunker.

"I wrapped your injuries at tight as I could, and used the cream as we were taught," one of the soldiers said to Chang.

"Thank you for the help Private. Take your RPG and try to see if you can hit the gun port of that machine gun bunker to our left. We have to try and take it out or no one is going to make it." They each had an RPG7 with them, and a total of four rockets each. Chang knew the RPG could not destroy the bunker, it was too heavily reinforced. His hope was to hit the firing slit; the explosion of the RPG would travel inside the bunker and potentially destroy the gun or kill the Americans manning it.

As Chang looked back over the beach, he saw the third wave was already starting to hit the beach. He also saw dozens of bodies bobbing in the water all around burnt and blown out amphibious vehicles and landing craft. The beach itself was covered in bodies: some were stuck in the concertina wire, others were missing limbs or even half of their bodies from the various mines, and some were simply blown to bits by the mortars and artillery rounds that had landed in their midst. As he watched, he witnessed more soldiers getting cut down by those machine gun bunkers. He knew they had to be taken out.

One of the privates popped up long enough to fire his rocket at the bunker. Unfortunately, it impacted about two feet below the gun slit. The second private jumped up to fire his rocket, but was hit by several bullets from the Americans in the trench line in front of them. He died instantly.

Chang grabbed the RPG from his fallen brother-in-arms and slithered several feet down the embankment. He waited a moment to make sure that no enemy fire was aimed in his direction, and then he propped himself up to take aim at the bunker. He knew that the rocket would fall a little as it flew, so he set his sights just slightly above the gun slit. He fired the RPG, and then quickly ducked just as a stream of bullets and tracers flew over his head. When he did look up, he saw that his rocket had hit the gun slit and the machine gun had gone silent. Then smoke started emanating from within the bunker as it started to pour out of the gun slit. They had done it; they had accomplished their mission.

With the machine gun bunker now silent, hundreds of naval infantrymen rushed through the paths that had been made for them by the first two waves of the assault. They moved quickly to close the distance between them and the American soldiers in the trenches. Several rounds of claymore mines were detonated by the Yankees as the

Chinese soldiers rushed forward, but without the second bunker, the lines were being overrun by sheer manpower.

Suddenly, dozens of Chinese soldiers were jumping into the trenches, fighting hand-to-hand with the Americans. Chang took another rocket from one of the dead privates and reloaded the RPG. He fired another round at the second gun position to their right. Chang saw a soldier open a side door briefly and fire a flare into the sky. Not knowing what this green glow meant, Chang took one more shot with the RPG, aiming at the steel door he had just seen the soldier shut; he was hoping to take him out.

Suddenly, the remaining American soldiers still in the trenches ran to the bunker and opened the now severely damaged steel door. In mere seconds, they were all inside the bunker. The Americans tried to close the door as best they could after Chang had hit it with the rocket. Seconds later, several Chinese soldiers blew the door open and rushed the entrance of the bunker. As they did, the entire thing exploded, killing everyone in it and injuring other soldiers nearby.

Chang looked to the two privates left in his squad. "Well done, soldiers! Continue on with the rest of the company while I wait for the medic to come and further address my injuries."

Without any hesitation, they immediately moved forward, joining the rest of the naval infantrymen and advancing past the first trench line towards the second line of defense much further back.

As Chang looked at the carnage that was before him, he thought to himself, "*If every battle with the Americans on their homeland is going to be like this, we are going to need a lot more men.*" He had to give the Americans credit, they fought like savage dogs. They had made the Chinese pay dearly to take this land from them.

On the coastline, several larger landing crafts pulled up to the shore and opened their doors to offload a heavy main battle tank. "*We sure could have used those things to help take out the gun positions,*" thought Chang to himself. As the tanks moved across the beach, they ran over dozens of dead bodies as well as those of the wounded who could not get out of their way fast enough.

Immediately after the MBTs offloaded, a wave of medical personnel sprang forward and immediately went to work tending to the wounded and loading them back on to several of the landing craft that were still at the beach. As additional soldiers and medics advanced to Chang's position, an officer came up to him and angrily asked him, "Why did you not advance with the rest of your company?"

Chang simply pointed to the bloody bandages on both of his legs, and a medic ran up to him. The officer hurried off and started to yell at another batch of soldiers he had found near the American trenches.

Chang was loaded onto a stretcher and moved to a landing craft, which then headed back to sea and to the troop transports. Chang's part in the war was over for the time being.

****

The PLAN infantry had secured Homer and Anchor Point, dislodging the Americans after twenty-one hours of continuous combat. They had moved ten kilometers inland before they were finally stopped by a battalion of American Pershing MBTs and several battalions of the older, yet still venerable, Abrams Tanks.

In the battle for Anchor Point, 14,373 American soldiers had been killed, wounded, or found to be missing. However, the PLAN naval infantry had been effectively destroyed as a fighting force. They had lost 41,235 soldiers who were killed, missing or wounded during the battle before the PLA began to land their force and assume the role of attacker. The PLAN had started the Alaskan campaign just three weeks prior, with 150,000 soldiers fully equipped with the new exoskeleton combat suits. Between the battles of Kodiak Island, the Aleutian Peninsula and the battle of Anchor Point, they had lost 86,438 soldiers. The PLA, by contrast, had lost less than 43,000 up to this point, but they still had not fully dislodged the American defenders from Kodiak Island.

****

Dr. Dewei Zhong was in a holding pattern off shore. He would be part of the last group to reach Anchor Point. The first wave of doctors were Tieh Ta practitioners, who specialized in trauma injuries; they triaged the patients and would get to work setting broken bones and treating the soldiers who had lost limbs. The Tieh Ta practitioners would also offer to assist those who were too far beyond treatment in ending their lives peacefully. Dr. Zhong had mixed feelings about this practice, but Buddha had been tolerant of monks who had committed suicide in such cases, and so he kept his mouth shut and followed along, knowing that those who received such an offer were struggling under great suffering.

As Dr. Zhong waited offshore, he smiled to himself thinking about how much more equipment the Americans would need in order to do his job. He was quite sure that death rates with the American doctors would be at least double what theirs were with the limited amount of equipment they had under their budget. Dewei didn't need all of those fancy gadgets in order to do his work. He could simply look at a patient's face and their tongue and have a very good idea of whether or not infection had spread in the body, if IV fluids would be necessary, and which medicines would be of greatest use in restoring balance to the body.

While he was reflecting, his landing craft suddenly bumped into the shore, and he almost lost his balance as his ship lurched forward. Once everyone caught their footing, they all rushed forward as one unit, lugging their bulky bags of supplies. As more and more of the scene came into view, Dr. Zhong was no longer smiling...what unfolded before him was horrific, even past the limits of what he had imagined in his mind. The sheer enormity of the agony in front of him was overwhelming. There was hardly a place to stand where there wasn't blood or the remnants of a soldier blown apart by an explosion. Dewei took a deep breath; if he allowed himself to think about it all, he was going to become useless. He needed to calm himself and focus on what was immediately in front of him.

Dr. Zhong set to work; once he started working with the patients, the automaticity kicked in, and he was able to be effective and swift. He moved steadily from patient to patient, administering a combination of traditional Chinese herbal medications and Western drugs, dressing wounds, starting IVs, and motioning to the medical transporters when a patient was stabilized enough to move back to the ship. Hours went by in what seemed like minutes, and then suddenly all of the wounded were cleared from the beach. Dewei returned to the boat, accompanying a patient who was not quite as stable as the rest.

As they took off towards the Middle Kingdom, Dr. Zhong continued his work. There would be very little sleep until they returned home and were relieved by other practitioners. Dewei moved swiftly from patient to patient, feeling the temperature on different parts of their body and giving instructions to assistants who would add or take away blankets. Dr. Zhong was a little more liberal with the pain medications than most of his colleagues; he knew that his fellow Chinese service men were very stoic in nature and that most would not ask him for assistance, but he felt that easing their suffering would be one way to bring better karma to himself. His movements were like a well-rehearsed dance; he did not waste time or energy, but steadily moved along, caring for others well into the night.

The final ships would come to collect the bodies of the dead, so that their families could give them a proper burial. If a soldier's body was too damaged to be returned to the family, the family was given a set of their dog tags, along with any cremated remains that might have been collected. The Chinese believed that this dignity in passing would help ensure that the souls of the departed would continue to look after and care for their loved ones after their death.

Changing Tactics

14 June 2041

White House, Situation Room

The Chairman of the Joint Chiefs, General Branson, had been discussing the casualties and the state of the war in Alaska with Eric Clarke (the Secretary of Defense) for close to half an hour before the start of the national security meeting with the President. Slowly, other members of the President's national security team were filtering in with their aides in tow. They were reviewing their portions of the brief with their aides as they prepared for the grilling the President usually put his team through. Henry Stein was usually tough but fair in the meetings; he wanted unfiltered information about the situation on the ground. He typically did not get directly involved in the minutia of decisions, but he certainly wanted a clear picture of what was happening. Having served in the Second Iraq war and worked in the Department of Defense for many years before starting his own business, he had an adept understanding of the complexities involved in both fighting a war and the bureaucracy of managing one.

****

In the Oval Office, President Stein sat in his chair talking with his Chief of Staff, Michael Montgomery (or

"Monty" as he was usually called). They had been talking about domestic priorities and issues with Jeff Rogers, the Senior White House Economic Advisor, and Secretary of Treasury, Joyce Gibbs, before the National Security meeting. Secretary Gibbs had been reviewing the state of the economy.

"As you know, Sir, the US has been experiencing exponential growth the past five years since you have taken office. The America First Corporation (AFC) has been a boon for the U.S.A. As millions of Americans have been hired for reconstruction and infrastructure jobs all over the nation, the country has begun to turn around." Jeff reviewed various charts and metrics with more detailed information, and Henry couldn't help but start to daydream during the explanation. The President had established AFC to become a sort of sovereign wealth fund for the country, allowing it to leverage the various resources on federal lands all across the country. The money being generated by AFC was being used to shore up Social Security and help fund other aspects of the federal government in addition to providing hundreds of thousands of jobs. AFC was the only company allowed to mine and drill on federal land. They also planted fruit and nut trees along federal freeways and highways all across the country. It beautified the highways across America and again provided tens of thousands of jobs and tens of millions of tons of food a month.

Monty brought his boss back to reality as he asserted, "The economic news is good, Mr. President. Despite the draft and the fighting in Alaska, the economy continues to remain strong."

"The economy is doing well enough, but we are still not producing enough materials needed for the war. The fighting in Alaska is chewing through equipment at a faster rate than we can replace it. The Russians are picking up their offensive again in Europe and General Gardner wants to invade the IR," responded the President with a sigh as he sank a little deeper in his chair.

Knowing that getting depressed about the situation was not going to make it any better, the President quickly readjusted to a better thinking posture, resolving himself to find a solution. "I believe we are starting to run late for the National Security briefing; let's head down and see what they have for us. When we are done, I want to return back to this discussion and figure out how we can increase manufacturing."

"Yes Mr. President," they responded.

Henry stood up and began to walk towards the door.

Monty quickly followed the President out of the Oval Office and was thinking about that very question. The auto-industry had retooled their manufacturing plants months ago to crank out tanks and other armored vehicles at a record rate. The massive transition to additive manufacturing was starting to revolutionize the entire manufacturing sector. The U.S. could mass produce the materials needed to build a fighter drone in less than ten days. The goal was to get that number down to five. General Motors was working on being able to do the same thing with most of the component parts for the Pershing battle tanks and other infantry fighting vehicles. America just needed time to make the tools needed to win this war.

The President strode into the Situation Room, signaling for everyone to stay seated as he walked to the head of the table and sat down. As Monty took a seat next to him, he began, "Let's talk domestic issues first if we can, then transition to the war." As he spoke, the President looked towards Jorge Perez, the Director for Homeland Security. At meetings like this, the President would often "call an audible," changing the order of the agenda; this forced everyone to be ready to give their portion of the briefing at any given time.

Jorge Perez had been the Director for Homeland Security since the President first formed his cabinet. He probably would have retired at the end of President Steins first term to slow down and take a job in the private sector, but the terrorist attacks had become a blight in the country, and then the war broke out, and he felt he could not leave his position at such a critical moment. "Mr. President, we have identified ninety-three additional foreign intelligence operatives across the country. Most of them worked for the Russians, with a few belonging to China. They were probably activated once the invasion began." As Director Perez spoke, several slides were shown with images of the more valuable individuals that had been detained.

"Most of the detainees were in the process of committing some act of economic or military sabotage to our forces operating in Alaska or British Columbia. We are working with the FBI to obtain as much information from them as possible about their plans as well as the names of any other individuals they may be working with," Perez said as he nodded towards FBI Director Jane Smart in acknowledgement.

Director Smart took her cue to continue. "As of right now, we have identified a couple of additional people they had contact with. The Trinity Program identified them, and we moved in as soon as the information was vetted. We have added several new names and search parameters to the program, so we should start to see some additional leads in the coming days."

Switching topics, Jane continued, "As to the protesters, we are seeing an uptick in demonstrations against the war across a number of major cities and metropolitan areas. By and large they are peaceful; the individuals who do try to incite violence are quickly being identified and if they were not actively engaged in felony crimes, they are given a choice between jail time and serving in the military. With such a high percentage of young people in the military or working, we are not seeing as many people on the streets as we have in the past."

The President thought for a moment before responding, "Thank you Jorge and Jane. I know these are trying times. I appreciate your efforts in continuing to maintain the peace and protecting the civilian populace. Let's move on to the war updates then."

General Branson took this as his cue to start his portion of the brief and brought up the holographic display of the Alaskan theater of operations. "Mr. President, the situation in Alaska continues to be precarious and fluid at the moment. The Chinese have fully secured the Aleutian

Peninsula, and have begun construction of dozens of airfields as well as reconstruction of the various port facilities they've captured. We are now starting to see a steady stream of aircraft and drones being flown in from China to these new airfields and a proportional increase in the number of air sorties against our own forces. Our satellites have also spotted several large troop and equipment transports heading to Alaska, so it would appear their second wave of reinforcements is now in transit," the General explained as he brought up images of the convoy.

"Our forces on Kodiak Island officially surrendered five hours ago. The commanding general and his forces held the island for two weeks, inflicting significant casualties--"

The President interrupted, asking, "--How many of our soldiers surrendered?"

"About 11,400 in all; the rest of the force was killed in action. We anticipate the prisoners being moved back to China in the near future," Branson said.

"General, see if the Chinese would entertain a prisoner swap. We have nearly 209,000 Chinese prisoners from the Middle East; see if they are willing to swap prisoners at say, 5:1, but go no higher than 7:1. If we can get our soldiers back, I want to get them back," the President directed.

"Yes, Mr. President," Branson replied as he nodded towards one of his aides who made a note of the request. Next, the general brought up the images of Anchor Point, Homer and Seward. "Mr. President, as you can see, the Chinese have secured most of the Anchor Point Peninsula, but not before suffering heavy casualties. The 32nd infantry was assigned to defend the beaches and the towns of Homer and Seward. We held the Chinese at the beach for nearly six hours before they finally broke through the first line of defense. It took them a full day to break through the second line of defense and three more days to break through the third line. They have been battling now for nearly ten days at our fourth line of defense."

Eric Clarke, the Secretary of Defense, interjected at this point saying, "The Chinese are taking horrific casualties, yet they continue to steamroll through our force. We estimate the PLAN naval infantry, which led the invasion, have lost nearly 120,000 soldiers killed, wounded or missing in the last fifteen days. The PLA has landed about 130,000 soldiers on the Peninsula now and that number grows by 30,000 a day. On the Aleutian Peninsula they have landed nearly 350,000 soldiers, as well as a large portion of their armored forces."

The President saw the concern on Eric's face and could see the others in the room were troubled as well. "Everyone, we knew going into this that the Chinese would sacrifice tens of thousands of soldiers, maybe even hundreds of thousands, in order to gain a foothold in North America. Our plan has always been to make them bleed and sacrifice land for time. Nothing has changed. We all have to remember that now that the Chinese are fully committed in Alaska (and the Russians too for that matter), the logistical war is now going to come into play. The Russians and Chinese have a limited sealift capability. They can only move so many men and material to Alaska and their other fronts. This capability is going to become strained and as it does, that is when we are going to start to cripple them." The President knew that the American Navy was going to have to shoulder the larger burden of stopping the Chinese.

Seeing as the topic had shifted to his area of expertise, Admiral Juliano, the Chief of Naval Operations, spoke up. "Sir, we believe we have identified the problem with our new torpedoes and they have been fixed. Our two Swordfish Underwater Drones (SUDs) have successfully maneuvered to our naval facility in Washington and are being refitted with the updated Hammerhead torpedoes. They will soon be back on their way to Alaska and the

Chinese supply lines. Our intent is to use them to specifically go after the Chinese roll-on, roll-off transports and the larger commercial shipping container ships that they are using to transport fuel and munitions. Each sub can carry eight torpedoes, and we are confident these subs will start sinking ten to sixteen ships a month, maybe more."

"When do the additional SUDs start to come on line, Admiral?" asked Monty.

"We will have a total of ten SUDs by the end of the year, and that number will triple the following year."

The President changed the topic of conversation to ask, "So, what is the situation with the Russians in northern Alaska?"

General Branson brought up a new set of holographic images, displaying the Russian advances. "Like the Chinese, the Russians have advanced off of the beaches and are starting to move inland. We have pulled most of our troops back to their secondary defensive positions. As the Russians advance, they are going to encounter a series of fortified positions, blocking every major avenue into the heart of Alaska on their way towards Fairbanks. The Marines are keeping them busy in the artic portion of Alaska and will be heavily engaged in central Alaska."

"Our ground operations are going as expected; the first several days were a bit rocky but as planned and predicted, things are turning out just as we thought they would with the exception to the air campaign. Our loss at Eielson hurt. We have fortunately kept the Chinese and Russian air assets from attacking the base while we rebuild the drone squadrons. We've also expanded drone operations at three different airbases in the U.S.; they will soon start to participate in a lot more air operations in Alaska."

"We've flown in 350 additional fighter drones and another 130 F22s to Eielson. We have successfully regained control of the skies over central and arctic Alaska. We are building two new drone airbases at Whitehorse in the Yukon territory; these new bases will be solely drone bases, with the fighter pilots operating out of bases in the southern States. This will minimize the potential loss of our critical pilots."

"All right, General Branson, we are starting to get a little deeper into the weeds than I would like to go at the moment. I'll leave the rest of the details to you and your fellow generals. I just want to know that our strategic plan is still on track, and it appears that it is. How are things fairing in the Middle East with General Gardner and his forces?" asked the President.

"General Gardner's forces have been consolidating all along the Israeli/Jordan border. They have successfully secured all of Lebanon and captured Damascus. Now they are starting to push out and secure the rest of Syria and plan on stopping near the Turkish border. The Israelis are ready to move on Amman and push the IR forces there back. Right now they are waiting for General Gardner and his staff to finalize the next offensive plan and occupation strategy. I've talked with General Gardner at length, and he believes Third Army and the nearly 800,000 IDF forces could capture Jordan, Saudi Arabia and Iraq before the end of the year. The question is--do we want them to move forward with this offensive or hold in place?" asked General Branson.

"What are everyone's thoughts on this?" asked the President, wanting to get a consensus.

Mike Williams, the President's National Security Advisor, spoke first saying, "We need to finish the IR off. They started this war and are responsible for millions of civilians killed across the country. Not to mention the two nuclear devices in Baltimore and New York City. If we leave them alone, we only allow them time to rebuild their country with help from the Chinese, and they will once again be a problem for us. We need to crush them now while they are weak and getting weaker by the day."

Jim Wise, the Secretary of State, added, "I agree with Mike. We need to finish our war with the IR. Before General Gardner and the Israelis attack, we could make one final offer to the IR leadership to surrender. I am not certain they would accept it, but if we can convince them to surrender, we could bring the war with them to an end much sooner without losing tens of thousands of additional soldiers."

The Director of the CIA, Patrick Rubio, spoke next, "The IR is in complete disarray. They are trying to hold down the country as best they can right now, but with power knocked out across most of the republic and communications limited, they are starting to lose control of the country. They are maintaining most of their military force around Amman, which is keeping them from using valuable resources to restore control to the rest of the country. I believe if we were to offer them terms of surrender they can live with, we could get them to accept it."

"What are the terms you suggest we offer them?" asked the President, his curiosity now peaked.

"They are in desperate need of food; we could offer them a few hundred tons of food a month for, say three years, while we work with them on demilitarizing their economy and country. They would be allowed to maintain a military force for defensive purposes, but we would remove their ability to wage war beyond their borders. We would also remove their nuclear weapons and other WMD capabilities as well as their ability to produce these types of weapons," Director Rubio said.

"I believe if we approached some of the senior military commanders, we may be able to convince them to remove Mohammed Abbas, particularly if we offer them this deal and perhaps some cash on the side. It would be best if we could get the regime to implode from within via an internal coup; that would be better than continuing the war and losing more soldiers and equipment," Rubio said as he sat back in his chair waiting for the counter-arguments to be made. It did not take long.

General Branson cleared his throat before speaking. "I have to disagree with Director Rubio. We need to so thoroughly crush the IR that they will never challenge us again or Israel. If we support a coup, all we swap out is a radical theocracy for a military junta that will re-arm and rebuild to challenge us again in another decade. No, we need to absolutely crush them and then remove their ability to wage war again," Branson stated passionately as he surveyed the room.

The President looked at the faces of everyone at the table before speaking, "There is merit in both of your ideas and we should look at both options. General Branson, continue with the military option. Pound the tar out of them from the air and continue to do what you can to make their lives as miserable as possible. Director Rubio, put out some feelers and see if any of their senior military leadership may be open to a potential coup. I want to look at both options Gentlemen."

"Let's move on to Europe. Where do we stand?" asked the President, wanting to move the meeting forward.

General Branson changed the maps on the holograph display. The portions of Europe that were Allied territory were colored in light blue, and the area controlled by the Russians was a light red shade. At different points on the map there were designations for the various units that were fighting, as well as information about how they were doing in their most recent skirmishes.

"Mr. President, General Wade is looking to orchestrate one of the largest tank battles since World War II, just west of Berlin. His goal is to lure them in and deal a decisive blow, knocking them back to Poland or even the Ukraine." Branson showed the plans for the upcoming battle as he talked.

He continued, "It's a tricky battle as our forces do not have full air supremacy over the battlefield. Once the

Russian army is fully committed, General Wade plans on using the bulk of his A10 Warthogs and Razorbacks to attack the enemy tank formations before committing all of his Pershings and M1A5 Abrams. While his forces are conducting a full frontal assault against the Russian lines, Field Marshal Schoen will lead his Panzer divisions in a massive attack against the Russian southern flank. The British and French armor units will attack the Russian northern flanks. If they are successful, they will have effectively destroyed the Russian armored forces in Europe."

The President asked, "What happens if they are not successful? How will this affect our forces in Germany?"

Knowing this question was coming, General Branson brought up General Wade's alternate scenario on the display. "Mr. President, as you can see here, our forces would be in a tough spot, and so would the rest of the Germans, French and British. We may end up losing most of Germany."

"Yet General Wade believes this is the best course of action?" asked Mile Williams, the National Security Director.

"If our forces stay on defense, then they will be assaulted and be in a constant state of reacting to the Russians, rather than forcing the Russians to react to our attack. The Pershings are an incredible offensive weapon, but remaining still has made them sitting ducks against the MiG40s." Branson showed some images of Pershings that had fallen prey to the attacks of the MiGs before he continued, "The General wants to get them into the war where they can do some good, rather than continue to lose a steady stream of them daily to high altitude bombing runs."

The President knew his military commanders were chomping at the bit to go on the offensive. America had been attacked mercilessly the last nine months and had suffered some horrendous losses--not to mention the nuclear bombs detonating in New York and Baltimore. However, the military was stretched incredibly thin right now. With the new offensive happening in Alaska, it was going to be difficult to contain the Chinese there, let alone keep an offensive line in both the Middle East and Europe replenished with fuel, munitions, food, equipment and replacement troops. The country was still retooling for war, and it was going to take time to draft and train a several million-person military from scratch.

"General Branson, I understand the issue facing General Wade and his forces in Europe. I appreciate the effort that went into developing these plans and the effort that has been made to position forces for this trap. However, I want General Wade to keep his offensive on hold. He may conduct limited offensive operations as needed to keep the Russians from penetrating his lines, but nothing more. Right now, we cannot afford to take a chance on losing most of Germany. The EU countries need time to continue to mobilize their forces and the Germans need time to crank out their new battle tanks and other military vehicles. We simply do not have the resources available to support his offensive right now," the President explained.

He continued, "With the operations going on in Alaska, nearly all of our new soldiers coming out of training and our equipment coming from the factory floors is going to General Black's forces. That said, I do want General Gardner to continue with his offensive against the IR. Unless Director Rubio is able to work out some sort of deal with their military leadership, General Gardner should continue as planned and move to occupy the country. What additional forces do we have available to send him right now?" asked the President.

General Branson looked through his tablet and pulled up some information. "We have three divisions completing their final train-up and equipment loadouts. We were going to send them to General Black's group in Alaska. One is a tank division while the other two are mechanized infantry divisions."

"What forces will General Gardner need most right now for his offensive?" asked the President.

"Presently, he has the needed forces for his offensive; if we send him additional reinforcements, it will help him during the occupation. I recommend sending him the two mechanized infantry divisions. He has armor but he'll need more infantry if he is to capture and hold territory," Branson explained.

"Then redirect those two divisions to the Middle East and get that tank division to Alaska," the President directed before continuing, "Ladies and gentlemen, I've kept everyone here long enough. Please execute your orders and be ready to provide an update tomorrow at the same time."

With that, the meeting ended.

****

Dr. Travis Perino had a home in Baltimore before the nuclear attack. If he closed his eyes, he could still picture the beautiful view of the harbor during the summer (he would often walk there with his dog after a long shift). When the bomb was detonated, he had been on vacation in Jamaica, so he had survived, but his, condo, his co-workers, his dog…everything was destroyed. It felt strange to him to not be able to go back and see it for himself; he understood that the radiation was dangerous and that "closure" was probably not the best reason for him to grab a HAZMAT suit and head to ground zero, but still, he wanted to mourn what was lost in a better way than watching news coverage of the event.

As a psychiatrist, Dr. Perino felt that he had something to offer to those that survived this horrible tragedy, so he left his tropical paradise on the first flight out and headed to Richmond, Virginia, which was one of the major hubs where the injured were being taken. Many were clearly in a state of shock, so overwhelmed by their experience that they couldn't even function. In such cases, Travis would sit by the patient and calmly reorient them to where they were; he did have a way of speaking to people that would bring a sense of peace, and he didn't rush any of the patients that were unable to speak. They would begin to recover with time and reassurance.

He worked with the nurses to lower the stimuli in the rooms for some of the more distressed patients; all of the beeping from IV machines, lights and general noise from so many people rushing about was quite distressing. Like many who enter a "caring" field, he poured himself out for those around him, never stopping to think about his own needs. It was only at the end of the day, when he was all alone in a hotel room and everything was quiet, that he would fall into a pool of his own grief.

Months later, he was still caring for those who had been affected by this terrible tragedy. He had stayed in Richmond to set up his own practice there; now those he was seeing were mostly dealing with the ongoing effects of post-traumatic stress disorder (PTSD). The signs were obvious: recurrent flashbacks or nightmares, insomnia, a heightened state of alertness/guarding, and triggering events that caused the person to go into "fight or flight" mode. His father had been a veteran of the second Iraq War, so he had seen it all firsthand. It was actually part of what had made him want to become a psychiatrist in the first place.

Back then, his Dad had been treated by doctors at the Department of Veterans Affairs, who basically just shoved him full of pills and sent him on his merry way. However, those medications were not without their side effects, and his father would often complain of headaches or seem to space out in the distance, unable to focus on the people in front of him. Sometimes, the VA would mess up his medication shipment and he wouldn't get his pills in time; those medicines aren't meant to be stopped cold turkey, and his father would lash out like someone who is a mean alcoholic. One day his mother had enough of the whole thing, and the two of them split.

Dr. Perino wanted to be a different kind of doctor. Yes, psychiatrists can prescribe drugs to help heal the mind, and he did, but he would also work with his patients on other forms of therapy as well; eye movement desensitization and reprocessing (EMDR) was probably the most useful treatment, but he also did cognitive behavioral therapy, taught coping strategies, and would generally do whatever it took to help get the patient back into a normal life again.

Listening to all of these stories of horrific experiences around Baltimore was taxing, however, and Travis had to do a lot of work with himself at the end of the day to let go of everything he had heard so that he would not hold on to it and carry it like a stone around his neck. He hadn't always been a runner, but he took it up to help himself de-stress. When the breeze was blowing and there was a steady swish of his feet, he could almost entirely block out all of the tragic things that he had heard about. Otherwise, he usually had to have on some music or television shows of some kind to drown out the scripts of the truly awful things he heard from the survivors.

He almost hated to admit it, but he was glad that the U.S. had responded with all of those nuclear weapons. While he knew cognitively that resentment is like drinking poison and hoping that the other person will get hurt, he was truly angry over this unprovoked attack that had shattered the lives of so many. When he heard another story of a mother who lost her child in the blast while she went to work ten miles away, he wanted the IR to pay for their sins.

****

At the University of South Florida in Tampa, Dr. Rosanna Weisz had served a relatively quiet and happy life, finally achieving tenure as a humanities and history professor. The university had a greater need for teaching history classes, but it was really the humanities that made her excited to get up in the morning; she loved to pour over books about art history, poetry, and philosophy. She was a simple creature in many ways, finding great happiness in a good cup of coffee, an intellectual conversation or an impressionist painting. Two years ago she had lived out her ultimate dream when she was able to visit Claude Monet's gardens in France and then backpack through Europe, taking pictures of many of the sites and historical places she had taught about for so many years.

Despite being a history professor, she had more or less stayed out of politics. She did vote, but she was not especially loyal to one party over the other, and she usually made her choices mostly on the basis of personal merit instead of how they aligned to a strict set of ideological standards. However, this war was changing her day by day.

Dr. Weisz had been utterly horrified when Baltimore and New York had been bombed; she immediately donated money to some relief funds and helped organize a blood drive at USF. She wished that she could do more, but she was not trained in any sort of first aid or counseling of any kind, and her skills in French and Latin weren't going to be especially handy for this situation. She wasn't exactly a part of any specific religion, but she considered herself to be spiritual, and believed in a higher power (even if she couldn't quite agree that God was the deity described in the Bible); in her own way, she would pray for all those who were suffering.

When the United States retaliated against the Islamic Republic with nuclear weapons, she was not surprised; however, the scale of the response was beyond anything that she could have imagined. Rosanna was crushed at the sheer loss of human life, and the immense suffering that had become a plague on this planet. She did not believe that evil should beget evil. She began to think of all of the families on the other side of the world that had been crushed by the actions of the U.S. government, and though she was not often the type to cry, she set her head down on her desk and used up a few tissues with her tears.

As she composed herself and pulled her hair back out of her face, she saw an inspirational quote from Gandhi that she kept on her desk, "Be the change that you want to see." She thought to herself, "*What change do* I *want to bring?*" In that moment, she realized that she needed to work to prevent any future such tragedies from occurring in the world. She wanted to work to create policies that would garner more peace for the nation and the rest of the planet. Dr. Weisz did something in that moment that she had never done before, and decided to become more than just a casual participant in politics. She set to work on plans for a political movement towards peace.

For months now, this meek, normally quiet professor had been working in her downtime to organize marches and demonstrations. A friend of hers helped her to set up a website, and suddenly her thoughts were starting to gain some publicity and some traction. She was very careful to make sure that all of her events were peaceful and civil. Anything else would have defeated the purpose of her efforts. She always started any speech with the same line, "I want to thank you for being here today; I am very grateful to live in a country where we can love our nation and still disagree with our leadership."

British Situation Room

10 Downing Street, London, England

16 June 2041

British Prime Minister Stannis Bedford had been monitoring the Chinese advances in Alaska with a bit of concern. The casualties that the Chinese and Americans had been taking were horrendous and frightening. The Americans were fighting with all their grit for their homeland while the Chinese continued to pour more and more soldiers into the meat grinder that was the Alaskan front. Bedford knew the mounting casualties in Alaska meant there would be fewer and fewer American resources allocated to Europe, which would make stopping the Russians that much harder.

Stannis was walking down to the Situation Room (located deep under the residence) to meet with his senior military advisors and get an update on the war and the next steps. He signaled for everyone to remain seated as he walked into the room, and made his way to the center of the table to take his seat. He saw General Sir Michael Richards, the British Army Chief of the Defense Staff; he was in charge of the overall British Defense Forces. Admiral Sir Mark West was there as well; he was the First Sea Lord and the man in charge of all naval forces. Seated next to him was General Sir Nick Wall, Chief of the General Staff for the Army, and last but not least was Air Chief Marshal, Sir Andrew Trenchard from the Royal Air Force.

These were the men responsible for the Defense of the British Isles, and for better or worse, most of Europe. Also in attendance were several individuals from the EU defense staff: General Volker Naumann, Chief of Staff of the EU Army, General Dieter Kessler, the senior Field Commander for all EU Military Forces, and their boss, Minister of Defense, André Gouin. The Americans would term this gathering of senior military leaders as a "coming to Jesus" meeting that was long overdue. The level of coordination and cooperation between the EU, British Forces and the Americans was not what it should be, and the war effort was suffering as a consequence.

Bedford sat down at the table and looked briefly at his tablet. He nodded towards an aide to bring up the holographic map of the front lines across Europe and the North Sea. "Gentlemen, thank you all for being here and for agreeing to meet with my military commanders. As you all are aware, the Chinese and Russians have launched a massive invasion of the American homeland in Alaska. This means that the Americans will not be prioritizing their war effort in Europe for some time. I spoke with President Stein a few hours ago, and he informed me that they will be playing defense in Europe while they focus on finishing off the IR in the Middle East and attempting to stop the Chinese and Russians from breaking out of Alaska. That means it will be upon us to take the lead in Europe."

"I have spoken with General Wade, the SACEUR Commander, and he has told me that he has approximately 860,000 US Forces in Europe and does not expect to receive many more forces for the foreseeable future. He has been ordered to defend Germany at all cost, but to limit his offensive operations until things stabilize in Alaska or the IR surrenders. I have spoken with General Sir Richards about our military force, and right now, we have 80,000 new recruits finishing training over the next two weeks and another 80,000 more the following month." The PM nodded towards General Sir Richards as he continued.

"Tomorrow we will be announcing another military draft; we are going to conscript two million men and women into uniform and will begin training them as quickly as possible. Minister Gouin, what is the EU currently doing as far as troop additions? How soon will the EU be ready to assume a larger military role?"

Gouin was a pragmatic man, and had been arguing for an increase in defense forces for several years now with Chancellor Lowden. Unfortunately, those pleas had fallen on deaf ears until it was too late. Clearing his throat before he responded, Minister Gouin replied, "As of yesterday, Chancellor Lowden issued an emergency draft across the EU member states to raise the size of the EU military, and he has asked all member states to increase the size of their own state-run militaries. Spain has announced that they are drafting 400,000 people immediately, France is drafting 800,000, Germany is drafting 2.2 million, and the Italians are adding 500,000. The EU army will be increased by 600,000 once the draft has been completed. However, it will still be months before these new soldiers will be trained and ready for battle. Under the current military training programs, it will take close to three months for the first batch of soldiers to complete their training. So we are looking at graduating about 210,000 soldiers every four weeks starting in two months."

General Dieter Kessler added, "The EU army has officially been released to my full command as of three weeks ago from Chancellor Lowden. I have begun coordination with General Wade, and my force of 600,000 soldiers is currently moving to reinforce the German army in

Austria and the Italian army in Slovenia. This is where General Wade wants our army to hold the line. I am confident that my soldiers can do that, and I do apologize that our Chancellor had not released our forces sooner, but we are here now and will start to take the Russians on."

General Sir Nick Wall joined the conversation. "The past is the past; we must focus on the present if we are to have a future. General Wade has said that his force, along with the bulk of the German army, will be able to hold the Russians at bay in the Berlin area. They have ceded the city to them rather than destroy the metropolis in the process of trying to defend it. General Wade and Field Marshal Schoen are looking to engage the bulk of the Russian armored forces near Berlin in the near future. We will be assisting them in that effort by providing two additional armored divisions and a massive increase in air support once the operation gets underway." General Wall highlighted the battle plans on the holographic map, along with the disposition of the enemy force.

Minister Gouin felt the need to reassure his British colleagues. "PM Bedford, I know there has been a lot of tension between our governments since the start of the war. I cannot change or fix the past, but I can assure you that I am now fully in control of the EU's military effort and things are going to change. We are fully committed to stopping the Russians and will not leave this to the individual states' armies to do on their own. Any help or assistance we can provide, we will."

PM Bedford sat back in his chair for a second taking in everything his EU colleagues had just said and was satisfied with their response. "Thank you Minister Gouin and Generals for meeting with us and for assuring us of your intentions. The UK is ultimately a small island nation, and there is only so much we can do. If the Germans had not retooled their economy for war and been such tenacious fighters, I think we would be having a much different conversation. As it stands, I believe there is still time to prevent the Russians from conquering Europe…We know what needs to happen, so let's end the meeting on a high note and move forward with a renewed resolve to work together and defeat the Russians," the PM said as the meeting concluded.

****

The war in Europe had been picking up steam again as the weather turned from spring to summer. The MiG40s continued to cause havoc in the air for the Allies, though the new radar systems the Americans were employing were starting to turn the tide. The Russians continued to pour hundreds of thousands of soldiers into Poland, the Balkans and Hungary, readying themselves for the summer offensive. It was just a matter of when, not if, they would attack. In the meantime, the Allies continued to prepare themselves to meet a numerically superior force.

Red Square

16 June 2041

Moscow, Russia

National Control Defense Center

Once it became clear that the war with the Americans, the European Union and the United Kingdom was not going to turn nuclear (or at least not yet), President Fradkov moved all military operations and activities back to the National Control Defense Center (NCDC) facility, just down the road from Red Square. The NCDC was a massive edifice that replaced the older Ministry of Defense building in the mid-2020s. For months, the war effort had been run out of the Presidential Command Bunker under the Kremlin, but as the war continued to drag on, moving the operations to the NCDC became more of a necessity; the number of personnel needed to manage a global war was immense, and this was the only facility that could truly meet this need. This center could control all military activities around the globe and run the operations of the entire economy and country (there was also a nuclear shelter in the basement and underground tunnels connecting it to a number of critical facilities throughout the city). President Fradkov began to spend more and more time at the NCDC.

President Fradkov walked through a series of doors, hallways and checkpoints until he finally arrived in the bowels of the NCDC where the war was being run. As he arrived, his generals and their staff jumped to attention like a bunch of school children who have been caught misbehaving by a strict librarian. He signaled for them to resume their duties and to take their seats. Fradkov sat at the center of the table and said, "Generals, we have a lot to discuss; let's begin. Where do our operations in Alaska stand?"

General Gerasimov, the head of the Russian military, began the briefing, "Mr. President, *Operation Red Dawn* has been a resounding success for our forces. Our initial landings at Nome and all along the western coast of Alaska have gone according to plan. Our insertion of dozens of Spetsnaz units in central Alaska have yielded significant results as well. One of our teams conducted a daring raid against Eielson Air Force base in Fairbanks, resulting in the destruction of six squadrons of drone pilots. They effectively eliminated nearly 70% of all American air force operations in Alaska for nearly 24 hours. This enabled the Chinese and our forces to quickly secure our initial objectives." As he spoke, General Gerasimov showed a number of aerial images of the damage done to the air base.

Sergei Puchkov, the Minister of Defense, interjected, "We should have Prudhoe Bay and the rest of the Alaskan oil fields secured within the next four weeks. General Gerasimov's forces have moved quickly, securing the majority of *Red Dawn's* primary and secondary objectives." Puchkov nodded towards the general in acknowledgement. "We have landed 190,000 soldiers, and are currently expanding several of the airfields that have been secured. We are now in the process of establishing several new ones. The majority of our helicopters have arrived, increasing our air assault capabilities significantly. I do not believe we are going to need to use our reserve force any time soon."

General Gerasimov inserted, "As you are already aware, the goal of the forces in Alaska is merely to support the Chinese invasion by securing the central and artic territories of Alaska, and the new Canadian States. They are not going to invade further south or support the Chinese beyond this limited scope. Once the initial objectives have been secured, we will leave a residual force of 80,000 soldiers and then move the remainder of our forces back to the Western Campaign."

Fradkov was elated to hear that things were starting to go their way in Alaska. The first three days of *Operation Red Dawn* were a bit dicey. The Americans had inflicted significantly more casualties at the various landing zones than they had anticipated. The Russian forces were facing the American Marines in central and northern Alaska; they were well dug-in and had prepared a multi-layer defense.

"Well then, let's move on to talk about Europe. How are things shaping up?" asked Fradkov.

"The loss of the 2nd Shock Army near Damascus has certainly hurt us, but it will not deter our advance into Europe or affect our invasion of Alaska. With the fall of Romania, the EU has lost its one oil-producing member, which of course makes them completely reliant on American oil and natural gas. As we continue to capture more territory, the noose around the EU's neck will begin to tighten."

General Gerasimov pulled up a map on the display before he continued. "As you can see here, the 3rd Shock Army is concentrating their forces in Poland and the easern half of the Czech Republic, preparing for a summer offensive. The 1st Shock Army has consolidated in northern Italy, Croatia, Slovenia and central Austria (now that Vienna has fallen). The plan is for the 1st Shock Army to pivot the bulk of their force from Southeastern Europe and advance through northern Austria in an attempt to seize Salzburg and threaten Southern Germany, the industrial heartland of Germany and the EU."

The General could have used graphics to demonstrate the movement of troops, but he preferred to use large sweeping motions of his hands for dramatic effect as he spoke. He continued, "The 2nd Shock Army is going to advance across two points: the first, central Germany towards Dresden and Leipzig, and the second, to the North of Berlin. They will drive to Hamburg, the deep water shipping port so critical to keeping the NATO forces supplied. The northern half of Germany is relatively flat, which plays to our advantage in terms of using our tanks. We have given this attack the codename Operation Red Anvil."

"As we speak, General Kulikov has already put into motion the beginning of Operation Red Anvil. The bombardments of the frontlines are taking place now, and his armored forces will begin to advance in seventytwo hours."

Fradkov pondered, "This will be the largest armored assault in history, won't it?"

"Yes, Mr. President." Minister Puchkov puffed out his chest with pride.

"Well...I guess that leaves us with the IR--our misbehaving stepsister."

No one wanted to speak to this point. The Russians had been paid nearly $3 Trillion NAD by the IR over the last ten years to build up and train their military force. The investment had caused an economic revival in Russia; however, despite the amount of equipment sold to the IR (and the years of training and mentoring the Russian military provided), the IR had nearly destroyed their entire military within seven-months (granted, they had been in constant combat with the Israeli and American Forces).

Puchkov dared to answer. "Well, sir, the IR possesses all of the world's most modern equipment to defeat the Israeli and American Forces; however, what they lack is an experienced officer and NCO cadre, not to mention a military ethos and warrior culture like that of the Israelis and Americans. If nothing else, we all know the Americans and Israelis to be exceptional military fighters--fearless in combat, and able to operate effectively in large and small units. For all the training that we and the Chinese have provided, the one thing that we simply cannot instill in the Arab Army is the character and attitude required by a true warrior. By and large, the IR Army operates in more of a mob mentality...this becomes disastrous when a unit or group leader is killed during a battle or engagement."

General Gerasimov picked up from here. "Fortunately for us, the Middle East campaign is not really a primary theater of operations; rather, it was meant to tie down American Forces and prevent them from employing those resources in Europe, or having the necessary forces to prevent our Russian-Chinese joint invasion of Alaska. We continue to maintain 150,000 troops in central and northern Turkey and a blocking force in the Caucuses. Most of these armies were loosely scattered across key strategic locations in Turkey to protect the Black Sea. Our situation there is stable at this time, and we have to consider our position there to be at a standstill."

President Fradkov was not at all upset by this response. Instead, he pulled out a bottle of vodka to share. Things were going very well for him and his comrades.

Tank Pressure Cooker

19 June 2041

Brandenburg, Germany

The 2nd Armored Division (2AD), also known as the "hell on wheels" division (they were given the nickname by General Patton himself back in World War II); it was one of many WWII divisions being reactivated to form the American 5th and 6th Armies in Europe. 2AD was one of only two divisions equipped solely with the venerable Pershing Main Battle Tanks (MBT)s in Europe. They had not seen combat as their sister division, 12AD, had at the German border. Their last battalion of tanks came in a week ago; they were finally ordered to move forward, just as the Russians began their massive bombardment of the frontlines. Anticipation hung in the air.

Within the 2AD, Colonel Mica Aaron, was the 66th armor regiment commander-- the second highest ranking officer in the division, next to the commanding general. He was a career officer, and a graduate of the Army's prestigious West Point. Colonel Aaron had been a brigade commander during the invasion of Mexico, and was in line to get his General's Star in the near future. When the Army reactivated the 2AD, he had been selected to be the brigade commander for one of just five Pershing brigades in Europe. Being single, he was able to devote his entire life to the Army and his trade, armored warfare. When it came to tank combat strategies, he was the best in the Army.

Intelligence indicated the Russians were going to start a robust summer offensive within the next couple of days, so the 66th AR was being deployed near Brandenburg to stop a potential Russian armored thrust. Since Berlin had been turned into a 'free city' to avoid having it torn to pieces in a house-to-house fight, it was now just a big obstacle in the way of both sides' armored groups as they maneuvered to attack each other without getting caught in the city. Colonel Aaron had 192 Pershings, 260 infantry fighting vehicles, and other armored support vehicles in his brigade (such as the armored ambulances, ammunition carriers, fuel tankers, etc.). His unit was facing at least two Russian armored divisions that had between 600 and 900 T14 and T38 MBTs (along with their support vehicles)...that meant nearly 4:1 odds against them.

Lieutenant Colonel George Lewis was the 66th AR's executive officer (XO); during the invasion of Mexico he had served as a battalion commander for Colonel Aaron...now he was being groomed to take over as brigade commander as soon as his promotion to Colonel came through. As LTC Lewis walked towards the Command vehicle, he could hear the artillery in the distance start to slacken. After nearly three days of being bombarded, the brigade was starting to get antsy waiting for the eventual tank battle that was shaping up to be one of history's most epic tank conflicts.

The IFV that was acting as the Command vehicle was crammed with computer screens, radios, and soldiers, all attentively watching events around the brigade unfold. LTC Lewis spotted Colonel Aaron and signaled for him to exit the vehicle so he could pass along the information he had just received from Division HQ.

Colonel Aaron cut straight to the chase, "LTC Lewis, anything of interest from division?"

"Sir, the drones and signals intelligence are reporting a massive troop and armor movement by the Russians. It is believed that once the artillery bombardment stops, the Russians will begin to advance," LTC Lewis said.

Looking back into the Command vehicle, Colonel Aaron asked one of his Captains, "Are the drones showing any armored movements towards our position yet?"

Zooming out with the drone camera that the Captain was controlling, he quickly looked for signs of new enemy activity. "Sir, I am starting to see at least one brigade-sized armor element moving forward. Behind that unit are a number of others lining up. It looks as if they are getting ready to launch their offensive." The Captain was clearly a bit nervous as he spoke, drumming his fingers faster and faster as he continued.

Colonel Aaron wasted no time. "Looks like division was right, order the tanks into their fighting positions now!"

Turning back to LTC Lewis, he directed, "I want you to get to the alternate Command Post and be ready to take over in case my CP is taken out, OK?"

"Yes Sir! We'll be ready, and I'll continue to monitor the armor units moving towards us. If we spot anything unusual, we'll let you know." Then LTC Lewis turned and began to run towards the vehicle that would take him to the alternate CP. The brigade ran two active CPs--in case one was destroyed, the other could pick things up and continue the fight without a loss in leadership continuity. This was something that had worked extremely well in Israel, where CPs and military leadership were constantly being killed. The casualty rate among officers and senior NCOs had been horrific, resulting in a lot of battlefield promotions, much like had occurred during World War II. This strategic decision to have an alternate means of running operations had proven to be a key factor in defeating the IR, so all throughout Europe, all the major battle headquarters were enacting this approach.

****

Staff Sergeant Marshal was the tank commander (TC) for Alpha Twelve, one of four Pershing tanks in second platoon, Alpha Company. SSG Marshal had just received word to move forward to their firing positions and be ready to engage the Russian MBTs that should be to their front. As they moved their tanks into the berm, PFC Tanner (who was manning the tanks' targeting computer) said in an excited voice, "Enemy tanks identified! Four-miles to our front."

Typically, when a tank unit establishes a defensive position, engineers will carve an embankment out of the terrain for the tanks to pull in to. This type of position keeps the majority of the tank protected, and only exposes the turret. This way, a tank can fire between two to four shots at one location and then back out of that spot and move to the next berm, repeating the process for as long as the battle lasts. This keeps the tank from becoming a stationary target and turning into a bullseye for artillery and air strikes.

SSG Marshal began to issue orders to the rest of his crew. "Prepare to engage!" he directed

Within seconds, the platoon commander (PC) called in on the coms, "Engage the enemy tanks now!"

At this point, the Russian tanks were advancing quickly across the countryside, trying to close the distance between their lines and the American positions in order to get within range of their own guns. The Pershings, with their railgun, had an enormous reach advantage over their Russian counter-parts. In flat and open terrain, the Pershing could hit targets as far away as twenty miles.

"Target identified! Russian T14 MBT," yelled PFC Turner.

"Fire!" shouted SSG Marshal.

A low winding sound could be heard as the railgun charged and then--BOOM! The projectile was launched from the barrel at Mach 10, creating an immediate sonic boom. Soon, dozens of sonic booms could be heard as the rest of the platoon began to engage the Russians.

"Target identified. T15 IFV," said PFC Turner. His voice sounded calmer now that they had engaged and destroyed half a dozen tanks.

"Fire!" Marshal ordered. "Gunner, fire at will. I'm going topside to get the machine gun ready to support our infantry.

The Russians fired dozens of their new artillery smoke rounds at the American lines. These projectiles had a special chemical in them that greatly reduced thermal images within the smoke. The Russians and Americans had recently developed similar weapons as a means of defeating each other's thermal scopes. Alpha Company had destroyed nearly 67 T14s before the Russians started to plaster the American tank lines with smoke canisters. The smoke was starting to have a serious effect on the Pershings…their rate of fire began to drop significantly. Russian T15 IFVs rushed forward with the tanks to get their infantry units as close to the American lines as possible; they were hoping to engage the Pershings with their anti-tank missiles. As the battle moved away from a long-distance shooting match between the tanks and anti-tank missiles, the Russians began to get close enough for their IFVs to start engaging the American infantrymen a hundred yards or so in front of the Pershings.

As the smoke finally started to clear, SSG Marshal saw several T15 IFVs heading directly towards the infantrymen positioned in front of his tank. He quickly sent a message to Tanner to have him focus on the closer IFVs and then go after the tanks once the immediate threat was taken care of. Just as Marshal finished sending his message, he saw an anti-tank missile leave its launcher, heading right for him. He quickly ducked into the turret, just as the projectile hit their armor. The missile didn't penetrate the armor, but the impact shook everyone up inside the tank.

Turner recovered quickly, and destroyed all three IFVs before their tank was hit by another enemy tank round. This time, the projectile bounced off the armor.

"Driver, back us out of here and go to the next fighting position now!" yelled Marshal. He did not want to become a sitting duck. Just as their tank pulled out of its position, several artillery rounds hit the berm. Had they stayed there even ten seconds longer, they would have been utterly destroyed.

They continued on in their fight, firing several times and then weaving along to their next location. As they pulled into their fourth firing position of the day, a T14 fired a Sabot round, hitting their left track. The impact destroyed the track wheel and crushed the track itself. They were now stuck, half in and half out of their new firing position.

"Guys, we're trapped! Turner, keep firing and take out those IFVs; we need to support the infantry. Driver, I want you out of the vehicle to get on the machine gun turret, so we can start providing cover to the infantry," Marshal said as he lifted the commander's hatch to start using the M2 .50 mounted on the turret. With the vehicle out of commission, there was no reason to have the driver sit in the tank with nothing to do.

SSG Marshal saw dozens of Russian infantry moving closer to the American lines. They were firing feverishly at the Americans, trying to keep their heads down while others advanced. Marshal turned the M2 towards the largest group of soldiers he saw, which were about 300 yards away, and immediately began to engage them, sending two to five second bursts from the M2. The .50 caliber slugs punched right through the trees and other objects the Russian infantry were using for cover. Just as Marshal turned to say something to his driver (who had crawled up to join him using the machine gun located above the gunner's hatch), his head exploded and his body went limp, falling back into the tank. He had been hit by a Russian sniper.

****

Sergeant Trellis and Private First Class Ye were forward observers for a self-propelled artillery battalion that was assigned to support the 66th AR. They were operating in Alpha Troop area, where they could provide artillery support to both Alpha and Bravo Troop.

"Here they come," said PFC Ye as he spat a stream of tobacco on the ground near his boot. He never took his eyes off the enemy tanks heading towards them.

"I see them. Let's call in the first set of rounds and get those tankers to button up. No need to make their life any easier," Sergeant Trellis responded as he reached over to grab the radio handset.

Speaking into the handset, Trellis advised, "This is Ghost 2, we have eyes on enemy tanks...count is roughly sixty...request one round high explosive (HE) at grid..."

"This is Reaper 6. We copy. One round HE...grid...." acknowledged the voice from the Fire Direction Control (FDC) vehicle, which coordinated all of the fire missions for the battalion.

"Shot out..." confirmed the FDC a minute later. This meant that the round was on its way.

"Splash," said the FDC, thirty seconds later. The artillery round was now less than five seconds away from impact.

"Splash out," replied Sergeant Trellis, watching the area where the round should impact.

BOOM! The round landed exactly where they wanted, a couple hundred yards in front of the enemy advance.

"Round right on target. Fire for effect. WP, three rounds out," said Trellis, calling in the next round of artillery fire. White phosphorus (WP) rounds were designed to ignite in an airburst about a hundred feet above their intended target; they would force the enemy tank commanders to duck back inside their tanks and button them up, in order to avoid getting burned by the WP in the air. The effect of this attack would be that the enemy commanders would not be able to see and identify targets as easily.

"Reaper 6, targets hit. Adjust fire. Drop 500 meters, adjust 200 meters to the right...fire three rounds HE ground impact out," said Trellis. This new artillery strike he was calling in was closer to the Bravo Troops' position.

"Sergeant Trellis, we need to move. That's three firing missions in this position," advised PFC Ye. He quickly moved to the driver's side door and opened it, climbing in.

"You are right. Let's ditch this taco stand before the Russians throw a few rounds our direction," Trellis responded as he quickly moved around to the passenger seat. Just as he was closing the door, they heard a loud whistling noise, and before either of them could react, three artillery rounds exploded near their vehicle, shredding it with shrapnel and instantly killing the two of them.

****

LTC Lewis watched on the monitor as the Russians continued to advance. He was surprised to see them continue to rush forward despite the horrific losses they were taking. Nearly an entire tank battalion had been wiped out in the first five minutes of the engagement, and a second and then third tank battalion took their place. The Russians were trying to overwhelm the American tanks by rushing as many of their own tanks and IFVs as possible.

Suddenly, the radio in LTC Lewis's helmet came alive, and he saw an image of Colonel Aaron. "Lewis, it looks like the Russians are about to break through Alpha Troop's position. I'm calling in additional artillery and I'm going to see if we can't get a few Razorbacks as well. I need you to guide Delta Troop into Alpha's position and plug that hole," Colonel Aaron ordered.

"Roger that Sir. We just sent a couple of drones to Alpha's position, so it shouldn't be a problem," Lewis responded, signaling for one of the staff officers to send a message to Delta Troop to tell them to move forward. In the meantime, they revved up their own tank to join the fray.

Colonel Aaron had held one of his tank company's back as a mobile reserve force in order to plug up any holes in their defensive line. Now it was time to call in an artillery strike. Colonel Aaron signaled for his FIST officer (Fire Support Team). The FIST officer's job was to coordinate artillery missions for the Regiment from his own artillery battalion along with the Forward Observers assigned to the various Troops. After losing several forward observers, the

FIST Liaison Officer (LNO) immediately called in an Arrowhead strike.

Essentially the Arrowheads were "smart" munitions, meaning they could be fired in the general vicinity of the enemy, and as the round would complete its arc heading back towards the objective, it would begin to identify specific targets. In milliseconds, the round would distinguish between a tank and an IFV, and would automatically target the tank unless it were programmed to do otherwise. It would even calculate which of the surrounding tanks had the least amount of armor and move to attack that tank first. As the round neared the target, it would detonate the first shape charge, which would hit the top of the turret or engine compartment. This first charge was meant to activate the tank's reactive armor, leaving a hole where it once was; then the second shape charge would fire into the newly created gap in the reactive armor and punch right through the turret into the crew compartment. This entire process would happen within milliseconds, with devastating effectiveness.

As soon as the artillery battalion fired off a three-round barrage, they quickly began to move to their next firing position. Russian counter-battery fire started to land where they had just been. Knowing that the Americans may have moved quickly, the Russians began to saturate the area with artillery fire, finding one of the self-propelled artillery vehicles and destroying it and two other support vehicles. The constant counter-battery fire from the Russians was making it incredibly difficult for the American artillerymen to support the tanks and infantry who were fighting tooth and nail on the frontlines.

After eight hours of fighting near Brandenburg, the Americans had to withdraw and cross the Elbe River, where they would make their next stand. Colonel Aaron's brigade had started the battle with 192 Pershings; so far they had lost 49. However, his brigade had destroyed 492 T14s and 590 T15 IFVs. They had effectively destroyed two entire Russian brigades while sustaining a casualty rate of 25%.

****

The UK's 16th Air Assault Brigade (AAB) was Britain's rapid response unit, much like the American 82nd Airborne Division. The 16th AAB was rushed to the Elbe River once it became clear that the Americans were going to have to retreat across it. They had been held in reserve in case this situation became a reality, and now it had. Their objective was to provide maneuver and fire support to the armored and mechanized infantry units as they moved across the various bridges and pontoon bridges before the engineers dropped them.

Sergeant Michael Stonebridge was a sniper with the reconnaissance section of the Pathfinder group. His spotter, Corporal Brent Scott, had been assigned an over watch position several hundred meters behind one of the bridgeheads. Their objective was to take out enemy infantry as they approached the area, or call in what they were seeing to their higher headquarters.

They positioned themselves under their ghillie suits (special sniper suits designed to camouflage these soldiers with the grass in the surrounding area, to the point that they would be virtually invisible while still). They began to deploy their spotting scope and their L115A3 sniper rifle. The L115 fired a .338 cartridge and had an effective range of 2,000 meters. For their operation, they had a 25x scope with a suppressor to help reduce the muzzle flash of their rifle when it was fired.

As they laid prone in their fighting position, they could hear the rumble of the battle move closer and closer to their position until they spotted the first sign of the American units retreating. At first, it was a collection of ambulances carrying the wounded; then came a battalion of self-propelled artillery, who quickly fired off a barrage of rounds once they crossed the river before scurrying behind the 16th AAB's position. Then came several battalions' worth of light and mechanized infantry; the soldiers looked exhausted and beat up, but determined to continue fighting. They immediately took up defensive positions all along the shoreline and began to prepare for the next assault. The final group to cross the bridges were the heavy armor units. Nearly four dozen Pershing MBTs made it across the river before the remaining Pershings still on the enemy side of the bank began to return fire and engage the advancing Russian units. Slowly and steadily, they all made it across the river before the engineers blew the bridges apart just as Russian Infantry Fighting Vehicles and other armored vehicles appeared at the outskirts of the city.

Sergeant Stonebridge immediately began to search for targets; his spotter found several soldiers positioning an anti-tank missile system on the roof of a building several blocks away from the bridge. It was a long shot, maybe 1,900 meters. He carefully took aim, adjusted for wind, moisture and every other aspect one does when preparing to fire a shot from maximum range. Their target was not the soldiers themselves, but rather the equipment they were setting up. A soldier could be replaced if killed--a critical piece of equipment could not. Stonebridge found what he was looking for, the laser guidance box on the missile system. He closed his other eye, let out a deep breath and squeezed the trigger. In the flash of a second, he saw the bullet hit the guidance box, exploding it into pieces. The Russian soldier who had been looking through it also died immediately.

As more and more Russian vehicles and soldiers poured into the area, the snipers found themselves in a target-rich environment. They quickly fell into a routine, firing four or five shots from one position before moving to another one and then repeating the process.

Brains of the Operation
NATO Headquarters
Brussels, Belgium

The Supreme Allied Commander Europe (SACEUR), General Aaron Wade, was sitting in his office reading over battlefield reports when Major General Charles Bryant from the British Army knocked on the doorframe and then entered his office. MG Bryant was the senior British LNO to NATO, and General Wade's right-hand man. General Wade had been the SACEUR Commander for only two days when the war with Russia started on Christmas Day of 2040. MG Bryant had been critical in helping General Wade make a successful transition to NATO, since he had previously been the CENTCOM Commander.

"Sir, we are starting to get the final numbers from the Russian offensive near Brandenburg. We are also updating the maps with enemy unit locations and strengths. I really think you should see this Sir," MG Bryant said, indicating to General Wade that he should come with him to the main briefing and map room.

Sighing deeply, General Wade nodded and got up from his chair; he began to follow Bryant down the hall to the Operations Center (OC). This was the room where all of the major decisions for NATO were taking place. The room was large; it was shaped almost like an amphitheater, with rows of desks that descended in a semi-circle down towards the platform stage at the bottom. Along the front wall of the room were enormous screens, broken down into several feeds. The first was a massive colored map with NATO and Russian ground unit identifiers, along with their strengths and dispositions. The second was the same type of color-coded map, except this one showed NATO and Russian air units. The third screen was reserved for FLASH messages, drone feeds or briefings, and the fourth was the naval situation.

Seated in each row of the amphitheater was a Senior LNO from each of the NATO member nations that had air, ground and naval combat units actively involved in the fight. There were also other specialists such as Special Forces, Communications, Cyber, Public Affairs and Military Police. From this room, the entire war effort was being run and coordinated; General Wade could issue a command and have that nation's military respond immediately without delay. The location had been established within the first few weeks of the war. Germany had nearly been lost during the first month of the war because of delays in France, Spain and Belgium; this situation was rectified quickly once President

Stein, PM Bedford and Chancellor Mueller from Germany got involved and established a clear chain of command and a location to serve as the OC.

"General Wade, as you can see from the map near Brandenburg, the Russians have pushed our forces to the Elbe River. After crossing the river and setting up our next defensive line, we blew up all of the bridges that cross the Elbe, across all of Germany. The Russians are going to capture Dresden, and they look to be pushing towards Leipzig. In the north they are pushing past Perleberg along Highway 14 heading towards Hamburg. I don't need to tell you how big a blow losing Hamburg would be." As General Bryant walked General Wade through the Russian advance, units and likely objectives, it was clear the Russians were trying to cut Germany up into thirds, making it significantly harder for NATO to defend against their attacks.

General Wade thought for a minute before responding, "We need to stop their advance towards Hamburg; we cannot lose that deep-water port right now. Here is what I want you to do…"

General Wade began to use his laser pointer. "I want to focus our aircraft, in particular our Razorbacks, in the north. Pull aircraft from the other fronts, along with all of our Razorbacks. I want to attack the Russians with everything we have in the north. I also want as much of our artillery as we can spare to be moved north in order to engage the Russians as well." He began to highlight a number of units, and drew a line for where he wanted each of them to be directed.

He continued, "The 12th AD has joined forces with the German divisions, and is fighting the Russians in central Germany near Leipzig. Since the Russians are not looking to move across the Elbe, I want the 2nd AD moved north to cross the Elbe at Lauanburg and advance to attack the Russians. They are going to take some losses, but I want them to hit the Russians hard in order to stop their advance. They will have nearly all of the Razorbacks in Europe (and the vast majority of our aircraft) to support them. Ensure that the artillery continues to advance with them as well," General Wade said.

"Sir, I recommend we also send the British King's Royal Hussars, the Royal Tank Regiment (RTR). They are near Hamburg right now; rather than leaving them there to defend the city, I'd like to have them advance with the 2nd AD," MG Bryant advised.

Looking through the information and then back at the map, General Wade thought a minute before responding, "Yes, send them as well to support the 2nd AD. Their 620

MBTs will be greatly needed. Oh--by the way, isn't that Britain's most famed tank regiment?" asked General Wade.

Smiling, General Bryant replied, "Yes sir it is. It's also the oldest tank unit in the world."

"Excellent, then begin to issue the orders. At the rate the Russians are moving, they are going to be at the outskirts of Hamburg in the next couple of days. We need to start our counter-attack before then. Can the 2nd AD and the Royal Hussars be ready to attack in 48 hours?"

"If the Hussars lead the attack, then yes, the 2nd AD can follow right behind them and pass through their lines once their regiments are all across the Elbe."

"Excellent, then make it happen. I also want our air forces to start pounding the tar out of them immediately. We need to try and slow them down a bit," General Wade said as he indicated the meeting was over. "I need to get something to eat before I collapse from exhaustion. I'm heading to the mess hall--would you like to join me?"

"I'll meet you there in a few minutes; I want to get these orders issued first," Bryant said. He immediately began to get things moving by signaling for a number of the various LNOs to come gather around him.

"I'll see you there then," Wade replied as he turned and began to leave the OC to head to the mess hall. The

NATO headquarters had an exceptional Dining Facility (DFAC) for the thousands of people who worked there; today the DFAC was serving skirt steak with baked potatoes. It was just the kind of "brain food" that General Wade needed.

Sky Full of Drones

20 June 2041
Lakenheath, England
Royal Air Force Base

Major Theodore Cruse (aka 'Cruiser') had just been promoted to Flight Commander of 2nd Flight, 5th Fighter Interceptor Squadron, 5th Fighter Wing stationed at Lakenheath. He flew the Air Force's F38A fighter drone aircraft, which had become the mainstay aircraft for the Air Force in the war. Cruse had joined the Air Force through the ROTC program at the University of Texas in Austin as a means of paying for his degree in aeronautical engineering. His long-term goal was to go into aircraft design and work for one of the big aircraft manufacturers. While on active duty, he had also been working towards his Master's degree in aeronautical engineering and aircraft design as well. With school and all of the officer training and flight courses, Cruse had yet to find time to have a girlfriend, instead focusing his limited time and energies on achieving his dreams. Then the war broke out, and he suddenly found himself flying near constant combat missions, first in Mexico and then in Europe against the Russians. So far, he'd lost three fighter drones while having shot down twenty-three enemy fighter drones and nine manned fighters, including one MiG40. This made him one of the first Aces in his squadron (and one of the few pilots) to have shot down a new Russian MiG. For his achievements thus far, he had been awarded the Distinguished Flying Cross and a Bronze Star.

On this the 200th day of World War III, Major Cruse was informed that his flight had been chosen to receive the new F41 Archangel fighter drone, which would be ready for service in thirty days. The F41 Archangel fighter would be the first fighter to leverage the new EmDrive propulsion system. After receiving his initial briefing on the new drone's capabilities, he could not wait to start training on the new platform. The pilots in his flight were pretty excited about being the first to receive the new aircraft as well.

After returning back to the squadron bay from their briefing about the F41, their Commander walked into the room and quieted everyone down so he could speak. "Listen up everyone. I know you all are excited about our new aircraft, but we have a high priority mission. The ground pounders are preparing for a massive counterattack against the Russians, starting in twelve hours. The Reds have been on a tear lately, heading towards Hamburg and central Germany. I want to draw your attention to the display." The Colonel turned on the briefing monitor in the day room and brought up a map of Germany, showing the current Russian offensive.

"Our squadron has been assigned to fly fighter cover for the ground attack aircraft and Razorbacks. They are going to be going after the Russian armor to try to butter them up before our armored forces start their counterattack. I want you all to turn in and get some sleep; we start flying in nine hours, and it's going to be a long couple of days. I'll see you guys in flight operations in seven hours. Dismissed." The Colonel signaled for everyone to stop what they were doing and get some rest. They would be getting little sleep over the next several days while the counterattack was underway.

Seven hours later, Major Cruse walked into the flight operations center and found the rest of his pilots there waiting. He walked over to the briefing lectern and began, "All right men, you all know the drill. We'll form up over London before heading across the Channel and take up our position over Brussels. Once we get the go ahead, we'll head towards Hamburg and begin to aggressively patrol the area for enemy MiGs. Chances are, we are going up against MiG40s, so be ready for them. Our fighters have been equipped with the new radars and missiles, so we should see them just like any other aircraft. Also, our missiles should be able to track them. This will be our first engagement using the new radar and missiles, so let's hope they work." As he spoke, the Major looked each of his pilots in the eye.

"Remember, the guys on the ground are counting on us to keep those MiG40s off their back. If your aircraft gets shot down, grab another from the reserve pool. Each pilot will have two drones available in the reserve pool, which will be loitering over Brussels."

Because the F38As were drones, a second and third set of drones were going to be flown to what the Air Force had established as an aerial drone pool, which usually idled a couple hundred miles away from a major air operation. This enabled the pilots to activate a new drone from the pool and get back into the fight quickly. The advent of fighter and bomber drones had completely revolutionized the way air combat was being fought; the drones were more maneuverable, and carried more weapons and fuel, which gave the pilots a much greater ability than the previous manned aircraft could offer. The Air Force still flew the F22 Raptors and the JF35 Joint Strike Fighters, though the reliance on drones in the future was clearly written on the proverbial wall.

As the briefing ended, the pilots began to walk towards their flight pods and complete their pre-flight

114

checklists. The flight pods looked very similar to flight simulators, though they were much smaller, more like an actual cockpit. As the drone flew and made tight turns, dove or climbed, the pod would mimic the maneuver, giving the pilot the very real sense that they were actually flying in an aircraft. The pod would even simulate the feeling of a missile or bomb detaching from the aircraft and the sounds and sensations of the onboard machine gun being fired. Making the pod feel as real as possible helped the pilots to react just as they would in a real aircraft, and kept everything from feeling so detached like a video game. This greatly enhanced the survivability of the drones and made them that much more lethal.

Within half an hour, Major Cruse's flight was airborne and loitering 40,000 ft. above London. Once all the aircraft were there, they began to move as a group to Brussels and wait for their orders to begin their patrol over Hamburg and the surrounding area.

"Major Cruse, this is flight operations. Do you copy?" asked a male voice over the HUD.

"This is Flight Leader Cruse. Go ahead, over."

"Your Flight has been cleared to begin patrolling over Hamburg; you are to patrol at 45,000 feet and engage any hostiles you identify. You are not to descend below

15,000 feet. Ground systems will be attacking enemy aircraft below that altitude. Do you copy?"

"Copy flight operations. We are advancing to Hamburg. Will maintain patrolling altitude of 45,000 feet. Will not descend below 15,000 feet, out."

Turning his coms to the rest of his flight, Major Cruse directed "All right gentlemen and ladies, we just received our go order. We are to begin patrolling above Hamburg at 45,000 feet; no one is to descend below 15,000 feet. Ground systems will engage enemy fighters below that ceiling. Acknowledge."

"Copy that," said the pilots as the group began to maneuver their aircraft to the new altitude and heading.

Fifteen minutes after arriving above the skies of Hamburg, the Airborne Warning and Control System (AWACS) aircraft that was operating two hundred miles behind their position spotted several dozen drones, along with at least ten MiG40s heading towards Major Cruse's flight. Within minutes, that number rose to over 120 drones and 20 MiG40s and 50 Su38s. The Russians were starting to flood the sky with drones and fighters as they spotted the massive armada of ground attack fighters and helicopters heading towards their ground forces. The battle for the skies was about to heat up again.

Major Cruse activated his Electronic Countermeasures (ECM) and began to engage a MiG40 that was maneuvering to attack one of his flight mates. He toggled his missiles and activated two of his AMRAAMs and fired. Both missiles leapt from his drone and began to head towards the MiG. At first the MiG pilot appeared to ignore the missiles, assuming that his stealth abilities would win out just as they always had in the past. Unfortunately for him, just as he realized it was not going to work, both missiles impacted against his aircraft, blowing him to pieces. This was the first air-to-air engagement with the new AMRAAMs and the radar systems that had been specifically designed to go after the new MiG40s. Within minutes, their effect was made known--all 20 MiG40s were shot down in quick succession before the Americans switched over and began to engage the enemy drones and Su38s. After nearly two hours of air-to-air combat and two additional drones, Major Cruse's squadron was ordered back to their bases in England. The American and British Air Forces lost 342 F38A drones, 63 F22s and 57 JF35s. The Russians had lost 58 MiG40s, 196 Su38s and 432 SU39FD or Fighter Drones. The Allies had not won the day, but they had provided enough air cover for 250 Razorback helicopters, over 350 F38B ground attack drones and 210 A10 Warthogs to maul the Russian armored advance as it headed towards Hamburg, just as the American and British counterattack began in earnest. The Russians had lost over 1,400 MBTs, 2,800 LDTs and 3,000 other assorted armored vehicles and IFVs.

Killjoy

21 June 2041
Cooper Landing, Alaska

While the American and British counteroffensive was taking place in Europe, the fight for Alaska against the Chinese and Russians continued unabated. The Americans had fought tooth and nail for every inch of land they gave up on the Anchorage Peninsula, finally falling back to a series of defensive works established at Cooper Landing on Highway 1 in the Chugach State Park. This location was just miles away from the city of Anchorage itself. The inlet leading to Anchorage was so heavily mined, the Chinese decided against moving any ships through it until after the PLA had captured Anchorage and they could bring in proper minesweeper ships to make the channel usable again.

On June 10th, the PLA had begun to land a large force of armor and troops on the west side of the channel across from Kalgin Island (once the Americans lost the city of Sterling along Hwy 1, it created an opening for them to move in). This second offensive force was having to fight through a lot of rough terrain; numerous American firebases and other defensive works were making the journey to Anchorage slow and bloody. The ideal way to get at

Anchorage was along Highway 1 and then cut behind the city, sealing it off from any reinforcements while the Navy and Air Force continued to pound them into submission. Their ultimate goal was to secure from Eureka to Valdez, effectively cutting Alaska off from the rest of the country. Then they could focus on rooting out the remaining Americans left in the State before advancing into the Canadian States and the rest of America.

The 12th Infantry Division, like the other divisions on the Peninsula, had fallen back to the massive defensive fortifications that the Corps of Engineers had built in Cooper Landing. The engineers had built several hardened trench lines along the approach to the low-lying mountain ranges. These trenches had multiple heaving gun emplacements, lined with M134 Miniguns, M2 .50 Cals, and 20mm Railguns. At the base of the mountain, the Army Corp of Engineers had constructed a small series of tunnels and tracks, mounting over a hundred 155mm Howitzers to the tracks so that they could fire several rounds and then retreat back under the protection of the mountain.

Once the enemy fought their way through to the base of the mountain, they would have to capture a series of trench lines and fortifications all the way up to the top of the mountain and into the valley on the other side, and then repeat the process again until they had cleared all five mountain ridges. General Black had over 180,000 soldiers defending this position while additional soldiers prepared the next layer of defenses further back around Palmer. If it looked like the Chinese were going to break out, then the rest of his forces in Anchorage would make a hasty retreat so as to not be cut off and surrounded. The same would go for the troops defending the mountain lines along Susitna, 20 miles west of Anchorage.

With the new radar and missiles systems that could track the Russian MiG40s, the number of high altitude precision bombings against the American laser and railgun defensive systems was finally coming to an end. This had been a serious problem; in the last six months, US Forces had lost nearly 60% of their anti-air, anti-missile defensive systems. The Allies had yet to achieve or maintain anything close to air superiority since the start of the war until the new radar had been built.

****

SSG Paul Allen had done his best to keep the soldiers in his platoon alive and to stop the Chinese from capturing Alaska. Unfortunately, his platoon had been mauled; while they had started out with 56 soldiers at the outset of the invasion, they were now down to 17. They had become a shell of their former self. The 12th Infantry Division had been pulled from the line and reorganized as new units and soldiers continued to arrive from the rest of the country. During this reorganization, the division took some time to recognize the bravery of the soldiers and units who had defended the landing beaches against the PLAN. SSG Paul Allen had been awarded the Army's Distinguish Service Cross for his actions during the initial beach invasion, one medal below the Congressional Medal of Honor. Three other soldiers from the division had received the same medal as Paul, along with nearly four dozen Silver Stars and over 150 Bronze Stars with V device for Valor.

Because SSG Allen had close to sixty college credits completed, he had been given a battlefield promotion to 1st Lieutenant, making him the executive officer for the company and the 2nd Platoon Commander (PC). His battalion had been selected to receive the new Raptor combat suit, which was finally set to make its debut. The 12th Infantry Division was going to be pulled off the line while two battalions at a time would be rotated back to the US to be equipped and trained on the new suit before being sent back to Alaska.

US manufacturers had been working overtime to produce the Raptor combat suits to get them into the fight as quickly as possible. The training to become proficient in their use had been determined to be around one week, with a second week to learn how to use it with a weapon and a soldier's additional combat equipment. The plan was to rotate several battalions at a time through training, and then slowly integrate them back in to the war. The highest priority for the Raptor suits was the Alaskan front, with the 12th Infantry Division being the first division to receive them. The US could not let the Chinese establish a long-term base of operations in North America. Having to fight on two additional continents was straining the US's ability to fight and win.

Captain Tim Shiller walked up to Lieutenant Allen. "LT, I just received word from battalion; they are pulling us from the line tonight before the Chinese start their attack. They want to get us to Ft. Benning immediately," he said with a hint of a smile.

"You're just glad we won't be here when the Chinese launch their next offensive against this place," Allen said with a smirk of his own.

"Aren't you? We've gone through enough hell these past six weeks. We need a break, some good steaks, women and beer. All of which we'll be able to get at Benning while we complete our training," replied Shiller.

Paul thought for a minute before adding, "Yeah, but as soon as we get the new suits, they are going to throw us right back into the meat grinder. You saw the specs on the new suits. They are going to throw us headfirst at the enemy, thinking we will be invincible, which you and I both know--we aren't."

Laughing, Tim retorted, "You're a real killjoy, you know that Paul? Go inform the rest of the men; we are leaving in half an hour. They are trucking us back to Palmer airport in an hour."

With that, Lieutenant Allen turned and walked towards the day room where most of the Company had been relaxing while they waited to find out if they were going to be moving to the Cooper Landing defenses or somewhere else. He signaled for everyone to be quiet so that he could speak. After the bantering calmed down, he announced, "Listen up everyone! We are pulling out of here and being driven to Palmer Airport. Before you guys start to speculate; we are being sent as a battalion to Ft. Benning to receive training on the new Raptor combat suit." The room suddenly erupted in cheers and jeers as they realized they were going to be leaving the combat zone and heading back to the "real world," even if it was only for a few weeks.

"Hey not to be a spoilsport in all of this, but once we receive the new suits and are determined combat ready, you can bet that we will be deploying back here and you can bet your paycheck we will be leading a counteroffensive against the Chinese." Now the room filled with groans.

"On the bright side, when we do get a night off, first round's on me boys," Allen said to the joy of his soldiers.

Decisions in the Dark

20 June 2041

Japan

The Japanese government was caught between a rock and a hard place with not a lot of options available to them. To date, they had not upheld their defense agreement with the Americans, aside from providing some intelligence and surveillance activity of the Chinese. In May, they were forced to intern the remaining American Forces in Japan or face a military reaction by the Chinese. To prevent the Chinese from viewing them as a threat, Japan signed a non-aggression treaty, which formally ended their mutual defense agreement with the US. Japan had conscripted nearly one million soldiers and began a doubling of their navy, but these efforts would take time to come to fruition; in the meantime, they had to defend their island with the forces they had at hand.

Prime Minister Yasuhiro Hata had been in power now for five years. He had become the PM right after President Stein had won his first election, and had developed a good working relationship with the American President. Japan had benefited greatly from the U.S. economic revival and from the Grain Consortium. The export of American natural gas had also helped to fuel Japan's own economic revitalization of sorts. Despite some angst among his own political party, PM Hata had been instrumental in the modernization of the Japanese Self-Defense Force (SDF) and the navy. With the rise of the Chinese military and navy, it became imperative that Japan be able to defend itself.

When China launched their surprise attack against America, Japan had almost joined the war immediately. However, it was the threat of immediate invasion by the Chinese (along with the destruction of the American Fifth Fleet in the Red Sea, and the American Seventh Fleet at Pearl Harbor) that prevented the Japanese from immediately coming to the Americans' aid. During the first several days of the war, the Chinese had effectively removed American naval power from the equation in the Pacific, leaving Japan isolated and alone.

Both sides had agreed to leave each other alone for the time being. As China gobbled up Southeast Asia, the Japanese continued to build up their own forces. Once the Chinese had launched their invasion of Alaska, it became clear to the leaders of Japan that America was not going to be able to come to their aid should the Chinese turn their military attention towards them. With the Russians laying siege to Europe and America being invaded, it was time for

Japan to reevaluate their standing with China and the U.S. and make sure they are going to be on the winning side of this growing global war.

What really changed the tide, turning Japan away from a position of supporting America, was the overwhelming nuclear response to the destruction of New York and Baltimore. The government had expected the Americans to respond with nuclear weapons; what they did not expect, was the near destruction of the entire Islamic Republic. Over 650 million people had been killed in the nuclear holocaust, and this was simply something the people of Japan and the government could not support. They publicly denounced the attack immediately and even offered medical aid to the IR. This further strained the American/Japanese relationship, but resulted in improved relations with China.

When China had approached the Japanese government about the creation of a greater Pan Asian Alliance, the idea had intrigued them. A loose confederation of nations that would rule Asia and lead the world into the 21st and 22nd centuries had a great appeal to PM Yasuhiro Hata. It could be his legacy achievement, bringing great glory, power and prestige to Japan. The cost to joining this alliance though was the complete betrayal of their friend and ally, America. If they opted to not join, then they would be frozen out of the new PAA economy, currency and potentially face military action.

After a lot of internal consideration, the PM and several of his closest friends, advisors and key members in the government, made the decision to secretly join China in the creation of this confederation. The young emperor of Japan had even gone along with the idea. The thought of Japan being able to be a leader in the greater Pan Asian Alliance was very appealing, even to an emperor who did not have a lot of political power. His spiritual guidance and support would go a long way towards convincing the rest of the population that this was in the best interest of Japan.

Occupation Offer

25 June 2041
Riyadh, Islamic Republic
Central IR Command Post

The state of the IR was near chaos across most of the country, with the exception of Indonesia. The IR had limited electric power and intermittent rolling blackouts were plaguing the Republic; fortunately, several Chinese nuclear-powered ships and a single nuclear-powered Russian cruiser were still in the Gulf and providing power to the IR. It had been six months since the US had carried out their overwhelming nuclear attack across the IR. It had resulted in the provinces of North Africa seceding from the Caliphate in a side deal they made with the Americans. The country was further hurt by the near total destruction of their critical infrastructure, highway and rail systems along with the vast majority of their major ports. There were critical food and water shortages across nearly every major city, with tens of thousands of people dying from thirst and hunger weekly.

Talal bin Abdulaziz was the Foreign Minister for the IR. He had been the one to contact the White House and the President when Caliph Abbas made his demands to President Stein and then detonated a second nuclear device in

America. The Caliph had made a calculated risk that the IR could survive a nuclear exchange with the Americans... he was wrong. The Americans had hit the IR with five 25 Megaton neutron bombs that effectively killed over 250 million people; another 200 million more people were killed in the subsequent conventional nuclear attack and another 200 million would eventually die from radiation poisoning. The loss of so many additional troops and equipment during the second invasion of Israel further compounded the losses for the IR.

Recently, Talal had been contacted by the American Secretary of State with an offer to end the war. Jim Wise had called him on a secure line and calmly laid out the details, "Talal, we know that your country is suffering greatly. We would be willing to accept an unconditional term of surrender from the IR; the U.S. would even provide the Republic with 100 million tons of food a month, for the next three years. In return, you would have to surrender your nuclear arsenal and terminate your military alliance and base rights with both Russia and China. In addition, there would be a 30-mile radius of land around the Israeli border where there would be an Israeli and American military occupation and monitors. You would be allowed to maintain a military force, of course, but one that is no larger than what is needed for territorial defense and internal security."

At first Talal dismissed the offer. "There is no way that the Caliph would agree to this," he replied.

Unabated, Jim Wise had replied, "Well, please think about it. We will give you some time to consider, but don't take too long; this offer may not be on the table if you wait too much before making your decision. I will send you an official dossier on the details of my proposal."

Talal couldn't help but think about the offer; having spent the better part of a week mulling it over, Talal wondered if it might be best to inform the Caliph of the offer and see if he couldn't perhaps persuade him to accept. The IR as a country was falling apart; if they did not do something soon, they were going to lose the country regardless.

Huseen ibn Abdullah Al Gubayel, the Director of Intelligence, pulled Talal aside as they were getting ready for a briefing. "The American and Israeli armies are starting to amass on their border. It appears that they will invade in the coming weeks." He seemed nervous, and he never seemed nervous. "There is little the army can do to stop it, despite whatever protests you may hear from General Rafik Hamza."

"What do you suggest?" asked Talal.

"Islam can still conquer the world; we will just need to wait," he argued.

Talal sat at the briefing table, waiting for the Caliph to enter the room. Everyone from the governing council was present, and judging by the looks on their faces. they all knew the IR was doomed. It was just a matter of time.

Caliph Muhammad Abbas walked into the room and took his seat at the head of the table in his diamond and jewel encrusted gold chair.

He cleared his throat before beginning, "Council members, we have much to discuss today. The state of our Republic is not going to survive unless we make some tough decisions." Caliph Abbas turned to look at his Minister of Industry, Muhammad bin Aziz. "What is the current state of our economy and infrastructure?" he asked.

"The Americans continue to bomb our bridges, rail and road junctions, with little to stop them. Every time we turn on our radars to attack their drones and aircraft, they are quickly destroyed. We have successfully shot down over 150 drones in the last two weeks, but they far outnumber our radar stations. Our losses are just not sustainable."

He took a deep breath before he continued, "As to our economy, we have rolling brownouts throughout the country. We have restarted all of our deactivated power plants, but each time a new one comes on line, the Americans quickly attack or destroy the infrastructure needed to transmit the power. Our only effective production taking place is in the Kuwait region and parts of Iran near the coast. The Russian and Chinese naval ships there have been extremely effective in engaging the American drones and cruise missiles that get near them. I wish I had better news to report, but I do not," said Minister Muhammad as he lowered his head.

Turning to his Foreign Minister, the Caliph inquired, "Minister Aziz, what additional aid can the Russians provide us to help get our power restored and stop the Israeli and American air forces from continually destroying our infrastructure?" He was hoping to hear *some* good news.

Minister Aziz brightened a little, responding, "My Caliph, the Russian Foreign Minister said they can increase food shipments to the Republic via Iran and through Azerbaijan. They can ship us roughly 5 million tons' worth of food products monthly. They are also going to send thirty mobile anti-missiles, and anti-aircraft laser defensive systems (along with the crews for them). Their goal is to help us establish a defensive pattern that should protect southern Iraq, Kuwait and most of Iran, allowing us a chance to rebuild our industrial capabilities. As for additional military aid, they said there is no additional military aid they can provide beyond the laser defensive systems. Their war in Europe is now their primary focus."

The Caliph thought for a moment, *"This will certainly help, but without military aid to stop the Allied air forces, they are going to continue to pound us into the stone age."* Aloud, he sounded much more optimistic as he replied, "This is good news; we can work with what they are willing to provide. What about the Chinese?"

General Hamza was not sure if his reply would satisfy the Caliph. "Now that the Chinese have landed the majority of their ground forces in Alaska, they said they can send an aircraft carrier battle group to the Arabian Gulf. They will have multiple anti-aircraft ships with them; they will be able to provide a lot of aircraft support while we rebuild our air force in Iran. As for ground forces, they are capturing numerous countries in South and Central Africa while the U.S. appears to be distracted with their main focus now in North America. Therefore, the Chinese have no additional ground forces they can send to us."

"What about food and other aid?" asked Talal, the Foreign Minister.

"They are not able to send us this type of aid at this moment," he replied.

General Rafik Hamza added, "Caliph, this aid and support is appreciated, but it will not stop the Israeli and American forces who are now, as we speak, readying to invade our country. There is very little we can do to stop them from capturing Amman or driving further into Saudi Arabia. They have already captured Damascus and appear to be readying an advance into Northern Iraq."

Knowing the military situation needed to be discussed, Caliph Abbas moved the discussion in that direction. "You bring up some major concerns. What are your suggestions?"

"Sir, I recommend that we withdraw our forces to three major points: Fallujah, Mosul and Riyadh. We can turn the cities into fortresses and fight the American and Israeli forces house-to-house if need be," General Hamza said, showing some of his plans on the holographic map for the council members to see.

Clearing his throat and signaling to speak, Talal thought this was as good a time as any to bring up the American proposal. "My Caliph, council members. I was contacted by the American Secretary of State not long ago. He offered us terms of surrender and I would like to brief them to you." Talal hoped he had not just signed his death warrant.

General Hamza was shocked. His face went through a gambit of emotions quickly as he looked surprised, then hurt, and then curious to know what had been offered.

Caliph Abbas on the other hand, had only one reaction. He seethed with anger and broke out into an anti-American, anti-Israeli tirade before he calmed down enough for General Hamza to intervene on Talal's behalf. "Caliph, I believe we should at least hear the offer before we turn it down." He looked around the room for support; several heads nodded in agreement, while a couple of members dismissed this notion altogether.

"What are the terms then?" demanded the Caliph.

"Yes, my Caliph. The Americans broke their offer down into incentives and requirements. I will go through the requirements first, and then the incentives, which I believe everyone will be interested in knowing about." He pulled out his notes before continuing, "Their demands were as follows:

1) The surrender of all nuclear weapons and end our nuclear program, both military and civilian

2) A 30-mile buffer zone of land around the Israeli border, along with the removal of all Arabs and

population living within that buffer zone. The Zionists will actually pay NAD 25,000 to each person above 18 years of age who is being evicted (snickers could be heard from this statement)

3) The demobilization of our military, turning it into a defense force meant only to protect our borders and provide internal security

4) An immediate termination of our military alliance with China and Russia. This would include the removal of all their forces from our territory and access to it

5) The IR would have an Israeli and American military occupation and observers for a period of fifteen-years to ensure our compliance with the terms of the surrender

6) An occupation force of 250,000 soldiers, which would be phased out over the fifteen-year period would be spread throughout the country to ensure our compliance. They would establish several permanent military bases, which would be handed over to us at the end of the occupation."

"Hmm...so these are their demands," said the Caliph, who definitely did not seem at all excited by the idea. "What are their incentives?"

"They are actually quite generous. They would provide the IR with 100 million tons of food products of our choice each month for three years, and then 50 million tons of food products for another twelve years. Their military engineers and contractors would also work with ours to reestablish power throughout the country. However, they also insist on our full support to protect their facilities and occupation forces. They said this would limit the need for them to intervene and find insurgent forces on their own" explained Talal, waiting to hear the overwhelmingly negative response that he believed was coming.

The room remained silent for a few seconds while everyone digested what Talal had just told them. General Hamza was the first to speak. "Caliph, the Chinese and Russians are limited in the assistance they can provide us. Our army is in tatters and our people are starving and dying of thirst. We are coming into the height of summer; things are only going to get worse. This is honestly not that bad of a deal."

Muhammed bin Aziz, the Minister of Industry, added, "If they are willing to provide us engineers and personnel who can help get power reestablished throughout the country, then we should take their offer. The war is lost, let's not lose the country too."

"Enough of this talk of surrender! We have fought too hard to give up now. You all are traitors for even thinking of surrendering!" screamed General Omar Rafi, the Special Operations Commander. He looked to his Caliph for support.

Admiral Jaffa Mustafa slammed his fist on the table, spilling a glass of water, "General Rafi is right. I have sacrificed my entire naval force, over one hundred and fifty thousand sailors. We have nearly destroyed Israel and cost the Americans dearly. I say we continue to fight and bleed them dry."

Talal knew if he wanted this deal to succeed then he needed to intervene quickly. "Caliph, Israel has been virtually destroyed. More than half of their population has been killed. The Americans lost two aircraft carriers and their entire 5th Fleet. We have killed over one hundred thousand American soldiers. We need to look at the long picture and know that this fight, this battle may be over, but the war is not. If the Chinese and Russians do defeat the Americans, then we can restart the war. If the Communists are defeated, then we abide by the terms of the surrender and we rebuild our economy. We restart our military after the occupation ends. Right now we need to focus on saving the country and remaining in power." Talal was very calm and matter-of-fact, contrasting greatly with his screaming counterparts.

The Caliph thought about what Talal said, realizing he was right. He still did not want to surrender though. It just went against everything he had worked towards and every fiber of his being. He turned to Zaheer Akhatar, his personal advisor, and asked, "What are your thoughts?"

Zaheer sighed deeply before responding, "The thought of surrendering churns my stomach, but Talal brings up some good points. We have to be pragmatic at this point my Caliph. We have control of a unified Middle East right now. We need to maintain that control and if we wait until the Americans invade, then chances are we will not only lose, we will lose control of the country and the power we now hold. We have all sacrificed too much to lose the nation we worked so hard to create. I recommend we accept the agreement and rebuild our country." Zaheer and Caliph Abbas had been friends for decades; they had been the ones that developed and executed the plans to unite the Islamic world. His advisor's words carried weight with the Caliph.

Abbas mulled over his thoughts, "*Zaheer is right. We may have lost this war, but we can still win the ideological war as long as the Americans do not break our country up.*"

The Caliph announced his choice to the group. "Everyone, you all have provided sound counsel. We have forever changed America and brought the war to their own streets. We have also thoroughly destroyed Israel, and it will be decades before they recover, if they ever do." Turning to Talal, he said, "Talal, I want you to respond to the Americans. let them know we would like to discuss the terms in greater detail, but in general, we are going to agree to them."

The meeting ended, with some members of the counsel incensed beyond words, and Talal shocked at how he had managed to survive this briefing almost entirely unscathed.

Unintended Consequences

26 June 2041

Washington, DC

White House Situation Room

Secretary of State Jim Wise was elated. It was a longshot trying to persuade the Islamic Republic to surrender. The military, of course, would rather keep the war going and thoroughly crush them. Jim, however, wanted to end this war so all of America's effort could be shifted to fighting the Russians in Europe and repulsing the Chinese invasion in Alaska.

As Jim walked into the Situation Room, he saw the various generals and national security advisors discussing the surrender. All eyes turned towards him. "You really did it this time," Mike Williams, the National Security Advisor, said in a jovial voice.

Smiling, Jim sat down. "It's not signed just yet, but you have to admit Mike--being able to shift those forces to Europe and Alaska is going to greatly aid our cause."

"I'm still against this agreement. They are just going to rebuild and we'll be stuck dealing with this again in 15 or 20 years," General Branson said in a not-too-congenial tone.

Just as the groups with differing points of view were about to start arguing the merits of the plan, the President and his Chief of Staff walked into the room.

"I can see that not everyone is happy about the news," the President said after quickly assessing the facial expressions of everyone in the room as he sat down.

General Branson spoke up first, saying, "It's not that we are not happy about the surrender; we just feel we will end up fighting this same war again later. The surrender leaves their government intact; the Caliph will use the time to rebuild, and we will end up repeating this conflict all over again."

Secretary Wise jumped in, "Not necessarily. First, we will have an occupation force in the country, as well as observers. As long as we do a good job of monitoring them, they will still take several decades to rebuild after the occupation. In the meantime, we have 15 years to help mold and change the IR from the inside out."

"Gentlemen, I asked everyone to pursue their specific courses of actions. The military was ready to invade, and the State Department secured the IR's surrender." The President signaled for one of his aides to bring him a Red Bull; he was still living on caffeine to get through the 20 hour days. Despite the President's own time in the military as a young man, he had never developed the habit of drinking coffee; he just didn't care for the taste of it.

"We are going to move forward with the surrender. The IR has agreed to our terms, terms that everyone in this room came up with and agreed to. General Branson, I want you to have General Gardner determine what units he wants to leave behind for occupation duty and a garrison for Israel. I want the rest of his force made ready for combat operations against the Russians and Chinese."

Sighing slightly but still compliant, the general replied, "I will issue the order immediately." Wanting to change the subject, he inserted, "We should talk about Alaska, Mr. President." He pulled up the holographic map of Alaska and the situation there. "As you can see, the Chinese have disembarked a large armored force near Susitna. We have a large defensive garrison there, so it will take the Chinese some time to get past them. They have also pushed our forces on the Anchor Point Peninsula back to Cooper Landing. This is a very defensible position, with several mountain ranges providing a layered defensive network for us. We have to hold it. If we lose that section, then they will be able to get in behind Anchorage, and more importantly, they will be able to drive straight across the lower portion of the state to Yukon and cut our entire Alaskan force off." The map showed several potential strategies the Chinese forces were expected to use and how they would affect the continued operations in Alaska.

The President asked, "What are we doing to ensure we continue to hold this position?"

"We are rotating the 12th Infantry Division out of the line and sending them to Ft. Benning to receive training on the new Raptor combat suit. Once they are trained, we are going to send them back to Cooper Landing and the Susitna Defensive line, and hope that they are enough to stop the Chinese juggernaut. Following their training, we will pull another division from the line and repeat the process. We need to hold those two anchor points, or our defensive positions in Alaska will become unsustainable."

The DHS Director, Jorge Perez, interjected, "Do we have enough military forces in the State? Are we able to send them additional reinforcements?"

"Well, I'm not for accepting the surrender of the IR; However, it does mean we will have substantially more soldiers and equipment that we can send to Alaska. We have four additional divisions completing their advanced training over the next two weeks. We had allocated three of them to head to Europe and the Middle East, with one heading to Alaska. I can shift them around now and send one to Europe and the other three to Alaska. Our bigger problem is maintaining air superiority. Our fighter drones are slightly better than theirs, mostly due to our ECM capability--but they have numbers on us. Plus, their J38 (which is essentially a fifth generation Su-38) is a real killer. The Chinese took the Russian aircraft and really improved upon it a lot."?

"It always seems to come down to numbers, doesn't it?" mused Monty with a bit of a sigh.

General Branson wanted to reassure everyone in the room. "We knew at the start of this war that the statistics would be against us. The Chinese have 2.3 billion people, and over the last six months alone, their Army has recruited an additional ten million soldiers. Given, most of these soldiers are green-- not nearly as trained as ours nor as equipped as ours. However, they don't have to be, they just have to overwhelm us with their numbers. We have some new weapon systems coming online here shortly; the Wolverine will be ready to deploy to Alaska and Europe in a couple of weeks, and the new Raptor suits are in as well. The first ten Archangel fighters will be ready in a month. As long as we can keep the Chinese from securing a permanent foothold in North America, our oceans will continue to be an advantage to us."

The President stood and signaled for everyone to stay seated; he walked around his chair and stood behind it, leaning over it slightly and resting his hands on top of it. "General Branson is right; we need to stay the course. This war is going to be a marathon, not a sprint. We need to continue to do what we are doing; we cannot lose hope or our will to fight."

He stood up a little straighter as he prepared to make an announcement. "I am also going to start making more regular speeches about the war. Starting every other Monday afternoon, I will hold a one-hour press conference with General Branson where I will go over the successes of the war. On the opposite Monday, I will be holding a press conference with Joyce Gibbs and Jeff Rogers to discuss the economy, jobs and infrastructure projects. As everyone knows, we are going to rebuild New York City and Baltimore from the ground up in new locations (since their present locations are unfortunately going to be unlivable for some time to come). I would like to detail the progress on these projects to the American people. The point is, these meetings are to inspire our nation with hope, and assure them that their government is doing everything in its power to protect them and to end this war, on our terms. With that said, I will get off of my soapbox and let everyone get back to their tasks. Dismissed."

The energy in the room was high after the closing statement by the President. The senior staff were starting to get beaten down with the burden of running the war and everything else, especially in light of the horrific casualties that were still pouring in. Nearly 103,000 Americans had been killed in the Middle East, close to 34,500 Americans had lost their lives in Europe thus far, and 24,543 Americans had died in the Pacific. In less than eight weeks of combat operations in Alaska, another 22,352 more Americans had already been killed. These were just the KIAs; the number of wounded was significantly higher. For a war that was less than nine months old, it was proving to be the bloodiest war in American history. They needed something to believe in again.

****

Same Day

White House, Oval Office

Secretary of Treasury Joyce Gibbs walked into the Oval Office to meet with the President, Jeff Rogers (the Senior White House economic advisor), and Monty, the President's Chief of Staff, to discuss the state of the economy. Fortunately, she had good news to talk about. There was legitimate reason to be optimistic; the economy was really starting to run on all cylinders. With the absence of Asian manufacturers, products still needed to be built and those products were now being made in America, South and Central America, the EU and the UK.

The America First Corporation (AFC) was a real boon for the country. As a sovereign wealth fund, it had helped stabilize social security and provided for a secured retirement for aging American workers. A person who worked their whole life could now rely on a social security retirement of $35,000 a year if they retired at 67, and $42,500 annually if they retired at age 73. AFC was also providing hundreds of millions of dollars a year for free college education for students who chose to pursue certain degrees in career fields where there was a national shortage such as nurses, doctors, engineers and other STEM (Science, Technology, Engineering and Mathematics) degrees.

The New American Dollar (NAD), was once again the world's reserve currency now that it was backed by gold, silver and platinum. Many countries who were not aligned with the Axis powers had switched their reserve currencies from Chinese dollars to the NAD as it had become a more stable currency. The US had also effectively wiped out its debt shortly after the war started. The government had seized all Russian, IR and Chinese government monies that were in US financial institutions at the start of the war, along with those of any shell companies that were associated with their governments. This included monies, buildings, land, companies, houses, cars, yachts, and other items of value. Once they had been seized and retitled, the government began to slowly liquidate these assets among private investors and American citizens. Victims from the IR's terrorist attacks and those who received some sort of collateral damage during Chinese and Russian military operations in America were also receiving money as compensation from the seized assets. It was a small step in trying to correct the many wrongs the Axis powers had inflicted on the American people.

As Joyce walked into the room, she could see everyone was already seated and ready. She walked over to the couch and sat next to Jeff Rogers, opening her tablet.

The President nodded towards the Secretary of Treasury. "Joyce, it's good to see you again. Jeff was just bringing us up to speed on a number of items. It appears we are going to have another good economic quarter."

"Yes Mr. President, it does," Joyce said while skimming through some notes. "Mr. President, I would like to speak with you about the new war bonds. As you know, we are financing some of the war through the war tax, the confiscation of assets from the Axis powers, and war bonds. I would like to propose we kick off a new war bond initiative by bringing in celebrities from across the country, along with some personal visits from you and the Vice President."

"Right to the point, I always liked that about you Joyce. I agree, let's see who we can get from Hollywood to help run the war bond drive and I will, of course, make myself available as well. I believe the Vice President has fully recovered from his injuries, so we'll get him involved as well. How many bonds do we anticipate needing to sell each month, rough estimate?" asked the President.

"As many as we can, but in reality, the war is burning through $4.31 billion a day. With the national debt paid off, we could run a new deficit, but I would rather not do that. Thanks to the war tax that Congress passed a couple of months ago, I think we can avoid that. I know you caught some flak for it, but that $3% sales tax is essentially covering the increased spending at the moment."

"The fact that Alaska is being invaded by the Chinese has really started to hit home with most folks. Foreign troops are on American soil and beating our own soldiers has sent a chill down their collective backs…and they should be scared," said Jeff Rogers.

"The situation will change once some of our newer weapon systems start to show up on the battlefield," Monty countered, trying to keep the mood of the meeting positive.

A Problem with Math

06 July 2041

Tel Aviv, Israel

Third Army Division HQ

Colonel Joshua Richter had been General Gardner's aide decamp since the start of the war in the Middle East; he had served with the general on and off throughout his career as an infantry officer and was being groomed to one day become a division commander. Richter caught his boss' attention to give him an update. "General Gardner, the Secretary of Defense's aircraft just landed, he'll be here in about 30 minutes," Richter said.

The Secretary of Defense and the Chairman of the Joint Chiefs were on their way to Tel Aviv, along with the SACEUR. The goal of this meeting was to discuss the occupation and the next strategy for defeating the Russians. Third Army now had 560,000 extremely battle-hardened soldiers, desperately needed in Europe. The Israeli Defense Force had also grown significantly, reaching 800,000 soldiers. The question now was where to redeploy the Third Army--how many soldiers from the IDF could they get to help assist in Europe or Asia?

"Excellent. Let's go join General Wade in the conference room while we wait," Gardner said, leading the way. Colonel Richter went with the general wherever he went, ready to take notes and issue orders for the general.

As the two officers walked in to the conference room, they saw General Wade in a heated discussion with one of his officers. "Sorry gentlemen…would you like us to come back?" asked General Gardner as he slowly came into the room.

They immediately stopped talking, and there was a moment of awkward silence. "No that's ok. We were just talking about strategy and what to do in Europe to stop the Russians," said General Wade.

"What's the issue? Perhaps we can help you out before the VIPs show up," said Gardner.

"I'm sure you've seen our read-ahead. The issue we are facing is one of numbers. The Russians have such a huge advantage in armor, light drone tanks and infantry fighting vehicles. I'm not even sure your additional armor is going to make much of a dent in it." General Wade looked like he had been beaten down by the war in Europe.

General Gardner walked over to the center of the table and activated the holographic map. He pulled up the pre-brief slides from SACEUR and began to study the map and the enemy unit strengths. He squinted a little as he concentrated, looking for weaknesses in their lines. Just then, the Secretary of Defense, Eric Clarke, and General Branson, the Chairman of the Joint Chiefs, arrived and walked into the room with their aides and staff in tow.

General Branson walked towards the other two generals and held out his hand to shake theirs, saying, "Generals, it's sincerely good to see you both. I am so happy we were able to arrange a meeting where we could have our primary battlefield commanders discuss strategy directly with us as opposed to through these holographic images."

"I couldn't agree with you more," General Gardner replied, shaking the Joint Chief's hand. The two Generals had worked together a number of times in the past, and though they were both infantry officers, General Gardner had pursued a career that led him to spend more time as a field commander and less time as a politician.

Eric Clarke, the SecDef, walked over and joined in the conversation, "It's good to see you both as well. I'm glad to see that you all have made it. I know it's been a rough war, and you all are busy and exhausted."

"That it has been. Speaking of making it, I don't know if you heard that we did officially determine that it was poison that killed my predecessor days before the invasion," General Wade responded as he moved to his seat at the table.

Eric didn't look surprised. "We thought so. In any case, I'm glad you have been able to take over smoothly. You have done a marvelous job trying to herd all of the cats and dogs that make up NATO and still manage to keep the Russians from gobbling all of Europe up," the SecDef said with genuine gratitude. Clarke was liked by a lot of people in the military. Though he had never served himself, he really listened to his military commanders and deferred to them when it came down to significant military strategy, weapons, personnel and the needs required to win the war. He was not a micromanager like a lot of the previous SecDefs had been.

After some coffee, tea and other refreshments were brought in, the group of military leaders sat down at the conference table and began to get down to business.

The SecDef opened the conversation by saying, "Generals, the President is incredibly pleased with everyone and the results we have achieved thus far. That said, the war is far from over…we may be entering a more dangerous period than what we just left. The Islamic Republic has surrendered, and for that, we are eternally gratefully for your efforts in driving home this victory, General Gardner. I know the President and I have not always agreed with your methods, but we cannot dispute the results you have achieved."

"As we look to transition, there are several things that need to take place. Right now, I need you to reassign 250,000 of your men for occupation duty. They do not all need to be combat troops, but they need to be able to perform the full range of occupation duties as needed and ensure we do not have a problem later on. I'll leave you to figure out the composition of those forces. Next, I'll need you to also leave behind an additional 35,000 soldiers here in Israel. They will essentially be your Quick Reaction Force (QRF) for the occupation and help secure Israel and assist with the reconstruction efforts that I am sure are already underway now that the war is officially over."

Clarke looked at the rest of the generals in the room and then at General Gardner before he continued. "You had your meeting with the IDF a few hours ago; I won't get a chance to meet with them until later today. How did your meeting go?" The SecDef was curious to know what he might be walking in to.

"The meeting went great; they have agreed to participate in the greater war against both the Russians and the Chinese. When I asked for a troop commitment, they said they could lend 250,000 soldiers, mostly combat arms. They are committing 90,000 soldiers to the occupation. About 210,000 will stay on active duty, and the rest will be placed back in a reserve status so they can begin to rebuild their country. They are currently working out the details on how to move nearly 2,800,000 civilians back to Israel from Southern Europe and the US." General Gardner was all smiles since he had essentially gotten exactly the troop numbers the SecDef and the President were looking for.

General Branson was also smiling from ear to ear, excited to hear that Israel would continue to support their US allies in the war against the Russians. "I will speak with the President, but I believe we can use some of our civilian airlift capacity to help the Israelis in relocating their people back to Israel. I know the President is going to sign an agreement tomorrow bringing Israel into the Grain Consortium, which will give them preferential buying power for food stocks. He is also working on an aid package, mostly building materials and such."

The SecDef replied, "This is all good news General. Now, on to more pressing matters. Europe and Alaska--we'll discuss Alaska first."

Changing the holographic map, the battle of Alaska came into focus. "As you can see, the Chinese have pushed our forces back to Cooper Landing. This is our last line of defense around southern Alaska. Fortunately, General Black has turned it into a real meat grinder for the Chinese. To the north, we have the Susitna defense, which thus far is holding out against a massive PLA army." Eric sighed before continuing. "The PLA have landed a total force of around 330,000 soldiers on the Aleutian Peninsula, with most of them heading to the Susitna defensive line. In the south, they have a total force of around 290,000 soldiers attacking Cooper Landing. Now we expect these numbers to double over the next two months, and then double again by the end of the year. Right now, we are estimating they will have a total force of around 2.3 million soldiers on Alaskan soil by December."

General Gardner broke into the conversation, adding, "It would almost make more sense for my Army to redeploy back to the US and get ready to go fight the Chinese than it would to move to Europe. If we lose Alaska, then the Yukon, BC, then the other northern states will easily fall. If the Chinese are able to spread themselves out, we could have a thousand-plus mile border or more to have to defend," he said.

General Branson just nodded, "You are correct. We came to the same conclusion on our flight over here."

General Wade looked a bit concerned at the thought of losing the Third Army; he had been counting on them. "Am I losing the entire Third Army, or just part of it?" he asked dejectedly.

"You are losing the entire Third Army," General Branson said, matter of fact. "You are gaining all of Third Army's air support, along with the Israeli reinforcements. Third Army will have air support via NORTHCOM and General Black's forces in Alaska." Branson signaled for Gardner to hold his objections for just a second longer.

"General, we are going to have your entire army rotate back to the US as a whole unit, at least what's left of it after you detail off the occupation force. You, and portions of your force are going to be conducting victory parades all throughout the country. Following the parades, your army will then be given a full thirty-days of leave before we reconstitute your force in the Pacific Northwest. We are also going to outfit your infantry forces with the new Raptor combat suits and the new Wolverine IFVs. When your forces do enter the war in Alaska, your army will be fielding the newest in military equipment. You are also going to be facing several million Chinese soldiers and we are expecting you to not just defeat them, but drive them back into the sea. Once in place, we will begin a phased withdraw of General

Black's Second Army so his group can go through the same refit."

General Gardner was going to object, but held his tongue for a minute thinking about the global situation. He took a moment to look at the map before returning back to face General Branson and the SecDef. "I understand the situation is not looking good in Alaska. It is not looking good in Europe either. My entire army could be the difference in defeating the Russians quickly or dragging the war out for a lot longer."

The SecDef knew Gardner would have objections, but it was his job to make him see the bigger picture. "Gary, the war with Russia is going to have to continue without your army. Your air units will make a tremendous difference, but the situation at home is far more serious. We cannot allow the Chinese to land millions upon millions of soldiers in North America. If they are able to do that, then we are in serious trouble. Your army is the most battle tested army we have right now, and once outfitted with the newest equipment, it will be our most lethal. We are going to leave most of your equipment here with the Israelis while the armored units are moved to Europe. Your entire army will be completely refitted with the newest equipment. We also have the Central and South American Multi-National Force that is starting to complete their training. We are going to slice off half of them to Europe, while the other half will be integrated with your army. This is a huge manpower increase, nearly 550,000 soldiers in addition to the 750,000 US soldiers that your army will be increased to. You will be commanding the largest single American army in its history."

Very few people ever called General Gardner by his first name, Gary, but the SecDef did so in an attempt to break through the military man's defense. They needed him on board with this plan, and more importantly, they desperately needed him to help work some sort of miracle and defeat the Chinese, just as he had defeated the IR twice in Israel.

General Gardner knew that ultimately the SecDef was right; he just did not want to leave Europe to the backburner. But if Alaska fell, then the situation back home would get significantly worse. "I understand the situation now. Are things really that bad in Alaska?"

The SecDef held his hand up to stop General Branson from speaking, and looked directly at General Gardner as he replied, "The situation is much worse, General." He sighed and sat back for a second before continuing, "If the Russians break out of Alaska, we are essentially destroyed in the Pacific Northwest. The President placed all of our eggs in one basket in Alaska--not that he had much of a choice. Right now, if they break out, the entire Yukon, British Columbia, and the rest of the Canadian States are completely open. We have virtually no military forces in those areas that could slow down the Chinese juggernaut. We have roughly 35,000 troops in Washington State, which has no hope of stopping the Chinese."

General Branson jumped in at this point. "We are graduating 30,000 new troops every week, but they are green--very little in the way of NCO or officer experience. We are forming new divisions as fast as we can, but we can only train so many troops at a time, let alone equip them with modern weapons and equipment. Bringing your army home gives us 360,000 combat-hardened veterans and a backstop in case the Chinese do break through Alaska before your army is ready. You are going to receive an immediate 550,000 troops from the Multi-National Force (or MNF as we call them) and 30,000 new troops a week from training. We want to hold your army back until you reach a troop strength of 1,250,000 soldiers, and then unleash you on the Chinese."

The SecDef continued, "Intelligence is showing a massive Chinese Task Force heading for the Hawaiian Island. We've evacuated the civilian population and left behind a nasty guerrilla force for them to deal with, compliments of the Marines and Special Forces. But we anticipate them securing the port facilities and airport (or what's left of them from that nuclear torpedo they hit us with during the first days of the war). They are reconstituting the PLAN infantry force, which led the invasion of Alaska. We are leaving you with a lot of footage and reports of the naval infantry for your people to study. Our intelligence shows that the PLAN is moving forward with expanding its force to 600,000, and is currently training that force right now. We anticipate them being ready for combat by the end of the year, maybe sooner."

Colonel Richter, General Gardner's aide, asked, "Do they have the sealift capability to support such a force?"

"That is a good question Colonel; as of right now no. They can only support about 160,000 troopers at a time. Everyone accuses China of being a cut-and-copy nation-- and frankly they are. They took our designs for our Marine Expeditionary Force, our amphibious assault ships and vehicles, and replicated them. They virtually hit us with our own equipment. They are expanding the capability rapidly. We just learned the other day that China and India have officially signed a non-aggression-pact, freeing up hundreds of thousands of soldiers and equipment they had been holding back in case they needed them against the Indians. To further complicate things, the Indians are going to start producing ships and other materials that the PLA needs for their war."

General Wade snorted. "Why would the Indians support the Chinese and not the Allies? The Grain Consortium is selling them tens of millions of tons of food stocks a week."

"Because their economy is still a wreck, and the orders the Chinese are able to place are going to be a huge economic boon to the Indian government. We are actively working with them right now to see if they will sever that activity and support the Allies instead, but we doubt they will," said the SecDef angrily. "The loss of the Fifth and Seventh Fleets mean we have virtually no naval force in the Pacific or Indian Oceans, so they view China now as the dominant power in the region and want to stay on their good side."

"As long as they do not actively join the war on the Axis side, I think we can handle it; there are ways for us to slow down their economy if need be (such as cyber-attacks). The main thing is, we cannot afford a war with two nations whose population is above two billion people. China is bad enough," said General Wade.

Looking at his watch, the SecDef interjected, "Generals, I have to meet with the Israelis, and I need to prepare for that conference. I am going to leave you all to your tasks and new orders; please implement them immediately. General Gardner, I look forward to seeing you back in Washington, D.C. soon. You'll be bouncing back and forth between your Command HQ in Washington State and DC for a bit, so you may want to invest in some airplane pillows." The SecDef chuckled as he got up.

With that, the various commanders left for their commands to begin implementing the President's orders and directives. General Gardner began the immediate task of identifying the units that would stay behind.

Raptor Rapture

30 July 2041
Tel Aviv, Israel
3rd Marine HQ

The 3rd Marine Expeditionary Force (3rd MEF), were finally relieved of their position in Damascus following the IR surrender. The entire 3rd Marines had been selected to stay with General Gardner's Army and rotate back to the US for a rest and refit before moving north to attack the Chinese and drive them back to the sea. For the men of the 3rd Marines, this decision could not have come at a better time. They were tired, dirty, beat up and downright ready for a long-overdue break. They had been fighting for nearly a year, first in Mexico and then rapidly deployed to the Middle East for an incredibly fast and intense war, resulting in several million people killed in direct combat.

1st Lieutenant Thornton had started the war as an E5 Sergeant; he was given a battlefield promotion to E7 Gunnery Sergeant, and then given a battlefield commission to 1st Lieutenant as the leadership in his battalion had been nearly wiped out. He had just gotten done with a staff call with Major Lee, the battalion commander (well, technically, he was now Lieutenant Colonel Lee, since he had just recently been promoted).

"Thornton, I know that you are getting ready to have some time off, and it is well-deserved, but we are going to need for you to complete an officer familiarization course after your leave. Lest you think we are singling you out, all of the battlefield-promoted officers and NCOs will be attending one of these courses. Even though the 3rd MEF may only be returning home for a short time, now we need to normalize some of our more traditional training."

"Also, congratulations are in order. You are being promoted again, this time to Captain; your new rank will be more befitting of your position as Company Commander. With the Corps still dangerously short on officers and senior NCOs, you are also going to be functioning as the battalion executive officer (XO) in case something happens to me or I need to be taken offline."

"Yes sir, thank you sir," replied Captain Thornton. He had made the mistake of making a less-than-grateful response to a promotion once before; he wouldn't make that error again.

Once he digested his own promotion, Captain Thornton had to pass along some news to the rest of the company.

"Listen up ladies and gentlemen. You all know that we are going to be headed out of this hole and headed home for some R & R."

Whoops filled the room.

Thornton signaled for the room to quiet down. "Well, we are all getting 30 days at our homes of record. Following the R & R, we will reform up and start attending two weeks of various professional development training courses. Then we have four weeks of intensive training on the new Raptor combat suit, and finally a two-week field training exercise (FTX) in the new suits. From there, the 3rd MEF will continue to train at our home station for another month before deploying forward to California to await further orders."

The men of the Company were excited; they had just survived a horrific year. Many of their friends and comrades had not been so lucky, and now it was time to return home, rest and recuperate before preparing for a new fight. This fight would be different from the others; it was a fight to defend the actual homeland on U.S. soil. Many of the Marines were ready to go fight the Chinese now; the adrenaline junkies inside them were chomping at the bit to get back into the fight.

Most of the longer combat veterans, however, knew the war would still be there waiting for them after their leave, so they were more focused on enjoying the downtime before the killing began again in earnest.

DARPA

15 September 2041
Operation Pegasus

Once the Chinese main army reached the American defensive positions at Cooper Landing in the south of Alaska, and Susitna in the north, they established their own lines of defense and began to settle in while the rest of their army and equipment was offloaded. The PLAAF continued to establish more manned and fighter drone airbases across the captured portions of Alaska, while the Russians continued to fight for control of northern and central Alaska. Because the U.S. Marines had established a wide network of firebases all throughout key strategic areas of central and northern Alaska, it was forcing the Russians to have to take them out one at a time if they wanted to continue to advance further into the interior of Alaska.

The reprieve from the continuous Chinese assaults was both a blessing and a curse. It provided US Forces the time needed to bring in additional reinforcements and refit General Gardner's Third Army, but it also meant the Chinese had more time to offload hundreds of thousands of soldiers and armored equipment. The PLA forces in Alaska now stood at 950,000 soldiers, with more arriving each week.

Despite months of heavy fighting in the air, neither side had established full dominance of the skies. Just as the PLAAF and Russians were starting to secure the air war, the Americans began to introduce the newest and most advanced fighter ever seen. The Archangels (F41s) with their EmDrive propulsion and "angelic" power system. The U.S. had few of these aircraft in service; the material requirements to build one was immense, but so too was their impact on the war thus far. America had not lost a single F41, and had already shot down over 430 drones and 93 manned fighters with just ten of these aircraft in service.

Leveraging the new angelic power system, the F41 was the first aircraft to make use of an air-to-air laser. When enemy drones or fighters would fire a missile, the F41 would simply shoot the projectile down and then target the enemy fighters or drones, destroying them at ranges as far as 150 miles. Because the F41 did not run on a conventional fuel system, they could stay aloft for as long as the pilot and weapons systems could handle, making them a very unique weapon (particularly if they could be produced in greater quantities).

What American defense manufactures lacked were the rare earth elements needed in a host of advanced manufacturing. These rare elements were becoming harder and harder to come by, with China owning nearly 90% of all known rare earth element deposits. The need for America to be able to extract lunar minerals was becoming more and more apparent as the war continued. The Moon contained a host of these rare elements, along with a new mineral called Veldspar, which could be found in the asteroid rocks that impacted the Moon quite often. The Veldspar could be refined down to create Tritium4, which was a critically rare element that right now was being synthetically produced, albeit in small quantities.

With the advent of the angelic power system and the EmDrive propulsion system, the President directed DARPA (Defense Advanced Research Projects Agency) to develop a prototype deep space mining starship that could leave and reenter Earth's orbit and fly to the Moon with the specific intent of locating these rare elements and bringing them back. The angelic power source would provide the power needed to run the first continuous thrust propulsion system. Once in space, it would leverage an improved ion engine that could propel the craft from Earth to the Moon in 16-hours. Once on the Moon's surface, the mining astronauts would immediately begin the process of establishing the first lunar base of operations and begin to identify, move and process the required materials and then arrange them for transport back to earth.

DARPA had been tinkering with the designs for such a ship for decades, and once the appropriate power source had finally been identified, they immediately set to work on building a craft around it. The ship was called the HULK, mostly because of its size. The ship would be 5,100 feet in length, 400 feet in width, and 600 feet in height, broken down into multiple cargo holds and an onboard smelter.

The ship would be run by a crew of six engineers, three communications specialists, two navigators and four other members to include the pilots. It would also carry twenty space miners from a company called Deep Space Industries, who would manage the smelter and actual mining operations. Because most of the ship would be automated, the large ship could get by with just fifteen full-time crew members to run the actual day-to-day operations. It also had a decent sized living and recreation area built in for the crew and miners to live in, and a set of laboratories, in which the scientists on board could conduct their space research and experiments. It could also be configured to carry any number of different types of cargos and equipment loads. A similar version for actual deep space exploration was also in development.

When the initial design had been shown to the President and his science team in July, he had immediately signed his approval to move Operation Pegasus forward. The construction of the HULK started immediately in Kentucky, and would take approximately nine months to complete. The location had been chosen because of its close proximity to a number of other manufacturing sites; plus, the President had promised to bring additional manufacturing to Kentucky to augment the loss in coal jobs.

During the past four years of the Stein Administration, the President had stayed true to his word on revamping the American energy program by expediting the conversion of coal-fired plants to natural gas and increasing the use of solar, wind, geothermal and wave energy. Of course, this transformation also meant a lot of Americans in the coal industry had lost their jobs, and the President was determined to ensure every one of them was able to cross-train into another career field, paid for by the government.

In collaboration with Deep Space Industries, DARPA had developed, a rock crushing machine that could bust up rocks in the near zero-gravity found on the surface of the Moon. The plan was for several Moon excavators to gather the identified minerals and then bring them to be broken down; once crushed, the ground materials would move through a conveyor belt system into a specialized loading bay where the materials would be processed through an onboard smelter and then turned into an initial refined material ready for transport back to the U.S.

In collaboration with DARPA, SpaceX had built a smaller cargo ship, which would gather the refined material and transport it back to the US before returning back to the Moon for another pick up. The smaller cargo ship was 1,200 feet in length, 200 feet in width and 300 feet in height, and built purely for hauling cargo. It could transport up to 120 tons of refined material from the Moon to the earth. It would also be used to transport necessary supplies from Earth to the Moon on its trips up. Key scientists had estimated that once the mining operations were fully operational, and materials started to consistently arrive on Earth, the defense manufacturers would be able to produce upwards of 1,000 Pershings and 200 F41 fighters every month.

Of course, the U.S. would not be watching anything in the daily news cycle about all of these space missions for quite some time, because the hope was that by keeping the whole operation clandestine, America would finally have a true leg up on their adversaries. All of the scientists and astronauts that were directly involved in the project had been assigned Secret Service details, and had been required to sign nondisclosure forms longer than the Great Wall of China.

Many of the scientists involved in Operation Pegasus were single, career-minded individuals who were able to leave for some time and easily explain their absence as business trips. Dr. Karl Bergstrom, who would be the lead geological astronaut in charge of planning the excavations on the surface of the Moon, did have a wife and two children. He felt horrible about it, but he had led them to believe that he was in the CIA; it was the only way to really explain why they were also being assigned Secret Service protection. His wife Amy, who was an independent and adventurous sort of woman, decided that the best way to handle this intrusion in her life would be to move to a more remote town in the mountains, where she could homeschool the children and work on her botany experiments in peace. While she didn't know the full truth of the situation, Amy did know that her husband's sacrifices were for the good of the nation; that was enough to keep her going.

The communications were a bit spattered (no Skype or FaceTime sessions would be available for them, even during the training period while he was still in the United States), but Karl did the best he could to send messages back home, and he would even sometimes create videos of himself reading books to send back for the children. Every time he would come back home, he would be surprised by how much his children had grown; these sacrifices were deep (like many made by members of the military and their families throughout generations), but they were crucial to ending the conflict in the world. Karl dreamed of a day in which his children would no longer live in a planet at war.

****

To further hamper the American war efforts, the Chinese continued to unleash wave after wave of cyber-attacks across all aspects of American life. Since the Chinese's successful attack against the American communications grid at the outset of the war, the government had quickly broken the energy grid down into dozens of smaller nodes to ensure that no one node or group of nodes could cause a cascading event that could spread across the entire nation. The Chinese had continued to target the grid on multiple occasions; some nodes had been taken down, temporarily knocking out power to a single state (or a portion of a state), but that was it.

The US was also waging a cyber war against China; however, they were not having even a shred of the amount of success that the Chinese had been having in disrupting the American way of life. So, to play to their strengths, the U.S.

was trying another way to combat these attacks; whenever an opportunity presented itself, the US Navy would launch a series of Tomahawk cruise missiles at the locations where the cyber-attacks were originating from. In some cases, they were successful and hit the targeted compound, but at other times the cruise missiles were shot down before they hit their mark.

****

The Navy's Swordfish Underwater Drones (SUDs) were also starting to have a greater influence in the Pacific. The Navy still only had a small number of these underwater drones, but they began to seek out and hunt specifically for PLAN transports, fuel tankers and cargo ships. The four SUDs in operation were sinking (on average) nine ships a month, which was starting to have an impact in the volume of supplies and equipment the PLA was receiving in Alaska.

While the Americans had introduced the SUDs in the Pacific, the Russians had introduced a very similar type of underwater anti-ship drone in the Atlantic. Like the SUDs, the Russians only had a limited number of these underwater vessels, but they were becoming extremely effective in finding enemy ships and sinking them. This was starting to cause a shortage in materials and other essential equipment needed for the war in Europe as key transports were starting to be sunk.

The war in Europe had become bogged down in Germany; the Russians had captured large portions of eastern Germany, while the Allies sustained their hold on the rest of Germany, as well as the region down through Austria, Slovenia and Croatia. The Russians continued to train hundreds of thousands of new soldiers, and kept the pressure on the Allies; they had not been able to force a breakout since their initial attack that captured Berlin and nearly captured Hamburg.

Smart and Bored

16 September 2041

National Security Agency

Neven Jackson was a twenty-three-year-old computer hacker who worked for the National Security Agency (NSA). He was not here by design; he had hacked the FBI database as a prank when he was a freshman at the Massachusetts Institute of Technology (MIT), and he had been caught. He thought he had shielded his activities, but he had missed something, and as a consequence, he was arrested and given a choice--either work for the government as a paid hacker, or go to prison for a very long time.

Neven, preferring a life outside of barred walls, had chosen to go to work for the NSA, and he had spent the last several years playing defense against Russian and Chinese hackers who were becoming more and more sophisticated in their attacks. Since the start of the war, he had been transferred to the "Red Team" and been given full permission to hack in to any sector of the Chinese economy and military systems and cause as much havoc as he could. This opportunity was like a dream come true. During the first several months, he had successfully shut down the power in two provinces for several days, caused the ATMs in one city to empty all of their money, and completed a number of other malicious activities.

Today, however, was a special day. Two weeks ago, he had been assigned the task of infiltrating the Chinese exoskeleton combat suit program, and yesterday he had successfully found a backdoor in to the source code (it was too bad that the Russians used a different operating system, or else they would really have something going). He had spent the better part of the day writing a zero-day code to be placed in the exoskeleton suits' operating system. Once the update was sent out by the program developers, this code would be dispersed to all of the combat suits that received the update. The code would then lie in wait, ready for it to be activated. Upon sharing his discovery with his superiors, they had worked with him to develop a special surprise. The next time the PLAN infantry attacked the Americans using these suits, they would suddenly find that the entire left or right side of the suit had been essentially disabled. This would confuse the ranks, making them think that the suits were experiencing mechanical problems, and throwing the scent off away from the real issue of a software problem. When the PLAN infantry did attack, their entire attacking force would suddenly find themselves stuck in malfunctioning exoskeleton suits at the worst possible moment. Of course, this attack could only be used once so finding the best opportunity to use it was going to be critical.

Trying to See Eight Moves Ahead

17 September 2041

Washington, DC

White House Situation Room

The President was becoming nervous after reading through the various intelligence reports and summaries of the numbers of Chinese troops arriving each week and their grand totals. As of that moment, there were nearly one million enemy soldiers on American soil. Now there were reports that millions more were on the way, and President Stein was unsure if even the mighty Third Army could stop them; they were still close to sixty days away from being fully ready for combat after their R & R and training, and no one knew how many more Chinese soldiers would be on American soil by then. General Black (the Second Army Commander, and overall Commander for all US Forces in North America) was doing his best to keep the Chinese bogged down. Thus far, his efforts had kept the Chinese from being able to break out of Alaska, but that would only last for so long.

The President sat at the head of the table with the rest of his National Security team and his senior military advisors trying to ascertain what their next move should be. "General

Scott, what is the DIA's assessment of what the Chinese may do next?" asked the President, wanting to get a better picture of the Pacific and Asia.

Lieutenant General Rick Scott prepared to speak. He had been the Director for the Defense Intelligence Agency for nearly three years; however, he and the President had a very checkered past. He had nearly been fired in the opening days of the war with China because of his disregard of what his other intelligence departments had been warning him about with regards to the Chinese. LTG Scott had believed (like many others) that the Chinese had too many economic ties with the US and Europe to risk an open war. Like everyone else on that ill-fated date, he was proven wrong when the Chinese launched a massive surprise cyber-attack against the American communications grid, taking AT&T, Sprint and many other internet and cable providers down for nearly two months. Verizon was the only internet and data provider who had survived the Chinese cyber-attack; they had essentially prevented the entire government and country from what would have been a full economic collapse. The CIA and the Joint Counterterrorism Task Force (JCTF) had also missed the warning signs of an imminent attack by China; it was for that reason alone LTG Scott was not relieved on the spot--that and his ability to work with British

Telecom and Verizon to quickly get America's cell phone and data providers back online in two months. He had been redeeming himself ever since.

LTG Scott finished his preparation as he brought up some images from his tablet to the holographic map at the center of the table for everyone to view. "Mr. President, there are two items of concern. The first is the massive troop movement we are seeing in the North China Sea; it would appear they have assembled a convoy of nearly 280 troop transports. Each transport can carry 3,000 troops; if they load them up with only troops, then they will be bringing 840,000 fresh troops to Alaska."

Audible sighs and groans could be heard throughout the room. "The second area of concern is the activity we are seeing in Hawaii. The Chinese have spent the last two months doing a lot of repairs to the facilities there, and they have repaired all of the runways on the island. They presently have a garrison of 20,000 PLA soldiers there, and they were just augmented by 30,000 PLAN infantry. The PLAN is currently moving their entire amphibious assault capability to Hawaii, along with four of their five carriers from Alaska. They have started a massive airlift of their PLAN infantry from the Mainland to Hawaii as well," LTG

Scott explained as he showed more images of what was transpiring.

"Are you suggesting that the Chinese are planning another amphibious assault, possibly against California or somewhere along the West Coast?" asked the SecDef Eric Clarke.

"Yes Mr. Secretary, it would appear so." Scott replied.

The President looked around the room and asked, "Any suggestions on where they may be heading and what we should do about it?" He was hoping to hear some good ideas from his brain trust.

Patrick Rubio, the Director of the CIA, chimed in, "If I were a guessing man, I would say they will look to land their troops in the Pacific Northwest, most likely in Oregon or Seattle. This would put them in position to cut off our entire force in Alaska and put our guys in to a terrible position for retreating."

"You don't think they would go for Los Angeles?" inquired General Branson, curious to know his logic in his assumption.

"No, I think they would like to avoid the urban areas and focus more on defeating our Army rather than capturing a symbolic trophy. We can trade land for time and maneuverability; they are most likely going to look to defeat our armies and then have free range." Director Rubio said.

The President asked, "Can we shift our SUDs to focus more around Hawaii and help to keep that amphibious group from going too far?"

Admiral Juliano, the Chief of Naval Operations (CNO) spoke up, "We can, Mr. President, but I doubt it will make that much of a difference; we just do not have the numbers. Personally, I do not believe the Chinese are going to launch another amphibious assault. I know the intelligence says otherwise, but the logistical capability of the PLAN does not support it. The PLA is chewing through resources in staggering numbers in Alaska. The PLAN support ships are having a hard enough time trying to keep up with them. Throw in another 840,000 soldiers into that mix, and they will be thoroughly overwhelmed. They just do not have the logistical capability to support two landing zones like that."

"So you think this is a diversion?" inquired the President.

"I do. I believe they are going to send their PLAN infantry to Hawaii and train them hard for a few months, making us think and believe they are going to launch another landing. In doing so, they will force us to tie up hundreds of thousands of soldiers and precious materials on the West Coast, as opposed to having them engaged in the fighting in Alaska. They know we rotated the Third Army in, and this is their attempt to neutralize General Gardner by having him chase a ghost invasion that will never happen." The CNO was very matter-of-fact in his response.

Director Rubio interjected, "Mr. President, I have to disagree. If we do not take this threat seriously, they could potentially cut our entire force off in Alaska, and if we send General Gardner's army in as well, then we have little in the way of forces that can be used to defend the West Coast."

The Admiral quickly cut in, "I understand your concern, Director Rubio, but the logistics do not lie; they could land those forces, but they would run out of fuel and munitions within a week. Then they'd have a large amphibious force on the ground with no ammunition. This is meant as nothing more than a distraction to tie our forces down." The Admiral was speaking with great force and conviction to hammer home his point. "Furthermore, it's not your people who are going to have to do the fighting Director. Our intelligence does not support the information the Agency has been pushing, and we categorically disagree with it as fiction." This last point was made in quite a sharp tone towards the CIA Director, to a point that the room suddenly filled with awkward silence.

Lately there had some friction between the Services and the Intelligence Community (IC). The CIA and DIA had really fouled up the intelligence about the IR prior to their sneak attack, and then again had been completely wrong about the Chinese. The Services had developed a real dislike for the IC outside of their own intelligence channels, and often brushed their assessments off or disregarded them entirely. The Army, Navy and Air Force shared intelligence seamlessly as they fought hand-in-hand; this intelligence sharing stopped or was reluctant when it came to disclosing anything with the CIA. Despite the fact that the NSA and DIA were military-run organizations, the Services still did not trust them because of their ties with the CIA. This distrust of each other's intelligence was becoming more apparent during each of the National Security Council meetings, and it was going to need to be addressed.

The President raised his hand to stop the parties from bickering further. "I agree Admiral; the PLAN logistics do not support a second large-scale invasion. However, that does not mean we can just ignore the PLAN infantry build-up in Hawaii either. For right now, we will not shift men or material around to the West Coast; we will move some air assets to attack their ships if they venture away from Hawaii, but that is it. Our main focus has to be on stopping the Chinese in Alaska and pushing them into the Sea," the President spoke with force and conviction in his voice, which commanded respect and attention from both parties. "I want one of our two F41 flights to be focused on defending the West Coast and harassing the Chinese efforts over Hawaii, while the other flight continues to stay engaged in Alaska. As soon as the third flight of F41s is complete, they are to head to Europe. We may not be able to commit a lot of ground reinforcements to Europe, but we can send them additional air support as it becomes available."

Shifting in his seat before continuing, the President redirected, "I want to discuss Japan and India next. I have a feeling more is going on between China and India than we would like to believe, and frankly, I'd like to know what the heck the Japanese are doing as well."

Director Rubio pulled some information from a folder on his tablet and brought it up for the group. "With regards to India, we do believe there is more going on. Since the non-aggression agreement was signed, the Indians have started construction of 86 new troop transport ships, 19 amphibious assault transports, 46 new attack submarines and two supercarriers. All of these appear to be of Chinese design and specifications. In addition to the naval ships, they have started manufacturing the Chinese main battle tanks, infantry fighting vehicles, munitions and other tools needed for war."

LTG Scott added, "Their ground forces have also started a series of training exercises. Most of them appear to be armored and urban warfare exercises, which leads us to believe the Indians may not stay as neutral in this war as we had hoped. Albeit, we have not intercepted any information suggesting they are going to join the Chinese, or obtained any human intelligence on that matter just yet, but their training cycle, type of training, military manufacturing and increases in the size of their military suggest that they are at least planning on a future military engagement."

The room sat silent for a minute digesting what they had just heard. Could it be possible that India would join Axis powers and turn on the Allies?

The President made a sour face before adding, "This information about India is troubling to say the least. The last time I spoke with the Indian PM, he was short and curt with me. He had expressed his outrage at our use of nuclear weapons against the IR. He further voiced his anger at the fallout that was landing across India. When I communicated with our Ambassador to India last week, he said they had seen a massive uptick in anti-American demonstrations. I believe we should plan on the Indians joining the Axis at some point, and continue to pray they do not. We should look at using cyber-attacks against any manufacturing production that is being used to support the Chinese war effort. No need to let them off the hook entirely."

Clearing his voice and then taking a couple of gulps from his Red Bull, the President asked, "What about Japan? What are they doing?"

LTG Scott shifted the map screen away from India and zoomed in to show Japan. "As of right now, we believe the Japanese are still planning on sitting out the war. They continue to train and modernize their forces; they have two additional carriers completing construction this month as well. It will bring their total carrier count up to five."

Director Rubio interjected to add, "On this front, I believe we have some better information. One of our sources within the defense ministry said that they have been ordered to ramp up plans for attacking the Chinese fleet at Hawaii." (Unfortunately, unbeknownst to the CIA and the American government, this high level source was not just a spy for the Americans, but a double agent for the Chinese. He had been feeding China intelligence about the American and Japanese relationship since the start of the war, which had greatly enabled the Chinese politically to counter every move the Americans attempted to make to strengthen their relationship or convince the Japanese to join the Allies.)

Perking up at this piece of information, Admiral Juliano asked, "What exactly are the Japanese proposing to do, and when will they reach out to us formally?"

"I am not 100% sure yet on both accounts; our agent only said that plans were in the works for the Japanese to attack the Chinese fleet assembling in Hawaii. The logic behind the attack is that if they can cripple the Chinese fleet there, then it relieves a lot of anxiety about them being able to launch an invasion of the Japanese home front."

The President smiled and said, "This is good news indeed. Will we have any of our carriers from the Atlantic that might be able to participate?"

Admiral Juliano glanced down at his tablet and flicked through a few tabs to find the one he was looking for before answering. "As of right now, we have two supercarriers coming out of mothball this month, two more by the end of the year. We will not have a fully operational support fleet though until around the end of the year. Right now, all of our ships coming out of mothball and the shipyards are staying on the East Coast where we can protect them, until we can put together a large enough fleet."

"We have the 6th Fleet still operating in the Mediterranean, and one carrier battle group operating in the North Sea, trying to keep the Russian fleet bottled up. I'm afraid we do not have a fleet ready to sail to the Pacific just yet in order to support any operation the Japanese may have planned," the Admiral said, clearly disappointed.

The President looked saddened as well. "Let's look to move our SUDs over to the Hawaiian area when and if this plan does pan out. Maybe we can get lucky and score a few critical hits; in the meantime, let's keep those SUDs sinking transport and fuel tankers. If no one else has any major points to discuss, let's end the meeting here, and we'll meet back again in a couple of days for our next update, unless something major happens," said Stein.

He stood to end the meeting, but Admiral Juliano moved to grab his attention. "Sir…not to be impertinent, but there is still something that we need to discuss."

"Oh? What would that be, Admiral?"

"It's Dr. Rosanna Weisz, Sir," replied Juliano. "Her protests are starting to gain quite a lot of traction. She has another one scheduled here in DC in two weeks. We don't want the war to be lost in the tide of public opinion."

"I see," the President responded. "What would you propose that I do in this situation?"

The Admiral straightened up (even more than his usual strict military posture) and asserted, "Sir, I think you should come out hard against this group. You can't let these people walk all over you; you have to show them that you are the one in power."

Director Rubio was aghast, "Mr. President, with all due respect to my colleague, I cannot imagine that would go well. Simply telling someone what not to think only makes them want to think about it more. It's like saying, 'Don't think about yellow elephants,' and suddenly, that's all you can think about. If you come at them harshly, it will only legitimize their position and give them more publicity."

"I see your point, Pat. Do you have any suggestions?"

"I don't know, Mr. President...I do concede that this is becoming a real issue. It wouldn't be such a problem if Dr. Weisz wasn't so...well...reasonable. She's about the most intelligent and non-crazy protestor I have ever seen."

The President furrowed his brows for a brief moment before turning to his Chief of Staff. "Monty, I want you to set up a meeting with Dr. Weisz and myself before this next protest. Bring her to the White House and give her a nice tour, and then let me meet with her personally. No cameras. I think I know what to do."

"But sir, by meeting with her directly, aren't you legitimizing her claims?" dared Admiral Juliano.

"If I want to slow this waterfall, I'm going to have to go to the source," replied the President. "We may have differing opinions, but if she truly is reasonable, I think I can at least bring us to a mutual understanding."

Admiral Juliano had said his piece, and so he deferred to the judgment of his Commander-in-Chief. The President dismissed the group, and then turned to walk out of the Situation Room.

F41 Flight

21 September 2041

Alaska

Susitna Mountain Range

12ᵗʰ Infantry Division

Lieutenant Paul Allen and his platoon had completed their training in the new Raptor combat suit several weeks ago and had redeployed back to Alaska. The Raptor was really unique; it leveraged a newer armor technology that was both lightweight and flexible. It was also a fully closed environmental suit, which meant it could operate in a host of different environments. The soldiers trained for weeks in the new combat suits, trying to become familiar with how to operate them while using their M5 AIRs and other equipment. Now they were prepared, and had been sent back to the fight at Susitna Mountain Range.

The Susitna defensive line was a massive fortified position carved into the low-ranging mountains of the area and was one of the last major obstacles the Chinese needed to capture in order to secure Anchorage. The Americans knew this, and had built a multi-layered defensive network of trenches, tank ditches, traps, and other obstacles meant to funnel enemy armor into pre-determined kill zones. General

Black knew the importance of this position and had placed nearly 185,000 troops in this one defensive position alone. Another 60,000 troops were held in reserve, and a mobile QRF of 45,000 troops was nearby as well. General Black also had 900 Pershing MBTs and 2,200 of the older M1A4 MBTs in the area as well. To the left and right flank of the mountain range was relatively flat terrain, which made it great tank country when not covered by the deep snow that usually falls in this particular area of Alaska five out of twelve months of the year.

Once the 12th Infantry Division (12th ID) had completed their initial training on the Raptor, they had been redeployed to the Susitna gap along with the new Wolverine Infantry Fighting Vehicle. The Wolverine was the newest IFV in the American arsenal, and was built specifically to augment the Pershing MBT. The Wolverine had the same chassis as the Pershing (and the same armor system), making it a very tough nut to crack. It had a 20mm anti-armor railgun turret and two twin barrel automated .25mm railguns; one mounted in the front of the vehicle just below the 20mm turret, and the second mounted in the rear above the troop carrier compartment. All three railgun systems could be used in either air or ground mode, enabling the vehicle to operate as not just an anti-armor/personnel killer, but also as an air defense platform. The IFV provided not just exceptionally armored protection to the twelve infantrymen it carried, but was an extremely lethal offensive and defensive weapons package.

The 12th ID was primed for combat when the word finally came down about the counter-offensive. The Chinese had been hitting the American lines relentlessly for the past five days. Now it was time for the Americans to introduce the Raptor and the Wolverine to the battlefield.

Captain Shilling came over the battle net saying, "Lieutenant Allen, the battalion is going to move forward in five minutes. Have your vehicles ready to move and stay frosty. They may be expecting us to attack soon." With that, he abruptly dropped off the net.

Allen thought to himself, "*Great. Nothing better than attacking an enemy who knows your about to attack him. This is already a cluster mess, and we haven't even started this offensive.*"

"Listen up everyone," Allen said over the platoon battle net, his voice managing to carry well over the low hum of the vehicles' electric engines. "We are moving out in five minutes. I want Sergeant Liner and Sergeant Lipton's vehicles to stay in air-attack mode through most of this attack. Your vehicles are responsible for engaging any and all incoming artillery, mortars, missiles and rockets heading towards the platoon and company's vehicles and positions. The rest of you, continue to look for armored vehicles and infantry and take them out. Those of you manning the twin machine guns, stay alert on those guns and engage any missile teams you see. If we have to dismount and engage the enemy, then remember your training and kill 'em all."

Outside the vehicle was a buzz of activity, as hundreds of Wolverines and Pershings began to spin up their engines and prepare to start what was going to the largest tank battle ever on American soil. Over 3,000 M1A4 Abram MBTs would be joining the fray as General Black made the first big attempt to push the Chinese back from the Susitna line.

****

Major Theodore Cruse's "Cruiser" flight had completed their training on the new F41 Archangels and had been flying combat operations over Alaska now for nearly two weeks. In that timeframe, they had shot down more enemy aircraft and drones than the Allies had in the previous six months. The F41 was about the size of an F18 Super Hornet, though it was shaped a lot more like an elongated diamond. Because the aircraft leveraged the new EmDrive propulsion, it could take off vertically or from a runway. It would also accelerate from zero to near Mach 10 in seconds, and stop in almost the same time. The aircraft could turn on a dime and had a ceiling of low earth orbit. It also leveraged a refractive armor casing that could deflect laser hits, giving the aircraft the ability to operate in nearly all environments. Where the aircraft was vulnerable was against conventional missiles and shrapnel. The aircraft was incredibly technical, complex and fragile, so if an explosion managed to detonate near it, debris could easily destroy the aircraft. It's speed and maneuverability were what kept it alive.

"Cruiser, are we going after that Chinese carrier yet or what?" asked Flapjack, one of the other F41 pilots in Captain Cruse's flight. Lieutenant Jordan Mina (aka "Flapjack") got his name because he ate twelve pancakes in one sitting during flight school at the local IHOP. The name had stuck ever since.

"Not yet. Our objective today is to clear the skies as best we can for the ground pounders. We have F38Bs and A10s providing ground support and about 90 F38As for air support with us. Stay on your toes guys; this offensive is important," Cruse replied.

"Angel Flight, Angel Flight, this is Overlord," called out the flight commander for the AWACS aircraft that were flying over Seattle. Her group had been coordinating part of the air battle over Alaska.

"Go ahead Overlord," replied Cruse, waiting for their orders.

"Angel Flight, we are tracking 250 bandits heading to Susitna towards our ground units. There is a separate air group forming up over the Chinese carriers that is heading towards our ground attack aircraft as well. We are vectoring you in to attack the enemy fighter aircraft heading towards our ground units. You are weapons free to engage."

"Copy that Overlord. We are receiving the data and coordinates now. Angels are moving to engage," said Cruse. He was eager to get his flight of five F41s into the action.

"Ok everyone, you heard the woman. Let's move to engage those enemy fighters quickly; I want them destroyed at range, and for you to cycle through targets as fast as you can. The pilot with the most kills today wins $1,000 NAD from me," he said to cheers. Everyone began to line their aircraft up for their attack runs.

The F41s were about 400 miles away from their targets at a remote airbase; they were going to accelerate to Mach 10 for a short period of time and then slow down to a near stop once they were within range of their lasers. They would fire a handful of shots, and then move about 70 miles in a different direction to another attack point and reengage the enemy. This maneuver would be played out over and over again to ensure no enemy planes or missiles were able to get within range of their aircraft.

****

Air Force Captain Dana Archer (Overlord) watched the radar screen at her console, tracking the five Archangels as they began to engage the enemy aircraft climbing to attack the Americans. Her AWACS aircraft was responsible for running the air-combat operation for the American offensive. This strike was going to be the largest attack of the war and as such, there were several AWACS on duty this morning to assist in handling the enormous air traffic that was starting to fill the air.

Captain Archer was an air battle manager, she was responsible for identifying targets for the manned and drone fighters and then directing them to their targets. Fighters and drones on all sides usually run passive radars rather than active radars when flying combat operations. This is done for several reasons: first, an active radar lights your aircraft up like a Christmas tree for enemy surface-to-air-missiles or SAMs and enemy aircraft running in passive mode. Second, passive mode allows your aircraft to fly through undetected unless someone turns on an active radar. Once the radar is active, it can then detect enemy aircraft in the area. All sides make heavy use of AWACS type aircraft to identify and then guide their sides fighters or drones to the enemy. This enables your aircraft to sneak up on the enemy before they know you are there.

****

Back on the ground, Lieutenant Allen's platoon was fighting its way to the Chinese positions while trying to stay close with the tanks. They had taken out dozens of Chinese anti-tank missile teams as they got closer to the Chinese lines. As their vehicles approached the enemy ranks, the Chinese soldiers began to retreat and scatter. The Wolverines cut the enemy soldiers down as they tried to run. As the Reds retreated, the MBTs and Wolverines quickly moved in behind them to both secure the Chinese positions and to chase down the retreating soldiers.

Captain Shiller received a message from Battalion that his Company was to stop, dismount and secure the Chinese defensive position for the follow-on forces. Shiller contacted his officers. "Lieutenant Allen, the Company is stopping here. We just received orders to secure the area," he said over the HUD.

"Roger that Sir. Stopping now, and securing the area. Any other orders, Sir?"

"Negative, and good luck Lieutenant."

Turning to look at the guys in the vehicle with him, Allen quickly found SFC Jenkins, his platoon sergeant. "Jenkins, new orders. We are stopping here with the platoon. The Captain wants us to secure the trench and bunker complex that we just drove over for the follow-on forces," Lieutenant Allen announced. He was not too thrilled with having to leave the safety of the Wolverine, despite the protection the Raptor suit offered.

SFC Jenkins just nodded and began to bark at the privates around him to exit the vehicle and begin to set up a perimeter. Lieutenant Allen radioed his other squads and made sure they knew the new orders and began to secure the enemy positions. The vehicles would continue to stay in the area; half of them would switch over to anti-aircraft mode, while the others continued to stay in ground mode to protect the infantry.

The vehicles stopped just past the bunker and trench lines, which were still smoldering from the recent assault. Dead Chinese soldiers, equipment and charred vehicles could be seen strewn in every direction; these were the remnants of a fierce and deadly battle. Aircraft, drones and hundreds of helicopters could be heard flying overhead, engaged in their own aerial dance of death.

As Allen exited the Wolverine, he could see a battalion's worth of tanks moving across the trench line his unit had just cleared. In an instant, two Chinese soldiers emerged from one of the smoldering bunkers and fired an anti-tank rocket at one of the tanks, disabling it. "Sergeant Jenkins, get some soldiers to that bunker immediately!" Allen yelled. "Have the troops start to clear the rest of them out. We can't lose anymore tanks!"

Five additional Chinese soldiers popped up from the ruins of a smoldering bunker and began to engage the soldiers near Lieutenant Allen as they dove for cover and began to return fire. Allen quickly raised his own rifle and fired a couple of well-placed shots, taking one of the Chinese soldiers out while his compatriots ducked back into the bunker. In an instant, a dozen of his soldiers in their new Raptor suits moved rapidly to secure the bunkers and trench lines. Within seconds, one of the machine guns in the partially destroyed bunker began to open fire on his men causing them to dive behind cover again. Fortunately, the gunner in the Wolverine nearby was paying attention, and she turned the turret towards the bunker. She fired a single round from the anti-armor railgun, obliterating the bunker. The other soldiers quickly moved forward and threw a couple of grenades in for good measure.

Slowly, the platoon cleared the rest of the bunkers with grenades. Several enemy soldiers surrendered, but they were few and far between. Most soldiers either retreated or fought to the death rather than be captured.

As the battle continued to rage on around them, the sounds of the tanks and artillery fire continued to move further and further away from their position. It sounded like the 4th of July fireworks display from back home, only these weren't fireworks. Bombs, rockets and mortars were exploding, killing and maiming people by the thousands an hour. Two hours after they secured the area, they spotted a large column of friendly light infantry moving towards their position. Within a few minutes, an officer identified himself to Allen's men and asked who was in charge. He was quickly directed to Lieutenant Allen's position.

The Major began to walk quickly toward Lieutenant Allen and the Wolverine he was standing next to with his platoon sergeant. "Lieutenant Allen I presume?" he inquired.

"Yes Sir. Are you my relief, Sir?" asked Allen in a hopeful tone. He wanted to get his men back into the main fight with their Raptor suits.

"That I am; I'm the battalion commander of the 3/5 light infantry," the Major responded. Curiosity took hold and he asked, "So are these the new Raptor suits we've been hearing about? How do you like them?"

Realizing that his small platoon was the only ones wearing the Raptor suits, Paul suddenly felt out of place among the hundreds of regular infantry moving towards them in their standard body armor.

"They are actually pretty great. Several of my men were shot while securing the area but the suit protected them. We took no injuries at all, which was amazing," Allen said feeling good about the accomplishment of his platoon.

"That is remarkable. Not sure when my battalion is going to get them, but I hope soon. So--back to business. Is there anything we should know about before your platoon leaves the area?" asked the Major, trying to get a better picture of what was going on.

"We captured a few prisoners; I have them over there near that blown-out bunker. They really put up a fight in those bunkers, so we had to level quite a few of them. Right now, our battalion is still moving with the tanks. They are about five miles in that direction. I'd work on getting this position ready to defend against another Chinese assault, in case we have to fall back. I don't expect that to happen, but my vehicles have been engaging a lot of air targets lately, so

I'd be prepared for anything." Allen did his best to give a good run-down of the situation and what to possibly expect.

Nodding as he made a couple of notes, the Major spoke on his mic to several of his officers, giving them instructions to relieve Allen's men and take possession of the prisoners. He also ordered his men to begin clearing the trenches of the dead bodies and to start to prepare a new defensive line. "Thank you Lieutenant for the information and your assessment. My men and I appreciate it. We'll have this place ready to meet the Chinese if they try and come back around," he said confidently. Then he turned around and began to walk towards the rest of his men, barking orders.

"Sergeant, get the platoon back into the vehicles; it's time for us to go catch up to the rest of our comrades," Allen said.

****

In the air, the F41s were having a huge impact as they continued to clear the skies of enemy drones and manned fighters. The F38B fighter bombers and Razorbacks continued to hammer the Chinese armor units, despite taking some heavy losses from Chinese surface to air missile (SAM) sites. In spite of the valiant effort by the Air Force, the ground war did not go nearly as well.

There were several moments where it looked like the Americans were going to break through and drive the Chinese back to the beaches; then additional reinforcements would show up and plug the holes in their lines. The fighting between the infantry and the armed forces was incredibly intense, with thousands of soldiers on both sides dying each hour as the fighting raged on.

The tank battle between the American and Chinese armored forces continued for nearly two days before the Americans were forced to withdraw when the Chinese reinforcements started a massive counterattack. The Americans had dealt a serious blow to the Chinese (who up to this point had thought that they would be able to drive the Americans out of Alaska by the end of summer), but in the end, they were just outnumbered by the sheer volume of tanks and drones the Chinese were able to throw at them. It did not take long before the Chinese were able to push the Americans back to the Susitna defensive line, right where the Americans had initially begun their summer offensive.

HULK

25 September 2041
London, Kentucky
Pegasus Spaceport

Operation Pegasus was proceeding at a rapid rate. With priority manufacturing and materials, construction of the HULK was moving along. The first several modules had been completed, and the front half of the ship was starting to take shape. The men and women who would be piloting the craft were currently in training at the Kennedy and Johnson Space Centers in Florida and Texas. A second group of volunteers was also in training for the second HULK that would be completed approximately twelve months after the first one.

Dozens of new manufacturing plants were under construction that would support both the construction of the HULK and the habitation modules that would be continually built and sent to the lunar surface. Space X's new transport craft was nearly fifty percent complete; they were also going to build a second transport, so at least two of them would be in service. That way they could continually bring modules and required materials to the lunar surface for those who would be living there, and return Tritium4 back to Earth, which was critical to the war effort.

The space port itself was turning into a magnificent structure; it had a landing and launch pad for the HULK and the transport craft that would be moving between the Earth and the Moon, along with several loading and unloading docking stations. Everything was being built to move the ships through a very efficient assembly line like process to minimize the amount of time the crafts would be required to stay on Earth before returning back to the stars. There was also a massive maintenance bay that was under construction. There was a terminal with a beautiful control tower being built as well. In time, people would be able to move to the lunar surface and live there full-time. Right now, the only people who would be allowed to live on the lunar surface would be those working on the mining operation and about 100 scientists of various disciplines who would be studying the effects of humans living in space and terraforming.

President Stein already had his eyes set on Mars; once the war on Earth had been won then he would focus the country's efforts on not just establishing a permanent colony on the lunar surface, but also on Mars. There were also designs for several deep space reconnaissance ships as well. These explorer ships would be sent to find other habitable planets and moons that could support life, and send the data back to earth. There were separate initiatives underway to explore some of the asteroid belts in the solar system to determine if they might contain any valuable minerals as well. It was highly suspected that these asteroids could be mined and reduce the need for mining activities on Earth. This could only have been made possible through the development of the EmDrive system and the improved Ion engine. The Angelic power system (which was essentially cold fusion) was also the core enabler for these technologies. For the first time in history, man was finally in the position to expand beyond earth.

******

Dr. Weisz was just finishing her tour of the White House; she had to admit that she found herself in awe when she was actually able to step into *the* Oval Office. So much history had happened here. It was something she had never dreamed she would ever be able to do in her lifetime. She certainly had never expected to meet directly with the President of the United States. However much she disagreed with him, she could not turn down the opportunity to talk to him face-to-face.

The young female tour guide (who reminded Dr. Weisz of her students) brought her to some of the back rooms that were a bit more non-descript. "This is where you will wait for the President. Is there anything that I can get for you? A coffee perhaps?"

"Well, I certainly won't turn down coffee," Rosanna replied.

She looked around the room nervously, trying to go over her game plan in her head. The seconds seemed like hours, but really it was only a few minutes before President Stein walked into the room, larger than life, and shook her hand.

"Mr. President," she said, "It is a great honor to meet you."

"I am likewise honored to meet you, Dr. Weisz," replied the President. She certainly hadn't been expecting that response. A look of credulity was not very well-concealed on her face. The President smiled in response. "You see, I've listened to your speeches. While I fundamentally disagree with you on a few factual points, it is very clear that you do love this country, and you are a patriotic American. That is someone I can respect, even when we don't think all of the same things."

"Mr. President, I am humbled that you would ask to meet with me in person. However, this nice tour and your kind words aren't going to change my opinions of the world and the horrible things that have happened."

"Nor would I expect them to, Dr. Weisz. What I hope it does convey is that I am taking you seriously," responded the President. Then he turned to open a folder in front of him.

"You have a PhD in humanities, correct?"

"Yes, Mr. President."

"And you also teach a number of history classes, as I understand it."

"Yes Sir."

"So tell me, what is your understanding of why President Truman chose to use atomic weapons in World War II?"

She felt like a student defending her thesis again. "Well, the answer to that question is complex. There were a number of issues at play. Some feel that nuclear weapons were used as a show of force to deter the Soviet Union, who were becoming increasingly threatening. Others feel that the public mood in the United States had shifted away from supporting the war, so Truman was looking for a way to end the war quickly…there are various factors."

The President nodded. "Those answers are not entirely inaccurate, and may have contributed to the decision, but I would like to submit a piece of history to you." He handed her an old type-written document on yellowing paper.

She wasn't sure what she was looking at. The President explained, "This is the estimate from General MacArthur of how many casualties there would be in a continued ground war against Japan."

Then she could see various military groups identified and the number of men anticipated lost on the right. The total at the bottom was over one million possible lives lost.

The President continued. "What you don't see here is that the anticipated loss of life for the Japanese was over seven million. I do not take the use of nuclear bombs lightly; however, at the end of the day, there were about 200,000 deaths compared to about eight million casualties."

Those words sunk in...there was a moment of solemn silence. "Sir, I can appreciate that. However, the response from the IR's attack on our cities was so asymmetrical--surely you must feel some sympathy for the human toll of this tragedy..." Dr. Weisz was hoping for even just an inkling of acknowledgement of her point of view.

"I do. It keeps me up at night, many nights. Honestly, I keep playing it over, wishing the circumstances were different, but when I do, I ultimately come to the same conclusion. You see, there is another picture that keeps haunting me." He pulled another photograph out of his folder; it was a horrific scene of mass carnage on the battlefield. Bodies were literally in heaps on top of each other. "What you are looking at here is a scene from the battle in Israel. These images were never made public in interest of human decency, but the Islamic Republic sent wave after wave of soldiers to attack us. Many of them were not well trained, and some were not well armed. Caliph Abbas simply has no regard for human life whatsoever. He had his political objective, and he did not care how many pawns were sacrificed on the altar of his success. I know so many died in nuclear explosions, but at the end of the day, I feel that I prevented further carnage, not just of our people, but of theirs."

Dr. Weisz was deep in thought. She wasn't exactly sure what to make of all of this. There was a silent pause while the President gave her a moment to ponder it all.

"Do you know Leon Trotsky, Dr. Weisz?"

"I am familiar with some of his works, yes."

"He made a statement that I still find very true. He said, 'You may not be interested in war, but war is interested in you.' I know that these few minutes we've had together may not have changed your mind about what has happened, but I hope you will see that there was more to my decision than just revenge."

"I certainly have a lot to think about, Sir."

Interrogator

1 October 2041

Fort McCoy, Wisconsin

US Army Prisoner of War Internment Camp III

During World War II, Ft. McCoy had been used as a Germany POW camp, in addition to a basic training facility. Now history was repeating itself, and the old National Guard base was reactivated to be an active duty military training facility alongside the POW camp, just as it had been in the 1940s. Ft. McCoy was located in the middle of Wisconsin, in a relatively low-populated area of the state, which made it ideal for a POW camp. The base was also training 12,000 new army recruits at any given time, graduating 1,000 new soldiers a week from their twelve-week basic combat training course.

Ft. McCoy did not house all of America's POWs, but it did house the prisoners identified as having some sort of intelligence value. Prisoners not being deemed as having intelligence value had been turned over to other POW camps that worked with DHS to provide tens of thousands of prisoners to be used on various work gangs and projects all across the US. The prisoners farmed their own food and carried out a variety of other physical labor services as both a means of keeping them occupied while also helping to rebuild the various areas inside America that had been damaged or destroyed in the war.

Chief Warrant Officer 4 (CW4) Josh Schafer was the senior military interrogator at Ft. McCoy. He was also the XO for an interrogation detachment from the 201st Battlefield Surveillance Brigade, 109th Military Intelligence Battalion. They had thirty-six military interrogators, nine DoD civilian interrogators, and forty-five contract interrogators to handle the 25,000 Islamic Republic, Russian and Chinese POWs currently being held at Ft. McCoy.

CW4 Schafer had just received a new high-value prisoner from Alaska, a Russian Colonel who had been an armored brigade commander before he was captured by US Special Forces. The men that brought him in kept laughing about how he had been captured while he was relieving himself in the woods, not far from his Command vehicle. The SF unit in question had been shadowing the brigade headquarters, and was in the process of preparing to ambush it when they spotted the commander walking in the woods alone. Not wanting to look a gift horse in the mouth, they grabbed him and then proceeded to ambush the headquarters unit.

The Russian Colonel had quickly been transferred to a rearguard unit, who had him transferred to Ft. McCoy once he accidentally made mention of the new Russian main battle tank and how it would crush America. Now it was incumbent on CW4 Schafer, to find out as much information as he could about this mystery tank. After spending a couple of hours looking over all of the intelligence and information available on the good Colonel, Schafer felt he was ready to meet him and begin to assess his new prisoner.

Schafer had been an interrogator for sixteen years; he had a BS in psychology and an MA in International Studies. During his career so far, he had fought in the Mexican invasion, and had interrogated numerous Islamic terrorists for the war effort. He had originally been assigned to the 3rd Infantry Division in Israel, but he had been wounded and sent back to the US to recover. Upon recovering from his shrapnel injuries, he was reassigned to the 109th MI battalion and sent to Ft. McCoy. This was his third month at Ft. McCoy, and already he had conducted over 150 interrogations and obtained an incredible amount of intelligence, particularly about the IR military leadership structure and who was loyal to the Caliph versus their country of origin. He was adept at sifting out the radicals versus the pragmatic military leaders. This information was critical in determining who the US and IDF could work with during the occupation, and who was going to present a long-term problem for them. By assessing who could safely be trusted as team players during the occupation of the IR, the U.S. was going to have much greater chance of keeping the peace.

Now it was about finding out what the next steps the Chinese and Russians were up to. CW4 Schafer pushed his chair back away from his desk and computer, grabbed his notepad and tablet, and signaled to his analyst and interpreter that it was time for them to walk to their interrogation booth and get things prepared for the interrogation. Their prisoner was going to be brought to them in about thirty-minutes, giving them plenty of time to get things ready. As they walked out of the Interrogation Control Element (ICE)--the building the interrogators and analyst operated out of when not working with the prisoners--they made their way across the street to the interrogation building. The structure that housed the interrogation booths was connected to the actual POW camp, making easy access to move the detainees in for questioning. Inside were thirty state-of-the-art interrogation booths, which were in use nearly 24 hours a day, seven days a week.

Each booth had a separate viewing room connected to it with a one-way mirror (this allowed for rule-keeping monitors to see the interrogation as it was happening). The rooms also had a number of high-tech pieces of equipment that greatly improved the interrogation process. There was a thermal camera, which helped to monitor the prisoner's body temperature and spikes in perspiration that occur when a person is nervous or lying. In addition to the thermal imaging, there were also half a dozen mini-cameras observing the prisoner; these cameras were looking for any ticks or tells the detainee might have. With the aid of computer software, micro-expressions could be judged to catch eyelid quivering when nervous, slight movements of the lips that might indicate lying, and the dilation of pupils to indicate genuine surprise. CW4 Schafer said a little "thank you" in his head to President Stein as they walked into the room; it was due to his emphasis on improved equipment that he was able to enjoy all of the technology he had at his disposal.

As Schafer and his analyst got their equipment and room set up, their interpreter began to look over the various questions and points of discussion they were going to discuss with the prisoner. This way, he could ask questions for clarification before the interrogation started if he needed to.

The thirty-minutes went by quickly, and before long, a knock could be heard at the door, letting them know their prisoner had arrived. The Colonel was wearing the traditional yellow jumpsuit that all prisoners wore; his name and rank were sewn on to the front and back of his jumpsuit, so he could be quickly identified.

Colonel Dimitri Petkovic was the 13th Guard's Tank Regiment Commander, part of the 4th Guard's Kantemirovskaya Division (one of several elite Russian armored divisions). He was a career officer who was being fast-tracked to become a division commander until his capture. As he sat down, he thought to himself, "*If only I hadn't waved off my protective detail that evening...all I wanted was a few minutes to relieve my bowels in peace.*" Images of his capture were flashing through his head, and he felt himself being thrown to the ground, gagged and tied up with zip ties. He remembered a series of explosions as they left; the Special Forces must have destroyed his headquarters unit.

Colonel Petkovic was optimistic about the possibility of being broken out of prison by his own Spetsnaz, or escaping on his own, until he was flown from a small firebase to Fairbanks and then to northern Wisconsin. So far, his treatment had been better than expected; he had been given medical attention when he needed it, and he was fed three meals a day. He had made the mistake of mentioning the new Russian tank and how it was going to destroy the Americans to a fellow prisoner, who must have told the Yankees (the Americans had placed several of their interpreters among the prison population to gather intelligence inside the camp; this had proven extremely useful). This little slip-up was probably why he had been flown to Wisconsin instead of staying in Alaska. Petkovic thought to himself, *"It doesn't matter. The Americans will ultimately lose the war; the numbers are against them no matter what new technology they create."*

The Colonel had been at Ft. McCoy for five days, nearly all of it spent in isolation. What little he had seen of the base when he was driven from the airstrip to the prison camp, did amaze him. He saw thousands of American men and women conducting physical training and other types of military training. Clearly, the Americans were trying to train a new army, but it was too late. The Russian and Chinese alliance had already trained millions of soldiers and were in the process of training millions more. He knew that as soon as his division's objectives would have been completed, he would have been heading back to the Western front to be equipped with the new T41 battle tanks. The Chinese were also training five million soldiers, specifically to assist the Russians in Europe. He felt certain of the inevitability of the victory on his side.

As Petkovic walked in to the interrogation room, he was not afraid. Of course, he was determined to do his best to resist; he had received interrogation resistance training, and he had been told that the Americans would not use torture, so that relieved most of the anxiety he might have felt. As the Colonel oriented himself to this new room, he saw a man in his late thirties standing before him.

"Hello, Colonel Petkovic. You can call me Mr. Smith."

Petkovic was sure that this name was an alias, but that didn't matter. There was an interpreter in the room with him, and a third person, a woman who sat in the back corner at a desk with a laptop. He assumed the woman was there to take notes for the interrogator, who looked all business. The interrogator shook his hand, and offered him some coffee or a bottle of water. Petkovic accepted both and thanked "Mr. Smith." There was no reason to be rude.

Schafer knew that they were going to be talking for several hours, and one trick of the trade that he had learned was to humanize the detainee and his relationship with him. This would make it easier to develop rapport, and enable him to obtain the information he was looking for. He had the prisoner sit down, and then began to attach several wires to his hand, finger and chest.

"Colonel Petkovic, I am going to attach several sensors to your body; these will help us determine if you are lying or telling us the truth."

"This is a lie detector?" asked Petkovic curiously as he looked at the instruments.

"Yes and no. We use the data to determine if you are telling the truth or hiding something. If you are less than truthful, I will know." Schafer was very matter-of-fact.

"All I am obligated to provide you with is my name, rank and service number," the Colonel said sarcastically.

Josh smiled before responding, "Technically, that is true. However, there are a lot of incentives I can provide to you that would make your stay here at the camp a lot nicer and more enjoyable, if you are willing to cooperate."

Petkovic sighed deeply before he replied, "What could you possibly offer me that would make me want to betray my country?"

"If you are willing to talk openly with me, then I can have you moved to a single person room, complete with TV rights and room service. You can pick what you would like to eat, and each meal will be delivered to your room, or you may eat in the cafeteria with the other prisoners who have chosen to cooperate."

"Those prisoners will never be allowed to return back to Russia; they would be shot for treason," said Petkovic in a serious manner. The tone of his voice implied that he knew from personal experience what happens to people that the State determines to be traitors.

CW4 Schafer had heard this before, and had a response ready. "You should know that when the war is over, those who want to stay in the US will be allowed to do so. Those who wish to return back to their country will be swapped for our prisoners."

Having presented the situation, Josh switched gears. He sat down and began to look through his questioning guide to start the interrogation. "Tell me about the T41 tank. What makes it so special?" Schafer actually had no idea if the tank was going to be called a T41; he was guessing at the name and figured this is most likely what it would be called.

"Hmm, so they know what the tank is going to be called. I wonder what else they know about it?" thought the Colonel.

"I have nothing to say," replied Petkovic with a look of determination.

Immediately, Schafer could see in Petkovic's eyes that he was going to be a problem; he was not going to talk easily. He thought to himself, *"That's fine. I still have my ways of making you talk."*

With a mischievous grin developing, Schafer answered, "That's fine."

Signaling for the guards to return, he directed them to hold Petkovic in his chair so he could not move. Then he lifted a syringe from a small black case that he had in the cargo pocket of his military trousers.

Petkovic's eyes went wide with fear and surprise.

"I had hoped we could have a normal conversation, two military professionals discussing a host of topics. However, if you want to be obstinate, then we have our ways of making you talk. I am going to inject you with something that is going to make every nerve in your body feel as if it is on fire. It is going to be excruciatingly painful. Fortunately, the pain can be immediately turned off if I inject you with a counteracting drug. However, I will only do so if you are willing to answer my questions truthfully." Schafer spoke in a cold detached voice. He had the look of someone who had done this many, many times before.

Prior to the outbreak of World War III, the President had authorized a secret military interrogation manual and a program that incorporated the use of pharmaceutical interrogations, using drugs to facilitate the cooperation of a detainee. There were two main drugs they used. The first, the "fire drug," would indeed cause the nerves in the detainee's body to feel as though they were burning in scorching flames. The second, the "lucidity drug," was very similar to a medication often given to patients before surgery to relax them, Ativan. It quickly loosened the mind's ability to resist. After some interrogation trials on US Special Forces and Navy Seals, the military had found that if you give the fire drug first, the lucidity drug worked even better (because the individual's mind would have been exhausted from dealing with the fire drug). Part of the qualification process of being able to administer this type of interrogation required the interrogator to have gone through the process themselves. This ensured that the interrogator knew the type of pain the prisoner was being subjected to.

Petkovic was given the first drug, and within seconds, it felt like his entire body was burning from the inside. He started to scream, and tried to wrestle himself free from the guards who held him firmly in his chair. However, their grip was firm, and they were unmoved by his cries for help…they had clearly seen this done a number of times before. After nearly ten minutes of not answering the interrogator's questions, the Colonel finally gave in. "I will cooperate, Mr. Smith!" he cried. "Just take the pain away!" he pleaded.

Schafer gave him the counteractive drug, and then quickly injected him with the lucidity drug. Within seconds, he could see in Petkovic's eyes that he was feeling relief and was ready to talk. Schafer calmly sat back down at the table. "So, tell me about the T41. What type of gun does it have?"

With the lucidity drug in his system, Petkovic responded almost immediately as if his sub-conscious had been laid bare. "It uses a pulse beam laser."

"How many shots can it fire a minute?" asked Josh, wanting to establish a rhythym.

"Two."

"How long until it needs to be recharged?" queried Josh.

"It can fire a total of fifteen shots before it needs to recharge."

"And how long does it take to recharge?" Schafer continued.

"It takes three minutes to recharge enough energy to fire a single shot; the laser can fire a shot every thirty seconds. It can fire through its charged battery in six minutes, but then it takes forty-five minutes to return back to full charge."

"What are the dimensions of the T41?" Schafer asked, continuing to roll through the questions on his list.

Petkovic continued to answer question after question for nearly four hours before Schafer ended the interrogation. Josh had obtained all the information he needed on the T41, and now it was time to write up the Intelligence Information Report (IIR) and get this information out to the greater intelligence community so they could decide what further information they would like from Petkovic.

Teach and Train

4 October 2041
Twenty-Nine Palms, California
Third Marine Headquarters

Following the various victory parades and time off, the Marines of the Third Marine Division reformed at their desert training facility in California, Twenty-Nine Palms. The division was conducting a series of armored training exercises and mountain warfare training, in preparation for their eventual deployment to fight the Chinese and Russian soldiers in Alaska. Fifth Marines, which was already fighting in Alaska, had sent several dozen advisors to help them get ready and to instruct them on what to expect when they arrived. They learned that the Chinese were making heavy use of artillery and armored forces in Alaska, much more so than they did with their forces in the Middle East.

The challenge US Forces were facing in dealing with the Russian and Chinese soldiers was one of numbers. Despite the tactical advantage the American soldiers held with the integrated HUD system and the M5 AIR, the Chinese relied heavily on overwhelming manpower. They would routinely overrun units and just move through them with human wave assaults. They would attack with waves of light drone tanks, supported by their heavy tanks, and then follow up with a sea of humanity and send in multitudinous infantry. While American armor was, more often than not, able to deal with the Chinese armor, the infantry would get overwhelmed, and this would force the American positions to fall back. Had the Americans not established such formidable defensive positions at Susitna and Cooper Landing, Alaska would have been lost many months ago. As it stood, it was only a matter of time until these positions collapsed. They were being bombarded nearly 24/7, and attacked by enemy drone bombers on a daily basis. The air defense capabilities simply could not keep up.

The introduction of the F41 had probably given these defensive positions new life. Despite their small numbers, they were making a huge impact, going after enemy ground attack drones and drone bombers.

Equipment updates were important, but the updates in key personnel were going to be essential in winning the war as well. Major General Lance Peeler had just been promoted to Lieutenant General, and given command of all Marine Forces on the West Coast. Despite being promoted, LTG Peeler was still going to retain command of Third Marines for the time being, until his duties required him to relinquish that control. His main focus right now was getting his Marines ready to fight the Chinese. His division had been given their replacements, and they were finally sitting at 100% strength. Now they were focused on training and preparation for their eventual deployment with General Gardner's Third Army. Third Marines had been assigned the task of helping the Army get the new South American Multinational Force (SAMF) from South and Central America ready to participate in the war. One of the key training areas the Marines focused on was marksmanship. They were especially drilling on firing discipline, as well as small and large unit maneuvers. In the type of fighting they would be facing against the Chinese and Russian forces, these tactics were going to be critical to know inside and out, as well as how to coordinate them with their colleagues.

LTG Peeler had been given six weeks to get the SAMF ready to fight. The Army had assigned one armored division to work with the SAMF on tank and armored warfare tactics, something General Gardner was an expert at. While the training continued, new divisions fresh from basic combat training continued to filter in to the Army and were rotated immediately in to the field training exercises. Third Army was growing in strength at a rate of 30,000 new soldiers a month, and had just broken the magic number of one million Soldiers and Marines.

In addition to the Third Marines, LTG Peeler was in the process of training three additional 60,000 man divisions for future combat operations. The Marine base at Camp Pendleton, near Oceanside, CA, was a buzz of activity. They were responsible for the training of three divisions of Marines, with nearly 5,000 Marines completing basic and advanced infantry training every week. They were quickly rotated to Twenty-Nine Palms, where they trained with the large maneuver elements before being sent to their individual assignments or deployed as replacements.

After thirty days of R & R, Captain Thornton was relaxed and ready to get back to work. While on leave, he had spent some of his time in Key West doing some scuba diving and fishing, unwinding those thoughts in his head away from the war and the military. Now it was time to get back to the business at hand, training his Marines for their eventual deployment to the frontlines. One of the key things Thornton had learned during his near-constant year of combat was the importance of being able to fire and maneuver while taking enemy fire. Because the Chinese made heavy use of human wave assaults, it was imperative to keep your head up and place well-aimed shots at the enemy, as opposed to hiding in your foxhole or popping up and down like a gopher. This was hard to teach a soldier as most people's instinct is to duck when they start to hear bullets flying nearby or over their heads. Thornton taught his Marines, "Remember, the enemy is just as scared as you are, and if you can throw more lead downrange at him or her, you might be able to get them to duck instead."

The other area of focus was to practice training with the new Wolverine armored vehicle. It was a much improved upon vehicle from the traditional Marine Light Armored Vehicles (LAVs); the Wolverine was impervious to small arms fire and could deflect most RPG rockets, which made it very versatile. The railgun system could operate in air or ground attack modes, making the Wolverine a truly multi-purpose fighting weapon. It was perfect for providing light infantry the support they needed or accompanying the tanks for infantry support.

Thornton had his finger on the pulse, listening to as much information as he could about the battle to come. From what he could tell, they were in the fight of their lives once they arrived in Alaska, so he did his best to teach his Marines not just tactics and techniques, but mental readiness.

SecDef Pow-wow

5 October 2041
Washington, DC
White House, Oval Office

Eric Clarke, the Secretary of Defense, had arrived early for his meeting with the President. The offensive operation in Alaska had not gone well, despite the enormous losses they had inflicted on the enemy. The Chinese just kept coming. The President was clearly starting to get concerned because if the Army could not stop the Chinese in Alaska, then chances were, they were going to break through their defensive line at some point and secure the entire state. That would be not just a political disaster for the President, but an enormous military one as well.

Julie Wells, the President's secretary, signaled to Eric. "The President will see you now."

Eric walked in to the Oval Office and saw the President sitting down on one of the couches, with one of his trademark Red Bulls nearby. The President looked tired and worn out, the stress was apparent in his face. The President normally looked determined and calm under pressure, clearly he was not feeling that way today.

Walking into the room, Eric moved to shake the President's hand, and then quickly took a seat across from him. "Mr. President, I assume you have read the executive summary of the Susitna battle report?" asked the SecDef.

Looking up at Eric, the President said, "I have; I must say I am disappointed. We had given General Black 20,000 Raptor combat suits, all of our Wolverines, and the first batch of F41s, yet still he was unable to drive them back." Looking down at the notepad again, and then back at Eric, he quipped, "He used 450,000 soldiers in his offensive, didn't he?"

"He had, Mr. President; they sustained some pretty heavy casualties as well." Eric was not sure if this directly answered the boss's question.

"We've sustained 93,000 KIAs in Alaska, another 191,000 wounded. These kinds of casualties are not sustainable in a defeat. If we had pushed the Chinese out of Alaska, then this would have been acceptable, but as it stands, we have only weakened our position there significantly. What is our next course of action Eric?" asked the President pointedly.

Pulling up a holographic map from his notepad, Eric began to point to several mountain ranges and national parks. "We are beginning construction of two new defensive positions; one at the Denali National Park Preserve, and the second at the McKinley Park Reserve. These positions are all along Route 1, and are stationed at strategic locations to provide us the best possible defensive situations. There are very few routes in and out of Alaska because of its treacherous mountain ranges and the heavy snows." Eric sighed deeply before continuing, "I have also ordered the construction of a series of defensive positions in the Yukon and upper parts of British Columbia. It may become necessary that we fall back further before the end of winter or next summer."

The President made eye contact that was almost aggressive, and pointedly said, "That is unacceptable. Our soldiers are now better equipped; they have better tanks and body armor, and we finally have an aircraft that rivals the MiG40. We cannot continue to lose more ground like that. What about the new recruits we are training?" Henry was clearly not happy, and was fishing for alternatives.

"We have thirty military training schools operational right now; each is turning out 1,000 troops a week. We are essentially training a new division every week. It is going to take time to get the men we need. The Chinese started this war with a six-million-man army; our sources now say they have drafted another ten million. The DoD is just not capable of fighting a war against both China and Russia at the same time. We really need the Europeans to fight their own war so we can pull our troops back home where they are desperately needed." As the SecDef spoke, he was not very confident that even bringing all the troops back from Europe would be enough.

The President knew Eric was doing all he could; he also knew that the DoD had been extremely depleted when he took office, and despite four years of heavy funding, they were only just now starting to get up to speed. His next response was a bit calmer, more measured. "Here is what I want to have happen then. Tell General Wade that the force he has is what he has. No more reinforcements are going to be sent to Europe. As units dwindle in strength, he is to combine them with other units, because there will be no more replacement soldiers sent. Second, all of the wounded that return from Europe are to be filtered into the new basic training facilities to help train up the new units and provide them with much needed experience and expertise. Third, I want us to expand the military training facilities. I want to ramp up training; we need to move it up from 30,000 a week to 50,000. I don't care how many National Guard and Reserve facilities need to be federalized and reactivated. Make it happen…and construct new basic training facilities if needed. I don't want to resort to forming militia units, but if we lose Alaska and they start to threaten the rest of the country, that may need to happen."

Eric could see that Henry was returning back to his normal self again as he began to dictate orders. The President was, if nothing else, an organizational genius. He surrounded himself with people who possessed the same quality, which was probably why America had not collapsed from the challenges that had been thrown at it.

"I'll get on it right away Mr. President. Have we heard anything new yet from the Japanese about them joining the war effort?" asked Eric.

"Secretary Wise said he does not believe they are going to come to our aid or join the war effort. As a matter of fact, the only assistance they have offered is jack and squat. They are happy to keep selling their cars and other goods in America though…at least they are ordering tens of millions of tons of food products through the Grain Consortium. We believe they may be stocking up in case the Chinese decide they want to start a blockade of the West Coast," Stein answered dejectedly.

Despite the Navy introducing the SUDs to the Pacific, the Chinese Navy remained dominant in the North and Central Pacific. The Navy was slowly destroying the

Chinese submarines, which had been a priority to clear out; now they were starting to shift focus to the shipping container ships and fuel tankers. This would hopefully hurt the PLA's logistical efforts and slow their progress down in Alaska.

The President expanded the holographic map of Alaska to include most of Asia, and then clicked on India. "What concerns me most, Eric, is India. I just read an intelligence report (and also received some cables from Jim Wise at State) about what India is up to. They have agreed to assist the PRC economically; they have begun to manufacture their fighter drones, and to transport ships and other war materials that they are having a hard time replacing quickly. To further add to this, the Indian government-- which already maintains a two-million-man army--has just announced an increase in their military force to nearly four million. That means that they are doubling their army. The question is why?"

"Perhaps they are just concerned about China--I mean the PLA did gobble up all of their neighbors, and the IR is now an occupied country," Eric responded, hoping this might calm the President's concerns.

"You may be right. In any case, the Indian army is incredibly outdated. Thank you for your efforts Eric. It means a lot to have people I know I can count on right now in these trying times.

The meeting ended with Eric heading towards the door and Katelyn Williams and Jeff Rogers walking in for the next meeting.

"Good afternoon Eric" they said as he left; he returned the greeting.

Motioning for them to sit, the President wanted to get down to business quickly. He had a telecom with the Prime Minister of Britain and Chancellor Lowden of the EU in a couple of hours, and he still needed to eat lunch.

Peddling a Pan Asian Alliance

10 October 2041

Beijing, China

Central Military Committee Meeting Room

Premier Zhang Jinping was reading over the final proposal for the Pan Asian Alliance that the Chinese government was going to pursue with the remaining countries in Asia, along with India, Japan and Russia. The trick was how to arrange a ruling committee that incorporated senior officials from all of the members (India, Russia and Japan with China) that everyone could agree on and accept. The Pan Asian Alliance was a dream of Premier Zhang's for many years. It was not until the start of World War III that he saw a real opportunity to make it a reality. The combined armies, economy and people of these nations would rule the world and lead it in to the 22nd Century and beyond.

The Americans had made it easier to form this alliance after their brutal use of nuclear weapons against the Islamic Republic. It was rather ironic that the IR detonating two nuclear devices in America had worked to China's advantage like nothing else could have. The nuclear hot war had shaken the military and political alliance between Japan and the United States. It had also created a rift between the Indians and Americans; since both Japan and India had been on the receiving end of a nuclear war, they were aghast at the complete disregard for human lives displayed by the American leader. In a single day, President Stein had ordered the death of over half a billion people in response to the death of six million Americans.

India had just recently agreed to support the PRC economically by providing China with various materials they needed for the conflict, and opening their manufacturing up to produce the machines of war needed to win. Premier Jinping was close to securing an agreement with India to join the Pan Asian Alliance. Even after their losses in their own nuclear war, India still had a massive population that could add strength to the union; India had nearly 1.4 billion people and an army of two million soldiers. Of course, once they joined, their military would be greatly enhanced and expanded with state-of-the-art equipment and additional soldiers.

Japan was still gearing up for war; they had thus far stayed neutral, though it appeared that they may join the war against China. That, however, changed when America unleashed hundreds of nuclear missiles on civilian targets all across North Africa and the Middle East. Publicly, Japan continued to relay to their American allies that they were still months away from being able to join the war, but secretly, they had been meeting with the Chinese. PM Jinping had special plans for Japan, pending they joined the alliance.

Zhang looked up from his papers, and saw General Fan Changlong, the vice chair of the CMC, and the man in charge of the PLA. "General Changlong, what are your thoughts on the Pan Asian Alliance?" asked the Premier.

Knowing this was a political test of his loyalty, the general thought about the question for a second before responding. In theory, he liked the idea, but in practicality, he was against it. It would be hard to get the other generals of the PLA on board with it, unless some sort of major concession was made. No one would want to relinquish power. With these conflicting thoughts racing through his head, he responded, "I believe it has merit. The question is--how do we get the others in the government to go along with it?" By responding this way, the general was also sort of fishing to see if there would be a concession offered that he could support.

"That is a good question. I had thought that we would run the alliance much like we run the CMC, by establishing a ruling committee. The smaller countries would each have one member on the committee, and India, Japan and Russia would each have three members on the committee—and of course China would have four, one more than the others. Decisions would be made through majority vote among the committee members, as it is done now through the CMC," the Premier said, believing this should be enough of a compromise to gain the support of the PLA.

Thinking briefly about what Jinping had just said, General Changlong realized this would completely marginalize the current CMC and the PLA. "What about the PLA? How would you handle them with this new committee?"

Knowing this would be a critical question to answer, the Premier had his answer ready. "Ah, yes. Two of the four members from China would be members of the PLA, the third position would be my responsibility as the Premier, and the fourth would rotate between the directors within the PRC. This would still give the PLA a heavy voice in the committee, while letting the civilian government still have equal power. How the other countries would choose their members is of no concern to China."

As Jinping spoke, he saw a slight smile on his general's face. In that moment, he knew he had the backing of the PLA to move forward with this proposal to the other countries. Of course, no one would know about Japan joining until the last minute…Japan was going to be China's Trojan horse.

Bait and Switch?

13 October 2041
Tokyo, Japan
Office of the Prime Minister

The Prime Minister of Japan, Yasuhiro Hata, was in a tough position. Their strategic ally, the United States, had suffered a string of military disasters in the Pacific, culminating with the loss of their military base in Guam, the destruction of the Seventh Fleet, and the loss of the Hawaiian Islands. South Korea had ended their war with the North and had united the Peninsula; then they quickly received a non-aggression treaty with China in exchange for staying neutral in the war. Of course, Korea could not offer the Americans any real military support of significance, so their non-involvement would not turn the tide of the war in the Pacific. That, however, was not the case with Japan. PM Hata struggled with the decision of who to support.

Since the start of the war, the PLAN had maintained a strong naval presence around the Japanese waters. The PLAN had threatened to attack the American bases on Japanese soil again if they did not intern the U.S. forces. It pained the Premier to do so, but he ordered all American

Forces in his country to be interned, and he did not come to the aid of his allies when they needed Japan the most.

During the opening hours of World War III, when the Chinese had initially attacked America, they began by disabling the American air and naval stations in Japan; they had shown how easily they could penetrate the Japanese air defenses. A lot of changes had been made to ensure this did not happen again, but it had already rattled the military leaders of Japan. They were no longer as confident as they once were that they could prevent the Chinese from dominating the skies above Japan.

Still, the PM had Japan prepare for war, conscripting one million additional men in to the Japanese Defense Force (JDF). The navy had just completed construction of two additional aircraft carriers, bringing the total number to five. Albeit, these carriers were small by American and Chinese standards; however, they could still carry four dozen aircraft, which was more than enough to threaten a carrier battle group. The real strength of the Japanese Navy though rested with their modern day battleships, which could carry 600 missile interceptors and 550 land and sea capable cruise missiles. These ships were designed with the sole intention of defeating the PLAN supercarriers and providing the Japanese Navy with a versatile weapons platform. The

Japanese had three of these behemoths in service, with no additional ones scheduled for construction.

Today was a day that the PM had been dreading for some time; he would attend a meeting with the Chinese Foreign Minister and a virtual meeting with the Chinese Premier Jinping to discuss what would ultimately be the future of his nation. This was the day he would have to decide which path his nation will ultimately take--stand with America in her greatest hour of need, or join the Chinese juggernaut and finish the U.S. off.

PM Hata was shaken from his world of deep turbulent thought as the Chinese Foreign Minister, Fang Yung, walked in to the room. He bowed towards the PM at an appropriate depth to indicate his respect before walking over to him. "Prime Minister Hata, it is good to see you. Thank you for agreeing to meet with me," said Fang.

The Prime Minister returned the bow before speaking. "I hope your covert travel here was not too inconvenient." He attempted to muster up all of the genuineness he could in that statement, although he did not mean a word of it. In all reality, he hoped it was a terrible trip in to Japan, having to sneak his way across the border so as to not be seen by the American spies.

"This is an important meeting, so it was no trouble at all. Please, let me set up the secured holographic device so I can connect us with Premier Jinping. He is eager to speak with us."

Hata tried very hard to conceal the sigh he let out before he responded. "Yes, let's get him connected. We have much to discuss."

Within a couple of minutes, the holographic device came to life, and the image of the man who was possibly the most powerful man in the world, the Chinese Premier, appeared.

"Prime Minister Hata, it is good to see you. Thank you for agreeing to meet with us, even if it is in secret for now," said Premier Jinping. "I will get straight to the point. We are moving forward with the creation of the Pan Asian Alliance. I can tell you that Indonesia, Russia and India will be members; we would like to add Japan to that list. Our collective populations will now exceed four billion people; our combined military forces are in excess of twelve million soldiers, with another eight million more in training." The Premier let PM Hata in on this bit of military intelligence, hoping that the sheer enormity of those numbers would sink in.

After pausing for dramatic effect, the Premier continued, "As you know, the PAA will be run in a similar manner to how we run the CMC here in China; each primary nation (which, of course, Japan would be one) would have three members on the central committee. The committee would, of course, control and run all of the countries that are part of the PAA. Decisions would be made by majority vote of the committee members, and would be binding to each member country. The smaller countries that join the PAA would only have one member represented on the committee."

Premier Jinping stopped for a minute to see if PM Hata had any questions. As he did not, the Premier continued, "We are forming this confederation to better coordinate our economies, our currencies and our military organizations. We are also going to be moving to a crypto-currency, similar to Bitcoin, which will help us regulate our currencies a lot better. As you know, we would like Japan to be a part of this greater confederation--you are, after all, an Asian nation. What questions do you have that I may be able to answer?" asked the Premier. He wanted to get down to the meat of the negotiations.

Hata thought for a minute before responding, "I understand the proposal, and I agree in principle that a Pan

Asian Alliance would benefit all of Asia. That said, you are asking us to not only turn our backs on our ninety-year alliance with America, but to launch a surprise attack on the West Coast. Even if I wanted to agree to this, I am not confident I could get my military leaders to agree to your proposal. I would have a revolt within the defense force." PM Hata had a slight tremble of concern in his voice.

"I appreciate your situation, and I understand this would be a hard sell. Can we agree that joining the PAA and Confederation would be in Japan's best interests at this junction in the war?" the Premier asked, wanting to start establishing some common ground with the Japanese PM.

"America is down, there is no denying that. Between your efforts and the Russians, you have really crippled the Americans. I will say this; if it is one thing the Americans are extremely good at, it's finding a way to come from behind and win. They have been known to snatch victory from the jaws of defeat on more than one occasion. Why do you believe so strongly right now that America can be fully beaten? They are conducting a massive retooling of their economy and the rumors we have heard of their advanced weapon systems are amazing, if true."

Jinping was ready with a response. "For a moment, let us put aside the argument of honor; as we know Japan has already betrayed America when you cast aside your initial defense agreement. In that situation, you made the best possible choice, considering the circumstances. I will be as direct and blunt with you as I can--if any of the information I am going to share with you makes its way to America, I can assure you there will be some severe consequences. That said, we have nearly two million soldiers on Alaskan soil, and we have another three million more waiting to be transported to North America. We also have another six million more men and women in military training right now who will be ready for service over the next twelve months. It is true that the Americans are starting to edge ahead of us in some weapon systems, but it comes down to numbers. For every eleven Chinese soldiers an American kills, there is a twelfth, thirteenth, fourteenth and fifteenth soldier to take their place. We are also going to open up a second front in North America by launching an invasion of the West Coast. As you can see, the Americans are going to die a death by a thousand cuts." As he spoke, the Premier shared a video slide of the potential military operations that were planned.

"In addition to the second front we are going to open up in North America, the Indian government will also announce that they are joining the PAA, along with Indonesia. Both countries will be committing a sizeable portion of their military to the invasion as well. As you can see, the sheer volume of our army will be enough to crush the Americans. Japan will, of course, be given several states to federally administer once America has been defeated."

As PM Hata sat and watched the video unfold, he couldn't help but think, *"If they can do this to America, how much more can they do to Japan? There is no way the Americans are going to be able to stand up to this large of an Army on their own soil, not while they are fighting in Europe too."*

Out loud, he responded, "You make a persuasive argument. I cannot deny the fact that your army has confounded the Americans and done what most armies have never been able to do--win on the battlefield. Putting aside your loss to General Gardner's Third Army in the Middle East, your invasion of Alaska has been a resounding success. If I can persuade key members of my cabinet and military go along with this, how soon would you want us to attack the Americans? Would I be able to get some military assistance here in Japan should I need help in keeping control of things? Many people in my country will not be happy that we are betraying the U.S. They may be angry about their unprecedented use of nuclear weapons, but do not mistake that anger as them being willing to easily betray an ally."

"I can authorize as many PLA soldiers as you would like, should you need them. As for the timeline for when you would attack, we have planned for the attack to take place on December 24th, the eve of their national holiday. Once Japan has formally agreed to join the PAA, we will discuss the attack in greater detail (and what Japan's part would be) at a later meeting. Of course, your decision to join the alliance would stay secret until December 24th, when you would launch your surprise attack."

"So once again, history would repeat itself as Japan would launch a surprise attack on America...ironic."

"Yes, the irony is not lost on me either, but your forces will be able to execute the needed surprise my troops would never be able to achieve."

There was an awkward moment of silence as PM Hata considered Japan's entire situation. He took a deep breath before he responded. "All right, I agree. Japan will join the alliance; we will attack the Americans when the time comes. I will begin to identify the people who will be loyal to Japan and marginalize the ones who may cause us a problem." Hata wanted this meeting to be over. Just because he had made this decision did not mean that he was happy with it.

Premier's innate stoicism kept him from betraying too much excitement at this victory. "Excellent. Japan will rise with China to become one of the dominant powers of the world and beyond. We'll continue to coordinate things secretly for the time being. Thank you for your time and for meeting with me." As he finished his response, he killed the connection.

"You will have to excuse me Minister Yung, I have much to do if I am going to bring Japan in to the fold of the PAA. We can meet at a later date if you would like, or coordinate things through the embassy," Hata said, indicating he would like to conclude their business for the day.

Standing up, Minister Yung said, "Of course. Please let me know how China can assist you in this transition; we stand ready to provide any support you may need."

Once he was alone, PM Hata sat down and immediately began to put together a list of people he knew would be loyal to Japan over America. Identifying where people's loyalties may lie became a lot easier after the Americans nuked the Middle East; they had really alienated themselves from the Japanese people with that attack. That, and their continued insistence that Japan join the war, knowing full well that Japan was not ready and would quickly become occupied by China...but what did America care? They had two great oceans separating them from the rest of the world.

The biggest challenge for PM Hata was going to be identifying who within the Japanese Navy he could trust and count on. Many inside the Navy were chomping at the bit to get in to the war; they wanted to come to the Americans' aid as quickly as possible. They had conducted decades of joint naval exercises with the US Navy, so they felt a close bond with them. It would definitely take some time to identify who would stay loyal to Japan versus coming to the Americans' aid.

Russian Reset

14 October 2041

Moscow, Russia

President Fradkov was sitting in his office, reviewing the tentative proposal that Premier Zhang Jinping had sent over. It was audacious. India had agreed to join, and so had Indonesia, now that they had abandoned the Islamic Republic. Fradkov mused, *"I like the concept and idea, but do I believe I could get my countrymen to go along with it? Besides, I rule this country--why would I want to yield any of that control to a governing council?"*

Sergei Puchkov, the Minister of Defense, interrupted his thoughts. "Mr. President, I presume that is the Pan Asian Alliance proposal you are reading?"

"It is. I am not one hundred percent sure this would benefit us in the fashion we would like. I do not like ceding our control to a ruling council, even if we would have three members on it," Fradkov responded as he took a sip of his coffee.

Puchkov thought about that for a moment before answering, "True, but there are some benefits. The pooling of resources and manpower would aid us significantly, particularly in this war."

Fradkov angrily jumped in, "Speaking of the war, what is going on in Alaska? Why have we not fully secured our sector yet?"

"The war is progressing, but resources are limited in Alaska. We only have so many air and ground units we can employ. Originally, we thought we would not need our entire force, or even our reserves; however, after several months of hard combat, we had to send the rest of our forces forward. Right now, we are going up against the American Marines, who have established a series of firebases and reinforced forts at key points throughout northern and central Alaska. We are having to fight them either one at a time or in small groups--in either case, it has slowed our advance down to nearly a crawl," Puchkov said as he brought up a number of images and maps on his tablet for the President to view.

Examining the maps, Fradkov asked, "So what can we do to move this along? The Chinese are landing hundreds of thousands of soldiers, and if we are not able to secure our objectives, they will secure them on their own and keep all of the gains." Fradkov did not want to yield any more to the Chinese than necessary.

General Gerasimov, the head of the Russian Military, interjected, "If you would like us to make Alaska the primary front, then we should halt our forces in Europe and focus our resources on Alaska. I could have our objectives secured before Spring if I could divert forces from Europe to the East."

"How *are* things going in Europe right now? Are we at a good stopping point where we could shift resources to Alaska?" inquired Fradkov. He was not wanting to lose his gains in Europe, but he was clearly looking for a way to do more in Alaska.

General Gerasimov opened his tablet up and brought up the map section. The holographic image appeared on the table and he began to go over the details of the European front. "First, let me review the ground operations, then the naval operations. We have captured the key objectives to keep NATO off balance: Leipzig, Berlin, and Hamburg. As it is, the EU countries are training a much larger army, and are currently converting their manufacturing over to war-time production. As we all know, this takes time, which is something they do not have. I can switch our priority to Alaska, but prior to doing that, I would like to launch one more major offensive in Europe--not to capture ground, but to destroy as much military equipment as possible by intentionally slugging it out with NATO (as opposed to looking for weak points in their lines to exploit). In destroying more of their materials, we would further slow down the timeframe of when they could launch a counter-offensive."

"As long as our additive manufacturing can continue to keep up with the losses, you are cleared to continue," replied the President. He coughed the cough of a lifetime smoker before continuing, "What about our naval operations?"

"The naval focus continues to be on the North Atlantic and interdicting the NATO supply ships from North and South America. The navy just received the first twelve underwater drone submarines; they are nearly identical in capabilities to the American SUDs. We also have twenty-two more attack submarines coming online over the next two months. We are slowly starting to strangle Europe as we continue to deplete the NATO navies and supply vessels," responded Puchkov confidently.

The President smiled slightly before replying, "Excellent. Then I want our focus to shift from Europe to Alaska. If we are able to help the Chinese apply enough pressure to the Americans, we can get them to buckle, and once that happens, they will pull their troops back from Europe. Then the Europeans will truly be on their own and we'll be able to finish them off." President Fradkov spoke with a certain giddiness that only comes from assured victory.

Alaskan Autumn

15 October 2041
Central Alaska

The battle for Alaska had raged on for the entire summer and well into the fall, with the lines changing very little after the first month of the invasion. Despite hundreds of thousands of Chinese soldiers using massive human wave assaults, they had not been able to break through the American lines. Both sides had been sustaining enormous casualties, and neither side wanted to capitulate. The Americans continued to pour tens of thousands of new recruits each month into Alaska, and had filtered in 100,000 soldiers from the SAMF. The South and Central American governments began a second draft, this time conscripting a total of three million additional young men and women to fight in the MNF.

As the first snowflakes began to fall, it became apparent that America was not going to be able to remove the Chinese before the end of the year, when the long winter settled in. They had hoped to bring the Third Army into the fight, but after several months of equipment delays, it was determined they would not be ready to redeploy as an army until closer to the end of the year. By then, the heavy winter snows would have settled in, making any armored advance or assault a lot less likely to succeed.

Meanwhile, the fight in central and northern Alaska between the Russians and US Marines continued to intensify as the Reds began to pour more soldiers into the battle. At first, the Russians thought they had it easy going up against a much smaller Marine force. They quickly found out why the Marines were called "Devil Dogs." They fought like men possessed.

The Russians were going up against the US 5th Marines; the 5th had been reactivated once the war with the Islamic Republic had started and the President reinstituted the draft. The last time the 5th Marines had been activated was during the Vietnam war back in 1966 (5th Marines were later deactivated in the end of 1969). Now they would be the force defending central and northern Alaska from the Russian invasion. The 5th Marines had grown from their original strength of 19,000 Marines to now 60,000. Three more Marine divisions were currently in training in southern California and South Carolina, and would add their own weight to the fight in the near future.

****

Sergeant Jake Lancaster was a Marine gunman attached to an infantry battalion on the front lines in Alaska.

His job was to provide counter-sniper support and take out any high-ranking Russian officers as they identified them. They had already taken out four Russian snipers in the last three weeks--it was not that the Russian snipers were sloppy at their trade--the Marines just had better equipment to identify where the enemy shot came from, which gave them a very precise frame of reference when searching for the enemy.

One of the Gunnery Sergeants in Alpha platoon had nearly gotten his head shot off while acting as a decoy for his own snipers. The Russian sniper had shot a hole in his battle helmet as he hoisted it above the trench line with a stick…he was understandably a little shaken up. "Sgt. Lancaster, have you found that sniper yet?" he asked through the HUD.

The report from the sniper rifle had given Sgt. Lancaster and his spotter the direction and location of where the shot had come from. It was about 1,600 meters to the left just behind the Russian lines. "Yes Gunny, we have spotted his location. I'm going to be taking the shot shortly; he's about to reposition and I want to catch him mid-move," Lancaster replied.

"Roger that. Let us know if you want any suppression fire before you shoot or once you start moving yourself."

As Sgt. Lancaster looked through his telescopic lens, he saw the enemy sniper slowly backing out of his firing position. He made a few last minute adjustments, and then centered in on the sniper's head. For a brief fraction of a second, the enemy sniper looked right at Lancaster, just as he pulled the trigger. In an instant, Lancaster's modified M5 AIR sent a .25mm projectile right into his enemy's face, exploding it as the sniper's body went limp. Suddenly, there was movement five meters to the right of the sniper as another soldier moved quickly to find new cover. Lancaster quickly moved his rifle to the new target and fired another single shot, hitting the enemy soldier center mass before he was able to complete his escape to a nearby foxhole.

"Sgt. Lancaster, look to the right twenty-five meters. We have movement in the gun bunker," said his spotter, who had found them another target.

Lancaster moved slightly to reposition his rifle; he quickly saw two figures manning a heavy machine gun. Suddenly they began to fire in the general vicinity of their location. The bullets began to fly over their heads, hitting nearby tree branches and shredding them into little splinters. He quickly took aim and shot the machine gunner, and then swiftly moved to fire at the assistant gunner. Just as they silenced the machine gun, they began to hear whistling as several mortar rounds began to land nearby. Suddenly, their world went black…a mortar round landed less than five feet from their position, killing them instantly

Too Little, Too Late

October 2041

New Deli, India

It had been nearly ten months since the overwhelming nuclear attack on the Islamic Republic had taken place, and India was still dealing with the nuclear fallout and repercussions of that aggression. Despite the Americans' best efforts to minimize the fallout, it was unavoidable that India would get hit with a large swath of it because of the jet streams that passed over the Middle East. India had been savaged by nuclear weapons during their several day war with Pakistan in the early 2030s, when both nations had made heavy use of nuclear weapons. The war had quickly escalated from a conventional fight to all out nuclear Armageddon, which resulted in the destruction of Pakistan as a country and a devastated Northern India. Nearly 800 million people on both sides had died in that war.

It was estimated that perhaps as many as ten million people or more may be made sick or have lifelong problems as a consequence of the fallout from this latest American nuclear attack against the IR. President Stein had spoken with the Prime Minister of India on a number of occasions, and had personally apologized for fallout that would have an adverse effect on the people of India. He had even offered to provide medical assistance, should it be needed. The gesture was nice, but it was too little, too late. Public opinion had soured against the Americans, with the vast majority of Indians siding with the Chinese assertion that America was no longer the sole superpower of the world and that the U.S. should not be able to continually make unilateral decisions in their own interests with no thought or consideration for other countries.

Large rallies and protests against the Americans had initially started out as small peaceful rallies, but had quickly grown into tumultuous anti-American rallies with many people shouting their support for China and complete with U.S. flag burning. The mood in the country had changed quickly, faster than the Americans had first thought or realized.

The Chinese had approached the Indian government in the spring of 2041 to discuss a large trade deal between the two countries. India had a large manufacturing base that was churning out products to be sent to Europe and North and South America. What the Chinese offered was far more lucrative than selling consumer goods to the Allies--China wanted India to turn its manufacturing capabilities towards supporting the Axis powers by manufacturing the tools of war China desperately needed. Chinese factories had no problem producing the needed ground equipment, but what they lacked was shipyards. The Indians, to the contrary, had several large shipyards currently not being used. They also had a large supply of relatively cheap labor to offer as well.

It was slow at first, but by the end of the fall of 2041, India had shifted most of their manufacturing capability over to producing the tools for war, along with all of the munitions needed to sustain and support a multi-million-man army. India and China continued to strengthen their political ties while deepening the divide between India and America. India secretly agreed to join the Chinese-led Pan Asian Alliance. They began to conduct a series of military drills and exercises to prepare them for war. Their formal announcement of joining would take place in November, when their navy and army would set sail for North America to join the Chinese-led invasion.

European Tide Shifts

October 2041

Europe

By the fall of 2041, the Russians had been fighting the American and European armies for nearly five straight months. The Germans had managed to produce their new Leopard IV tanks, leveraging the same railgun technology that the Americans used in their Pershings. The British were also catching up, completing their Challenge IV tanks. Just as the Allies had finally gained the upper hand, the Russians unveiled the first tank to make use of a pulse beam laser. The laser on the new tank had an effective range of nearly 60 miles, which was 20 miles farther than the Allies railgun could reach, and it could also be used in air defense mode. As Josh Schafer had learned, the weakness in the T41 was its energy consumption. Despite this, the emergence of this new tank made an immediate impact on the battlefield as the tank could sit back behind the attacking force and snipe at Allied tanks while the Russian T14 Armatas and T38s moved forward to engage and overwhelm the Allies.

October 1st proved to be a bloody day for the Allies; the Russians had launched a full frontal assault against the entire Allied line. They made use of over 12,000 tanks and

50,000 infantry fighting vehicles, backed up by nearly 200 of their new T41 pulse beam tanks. Despite a valiant effort by General Wade's 5th and 6th Armies, they were forced to withdraw back to the Rhine River, sacrificing most of Germany. The Allies managed to hold southern Germany and the areas around the Fulda Gap and Frankfurt, but they had lost Hamburg and most of the northern territory in the country to the Russians. With a large bulge in their lines, the Allies were having to make some tough decisions. They could continue to fight and defend southern Germany, but they might lose the Netherlands and Belgium in the process.

The British, for their part, had moved most of their ground forces to join with the French in defending the low countries, in order to help relieve the Americans from having to defend most of Europe on their own. With the war turning into a bloody slugfest in Alaska, the US was just not training soldiers fast enough in order to send reinforcements to Europe to stop the Russian advance and also effectively deal with the invasion of Alaska. General Branson had argued with the President to shorten the basic combat training for new recruits from twelve weeks back down to eight so that they would have additional soldiers to send to Europe as well as to Alaska, but the President had insisted upon keeping it at twelve weeks, arguing that a better trained soldier would kill more enemy soldiers than just sending them to the front right away.

The 2nd Armored Division (otherwise known as the "Hell on Wheels division") was given the task of launching a counter-offensive with Field Marshal Schoen's Panzer divisions. The Germans had produced one full armored division's worth of the new Leopard IV tanks, 280 in total. They would be complimented with the 2nd AD and their 520 Pershings. They would be supported by two mechanized infantry divisions as they attempted to break through the Russian lines and tear in to their rear positions, which would stop their continual advance.

The divisions had maneuvered around Frankfurt under heavy air cover to the German city of Fulda. For decades, NATO Forces had trained to fight the Soviet army at the Fulda gap; now they would put those plans into action as they moved their divisions to attack position. The initial assault would be supported by nearly 600 F38A fighter drones, 350 A10 Warthog ground attack aircraft, and 400 F38B ground attack drones. The goal of the air force was to hammer the Russian tanks and create a hole for the 2nd AD to punch through for their attack. At approximately 2a.m., the aircraft began to engage the Russian positions. As this was happening, the armored divisions began to spool up, getting ready to launch their attack.

Despite advancements in technology and the modernization of the Russian army, the Americans still owned the night. Nearly every major American operation started between 0100 and 0400 in the morning. Generally speaking, it is significantly harder to coordinate a massive movement of troops and vehicles in the dead of night than it is in the day; however, the Americans trained extensively in night operations to the point that they almost functioned better as a unit in the dark of night than during the daylight.

As the ground attack planes began to wreak havoc on the Russian armored units near Hofbieber and Hunfeld (10 kilometers north of Fulda), the 2nd AD launched into action like a coiled spring. They hit the Russian lines at nearly 50mph, blowing right past the first line of defense, and swiftly moving directly in to the reserve units, who were still recovering from the air attacks. Field Marshal Schoen's divisions followed the 2nd AD's advance and began to roll the Russian lines up across a 15-kilometer front. They continued to move rapidly along Route 84, heading straight for the Russian supply depot at Eisenach. By 0500 hours, four hours in to the attack, 2AD had captured Eisenach and was pushing past it towards Erfurt, with their ultimate target of capturing Leipzig. Once they had pierced their way through the Russian garrison at Eisenach, there was little in the way of resistance as they headed along Route 4 to Route 9, which would lead them right to Leipzig.

The Air Force was providing near-constant air cover over the advance, minimizing the effects of the Russian Air Force as they attempted to attack the American armored units. The 230 Razorback helicopters were supporting 2AD, dropping Army Rangers all along the route at critical junction points in advance of the armored units. As the Razorbacks found enemy armor units, they engaged them relentlessly.

The German divisions split off from the Americans and headed to Kassel Gottingen along Route 7 to block a Russian counter-attack, while 2AD continued their advance towards Leipzig. The challenge for 2AD was as that they advanced, their supply lines would continue to stretch, and since they were not stopping to engage every Russian unit they came across, they needed to bring a lot of their supplies, fuel, tank munitions and the like with them as they advanced. As the Razorbacks dropped off their loads of Army Rangers and expended their munitions, they would return to pick up another group of infantrymen and head back out to their next drop points. The Americans were going to try and saturate the area with platoon size elements from Fulda to Leipzig, mostly along the major supply lines.

While this was taking place, the rest of NATO launched their own counter-attack all across the Russian lines. If their plan worked, the Russians would be forced to withdraw from most of Germany or face the possibility of one of their Shock Army's becoming cut off and surrounded. It would be tough for NATO to keep an 800,000-man army group contained for long, but they could inflict significant casualties. They key to getting the Russians to withdraw was to leave the Russians an exit path for their forces to escape, and hope they would take it.

****

During the following twenty-four hours, the Russian 1st Shock Army, which had led the invasion of Germany, suddenly found themselves with one American armored division situated in Leipzig, and three German divisions between them and Leipzig. Faced with this reality, General Kulikov made the decision to order a full withdrawal of Russian Forces, just as NATO was launching their counter-attack across the lines. Now it was incumbent upon his field commanders to conduct a fighting retreat and hold some semblance of order as they fell back to the Elbe River, where they would make their stand. As units continued to withdraw, General Kulikov did order the destruction of as much critical infrastructure as possible in the major cities. This included dropping bridges, and imploding subways, rail hubs and factories. If they were going to have to yield most of Germany back to the Allies, then they would do their best to leave them with rubble.

****

Colonel Mica Aaron, the 66th armor regiment commander (66th AR), sat in a chair outside of his command vehicle, taking a few minutes to eat an MRE before Commander's call, the nightly meeting where he issued new orders and information from division down to his battalion commanders. His regiment had been the tip of the spear when the 2nd AD attacked the Russian lines. Twenty-four hours later, his regiment had entered the outskirts of Leipzig and had moved quickly through the downtown, making their way to the northern suburbs before settling in to a defensive position. Colonel Aaron immediately ordered his air defense units to fan out and set up their operations. He did not want to get his tanks mauled by Russian aircraft or helicopters. He had already lost one third of his tanks in the last twenty-four hours. He could not afford to lose any more, or his regiment would become combat ineffective.

One of the captains stepped away from his computer terminal inside the command vehicle and signaled for his boss' attention. "Colonel Aaron, the Mayor of Leipzig is at the perimeter; he has asked to speak with you. He said he has some urgent information for you."

Sighing and sort of grunting as he was forced to put his MRE down, Colonel Aaron turned towards his Captain and ordered, "Send him forward. This had better be good…he's interrupting my dinner." It had been nearly a day since he had had time to eat anything, and his body was starting to feel tired and worn out without fuel to keep him going. One can only survive on coffee for so long.

The Mayor of Leipzig was a short man; he approached Colonel Aaron and held his hand out to shake his. "Colonel, the people of Leipzig cannot thank you enough for liberating us from the Russians. I have some important intelligence to share; some of our police officers have spotted a Russian armored unit moving towards the eastern part of the city. So far they have counted twelve enemy tanks, but there could be more." The mayor was eager to relay his information to the American soldier, hoping he was not too late to make a difference for his city.

Turning away from the mayor for a minute, Colonel Aaron directed his comrade, "Captain Tully, have the drones move towards the eastern part of the city. See if you can spot some Russian armored units. Also, get on the radio to the battalion in the local area and have them dispatch some tanks to investigate the area. I do not want enemy tanks to infiltrate our lines." He turned back to the mayor to thank him for his information.

The mayor was then escorted back to his vehicle. Several soldiers followed him in an armored vehicle back to city hall; the squad would work as a liaison between the police, mayor's office and the regiment to help relay potential threats to the regiment and to the division as a whole.

****

Captain McQueen was the commander of Alpha Company, one of the tank companies that was part of the 66th AR. He had just received orders for his company to move to the northeastern side of Leipzig to identify and engage what appeared to be a Russian company-sized unit of tanks and light armored vehicles. As they drove their tanks through the main streets of the outer suburbs of Leipzig, they eventually identified the enemy line. They were lying in ambush on the other side of a river, adjacent to a bridge. His company had not been seen yet, so he ordered his tankers to move in to the side streets as he attempted to find another way across the bridge, at a better angle from which to engage them. His sent word to the infantry platoon that was with him to dismount their vehicles and set up a perimeter around the area.

Over the next twenty minutes, his tanks filtered into various firing positions, each identifying a different target to engage. Just as he was about to give the order to fire, a Russian attack helicopter appeared out of nowhere and fired an anti-tank missile at one of his tanks. Before anyone could react, the helicopter ducked behind a building and the missile streaked away, heading towards the tank. Within a fraction of a second, the tank's anti-projectile system activated, and fired a barrage of small tungsten balls in the direction of the missile. Fortunately for the tank crew, the missile was shredded before it could impact against them.

It was in that instant Captain McQueen ordered his tanks, "Open fire!" They quickly destroyed six enemy tanks and began to look for new targets.

Suddenly, four more Russian attack helicopters appeared and fired off a volley of four anti-tank missiles each. Now his six tanks had sixteen missiles heading towards them. McQueen quickly began to engage the helicopters with their railgun, hitting one of them and causing it to spit smoke and flame out of one of its engines. One of the infantrymen attached to his company emerged from the side of an alleyway and fired off a Stinger4 missile, hitting one of the helicopters and blowing it out of the sky. The remaining two helicopters quickly ducked for cover. The sixteen missiles continued to streak towards the tanks at lightning speed. The tanks' anti-projectile systems began to go to work, throwing a wall of tungsten between them and the incoming missiles. Thirteen of the sixteen missiles were destroyed; however, the remaining three missiles impacted against three of McQueen's tanks.

One tank survived relatively unscathed as the missile hit the front armor (which is the strongest part of the tank). Another tank was not so lucky, as the projectile landed near the roof and the entire vehicle exploded in a ball of flames. The third tank was hurt but not destroyed, sustaining minor damage to one of its tracks.

Then Russian infantry from across the river began to open fire on the Americans' position with heavy and light machine gun fire. Several of the American infantrymen were hit by the initial volley, and screamed out for a medic. Captain McQueen quickly grabbed his radio. "This is Captain McQueen. We have encountered the Russian positions, and we are under fire by tanks, infantry and attack helicopters. I need the QRF to get over here now and bring a Medevac for my wounded soldiers!"

His battalion Commander responded, "Copy that McQueen. The QRF is in route to your position, and we are sending an ambulance to collect the wounded. Artillery support is available if needed."

"Acknowledged," replied McQueen. He quickly had his tanks move to a secondary position until additional help arrived; after they had reinforcements, they would try and attack the Russian unit on the other side of the bank again.

Every moment seemed like a century as they paused in anticipation. It took twenty minutes for the QRF and the ambulance to show up. Two of McQueen's soldiers had died from their wounds, waiting for the ambulance. He was seething on the inside that a helicopter had not been available; had there been one, then his men might have survived.

The QRF was certainly something to be grateful for, however. It came equipped with six more Pershings and two platoons of infantry. They quickly formulated their new plan of attack; they would hit the other side of the river first with a barrage of smoke rounds, swiftly followed up with several high-explosive airburst rounds. Then they would have one of the infantry fighting vehicles race across the bridge, quickly accompanied by one of the Pershings. If the bridge did not blow up, then the rest of the Pershings would race across it to support the lead element.

After coordinating their artillery strike, they readied themselves in their vehicles, waiting for the rounds to land and signal the start of the attack. Meanwhile, the Russians on their side of the river bank were shooting anything that moved...they were jumpy. An American spotter drone had discovered five additional tanks and twelve light-armored vehicles lying in wait on the other side of a number of buildings. They quickly relayed that information to the tankers below, giving them a bird's eye view of where the enemy was hiding. Then, the screams of the artillery rounds flying over their heads began to sound. Seconds later, the smoke rounds began to detonate, throwing dozens of smoke canisters everywhere. This was followed by a barrage of twelve high-explosive rounds detonating over the Russian positions, killing a number of their infantrymen and destroying several light armored vehicles.

McQueen issued the order to his vehicles, "Move out!" In an instant, one of the American IFVs darted across the bridge unchallenged; then a Pershing quickly followed suit and began to engage the hidden Russian vehicles. Since they had survived their deadly game of chicken, a second Pershing rushed across the bridge to support his platoon mate. As a third Pershing was about one third of the way across the bridge, there was a sudden and loud explosion...the entire bridge was blown apart. The Pershing fell in to the river below and quickly sank until its antennas were all that could be seen. The river itself was not very deep; however, it was nearly impossible for the tanks to travel down the bank, into the river and up the other side.

Now McQueen had an IFV and two Pershings trapped on the other side of the bank. Using the spotting drone, he had his FIST LNO provide direct artillery to support to their comrades. Hopefully, this would keep them alive long enough for him to find another way across the river.

Looking at a map, he saw a park not too far from their location, where the river appeared to run through. McQueen was banking on the depth of the river being much lower there, passable for his tanks and IFVs to cross. Once across, they could maneuver behind the Russian units and finish them off, rescuing their trapped comrades. He ordered his Company and the QRF to follow his vehicle on their way to the park. Upon entering the grounds, they saw exactly what they were hoping for--a low lying bank on both sides of the river as it narrowed through the park. He ordered the vehicles to advance across the river and immediately fan out, looking for enemy soldiers and vehicles.

It was a strange sight, seeing three dozen armored vehicles tearing through a city park, running over park benches and anything else that got in their way. They quickly forded the river and immediately began to move to contact with the Russians. Scanning the images from the spotter drone, they could see that the Russian armored vehicles had changed to a new position, but were still in the same general area. Within minutes they had maneuvered around behind the Russian units, and had begun to engage them. They quickly set a loose perimeter and had the Russians surrounded, with the river bank to their backs now.

The battle was violent and quick, with the majority of Russian vehicles being completely destroyed. The Americans captured 63 prisoners, most of them wounded. All told, McQueen and the QRF had lost four Pershings, six IFVs and twenty-one soldiers killed, with another nineteen wounded. It had been a tough skirmish and they had really flattened this little area of the city in the process, but at the end of the day, they had secured their objective and removed a potential threat to their rear area and supply lines.

Grid Attack

31 October 2041
Ft. Meade, Maryland

Neven Jackson had found a way into the Chinese exoskeleton operating system and placed a zero-day malware protocol in place to disable them at the worst possible time, during an invasion when many thousands of soldiers would be wearing them. Now he had been given the task of supporting the NATO counter-attack in Germany against the Russians.

Neven was a gifted hacker, something of a prodigy. He also got bored quickly if he was not challenged, so his superiors had dreamed up a new experiment for him. He was to hack into the Russian air defense system and bring it down. He had two days and an unlimited supply of energy drinks and M&Ms to accomplish this task. In just five hours, he had found his way in. It was complicated at first, but once he found out who built the system, he looked around until he found a supplier to the air defense company who did not have a very good IT security structure but still had access to the systems. He had hit pay dirt with this one. Not only did the supplier have access to the defense contractor, it had nearly unfettered access. This was almost too easy.

He quickly navigated through the various security systems, ensuring that he was covering his tracks with each successive move, deleting logs and digital footprints as he weaved his way through the net. After spending nearly an hour looking through the various programs and projects with a Russian linguist sitting next to him, they found the specific program they were looking for. With a few clicks of his mouse, he was in. Neven alerted his supervisors, "Hey, I'm in. What do you want me to do now?"

His boss had thought this project was going to be nearly impossible, but somehow Neven had managed to break through the system in less than six hours. Now they had to coordinate with a few others and determine what in the air defense system they wanted to attack and when. It would do no good to take the system down if the Air Force and Navy were not ready to exploit the vulnerability.

The intelligence at hand revealed that the Russian air defense system for the country was broken down into various sectors, so they were able to develop a more precise cyber-attack. The goal was not to take down the entire Russian air defense; this would cause the Russian government to go into a panic, and potentially escalate the war from a conventional one to nuclear warfare, which they wanted to avoid. Instead, they would take down the air defense zones covering Germany, and then place backdoor access and zero-day malware in every other air defense zone across Russia. When the time was right, they could shut down an air corridor for aircraft or cruise missiles to fly through, undeterred. However, that attack would have to wait.

On the morning of the NATO offensive, Russian air defense operators all across Germany suddenly saw their computer screens go blank and then turn back on to show massive air armadas flying in from across the North Sea and Denmark, and then across Southern Europe. Just as the operators were scrambling all available aircraft to those locations, their screens flickered again and the images were suddenly replaced with a photo of David Hasselhoff, shirtless, laying on the ground with a bunch of puppies. The Russian operators did not know what to think or do.

The cyber-attack against the air defense grid had worked marvelously; it took the Russians nearly sixteen hours to get their backup system up and running. In that timeframe, the NATO air forces had mauled the Russian armored units all across Germany, destroying numerous enemy air bases and shooting down hundreds of enemy aircraft. The air campaign had been a huge success, making it possible for Field Marshal Schoen's Army Group and the

2nd AD to punch a massive hole through the Russian lines and secure a new line that stretched all the way to Leipzig. This forced the 1st Shock Army to have to fall back to the Potsdam area, sacrificing months' worth of gains they had previously made.

Fighting Retreat

November 2041

Alaska

By the end of October, the Chinese had managed to land nearly two million soldiers in Alaska. Prior to the full onset of winter, the Chinese had made one final hard push to capture the Susitna defensive line and the mountain ranges at Cooper Landing. During the ten-day battle that ensued, the Chinese were able to break through the Susitna line and drive the Americans back to the outskirts of Anchorage. With their northern flank collapsing, General Black was forced to withdraw his forces at Cooper Landing in order to avoid having them being surrounded and cut off. He ordered a full retreat of the American Second Army, falling back to the eastern most part of Alaska and the State of Yukon.

Despite a valiant effort by the 5th Marine Division, they were ordered to withdraw with the rest of the Second Army so that they did not get cut off. The Russians had been nowhere near capturing Fairbanks, but with the loss of Anchorage, it would not be long before the Chinese were able to roll up and cut off the Marines from being able to retreat. Being a Marine himself, General Black was not about to leave behind an entire Marine division.

****

General Black had pulled the Second Army back to Glacier View, about 40 miles east of Anchorage. He had also pulled the 5th Marine Division to Cartwell to act as a blocking force while the 12th Infantry Division moved to Fairbanks. They were hoping to keep the Russians busy while the engineers continued to destroy Route 2 and implode several of the mountain passes, making it much more difficult for the Russians to transport their army or supplies. Since the 12th was the one division that was fully equipped with the Raptor combat suits and the new Wolverine IFVs, it would be incumbent on them to buy the engineers the time they needed to complete their work and then conduct a fighting retreat down to Cartwell in order to link up with the Marines.

Lieutenant Allen did not feel comfortable at all with their new assignment. Their division was essentially being thrown out there as a glorified speed bump against a Russian army that outnumbered them by nearly 28:1. The Russians had shifted their focus from Europe to Alaska, which meant more troops and resources had arrived in Alaska over the last few months. As the Marines pulled out, the Russians slowly moved in.

Lieutenant Allen's platoon had been given a hilltop a couple of miles away from the Fairbanks Airport to defend. Below them was the road junction between Route 2 and Route 3, a key throughway for moving around the interior of Alaska. Their platoon would be one of the first sections to be hit when the Russians showed up. As the remaining Marines moved through their lines, they passed along as much information as they could about the Russians they would be facing. They learned that several of the Russian units were using their own exoskeleton suits.

Allen immediately ordered his platoon to begin digging in, setting up prepositioned artillery plots, claymore anti-personnel mines and plenty of ammunition. Fortunately, an engineering platoon joined them and immediately began to construct a number of artillery bunkers. Intelligence said they probably had a couple of days, maybe a week at most before they could expect to see Russian units starting to show up in force. The engineers dug out several "hull down" positions for the Wolverines to settle into so they would have some protection from the inevitable artillery while still being able to provide accurate ground and air defense support.

Within a day, Russian drones, fighters and helicopters were spotted flying within the air defense zone; with their fifteen-mile range, the Wolverines put their railguns to work to create a virtual shield in the sky. The Russian aircraft retreated; they returned in short bursts to launch standoff missiles and cruise missiles to attack the American positions. Fortunately, the Wolverines were easily able to shoot the projectiles down as they flew.

Five days into their defensive operation, Allen's platoon encountered their first Russian soldiers. The spotters determined that this was a small platoon, no more than forty fighters; they must have been there as a sort of probing force, scouting out the area. That small of a group barely put up any fight to Allen's crew in their exoskeleton suits; however, it was only a matter of time before more soldiers arrived.

SFC Jenkins approached the back of the Tactical Operations Center (TOC) to see if he could find Lieutenant Allen. Jenkins thought the LT was a good guy--a lot younger than he was, but so were most soldiers in the army these days. At least the LT had seen plenty of combat, so Jenkins was pretty confident that he knew what he was doing when he gave orders. Unlike most of the new lieutenants who had just graduated ROTC or were being rushed through officer training school, at least the mavericks (the guys who received battlefield promotions) knew what they were doing.

As Jenkins turned the corner around a cluster of computer consoles, he spotted LT Allen talking to his CO.

He walked over towards him to get his attention. "Excuse me Lieutenant, our scouts have spotted a large unit of soldiers heading towards our position. The First Sergeant said to come get you." As he spoke, SFC Jenkins pulled out a fresh cigarette.

Every time LT Allen faced a battle, he could feel the adrenaline pumping through his body; his heart started beating faster, his hands became sweaty, and it felt like butterflies were flitting through his stomach. He wasn't a coward, but he had a healthy respect for the seriousness of the situation. He tried to conceal these reactions; as he turned back to Captain Shiller, he was as cool as a cucumber. "It looks like I better get back before the fireworks start, Sir. Is there anything else I should know before I head off?"

Captain Shiller shook his head. "Just remember, we have very limited air support. Rely mostly on your artillery. I've been assured that if we really need air support, there are some Razorbacks in the area that we can call in. However, they are limited in number, and they are supporting the entire front. It will really depend on what you are facing as to how quickly and how much support may arrive. Good luck, and hopefully I'll see you at the next commander's call tomorrow, if they don't hit us too hard today."

The Captain turned and began to bark orders to the soldiers nearby to get ready for the pending attack.

As Allen and the SFC Jenkins walked quickly back to their platoon positions, Allen asked, "Where is the First Sergeant now?"

"He's at bunker one; he was making sure everyone had eaten when the report came in from the scouts." Jenkins read through some information on his tablet before continuing, "They have spotted about a brigade-sized element heading our way. It looks to be about one armor battalion and two light infantry battalions. One of the infantry battalions appears to have the exoskeleton suits—that's going to hurt. At least the others are just regular infantry." SFC Jenkins continued puffing away on his cigarette as they walked, snuffing it out with his boot as they got closer to the frontlines. He realized that there was no reason to give up his position to a sniper by walking around with a lit up cigarette. Besides, he would have to be suiting up with his helmet shortly.

"Are these tanks something we should worry about, or can the Wolverines handle them?" asked Allen. He wondered if they were going to need that air support already.

"They appear to be T14 Armatas--not the T38s or T41s--so we should be fine once they start to show up," Jenkins said confidently.

The T14 Armata was a formidable tank. It first came on to the scene back in the 2010s, but it had gone through several generation upgrades through the years. However, despite using reactive armor, it still could not stop a 20mm projectile traveling at Mach 10, which made it vulnerable to American attack.

As the two of them approached bunker one, they could see the First Sergeant talking on the radio to the scouts. Off in the distance, they could hear the low rumble of the enemy tanks as they approached through the valley.

When they got a little closer, they could hear what the First Sergeant was saying. "Copy that. Sending artillery to Tango 5 and Tango 7. Standby." Then he picked up a different radio handset and began to relay the information to the Fire Support Team LNO. Within a couple of minutes, they could hear the distant sound of three artillery guns firing; seconds later, they could hear the whistle of the rounds as they flew over their heads headed towards the pre-determined targets.

Off in the distance, they could hear the explosions as the artillery rounds began to land on the other side of the valley. They could see several glowing fireballs rise high into the sky, indicating direct hits on tanks, fuel tankers or ammo carriers.

The radio crackled to life, the scouts came over the wire, "Gun bunnies, direct hit! Fire again, same trajectory."

The First Sergeant picked up the radio set again and called the FIST, "Last rounds were direct hit. Fire for effect. Intermix the rounds with WP and airburst rounds." This call to fire for effect meant that the entire battalion of eighteen guns would fire between three and five rounds each to blanket the area.

Within seconds, they could hear what sounded like a freight train flying over their heads heading towards the enemy positions. They could hear the concussions as the rounds began to impact on the other side of the valley. Shortly after the barrage was launched, a second set of whistling could be heard; the Russian artillery guns began their counter-battery fire, trying to hit the American guns that had just savaged their armored counter parts. The battle for Fairbanks had started in earnest.

A few minutes later, the lead enemy vehicles could be seen coming around the bend. They were no more than five miles away, and began to fan out into the valley heading towards their position. Artillery smoke rounds began to land all through the valley, blanketing it in a thick canvas of grey clouds that hung heavy to the ground, covering the advance of the enemy armored vehicles, tanks and infantry. Inside the Wolverine IFVs, the gunners quickly switched to their thermal imaging so that they could track the Russian tanks and IFVs heading towards their position. They quickly began to engage the enemy ranks.

Russian anti-tank missile teams began to fire off dozens of missiles in an attempt to take out the Wolverines. Fortunately, most of the Wolverines were in a hull down position, leaving only their turret exposed. As the missiles approached the Wolverines, the anti-tank missiles sprang into action, creating a veritable wall of protection approximately 1,000 feet away from the American lines.

Lieutenant Allen shouted at his soldiers, "Put on your helmets, and close up your suits, now! It's time to show the world why the 32nd INF was the best in the world."

In short order, hundreds of Russian soldiers were within five hundred yards of their position, desperately trying to close the gap to get in range of their own weapons. Wave after wave of Russian infantry charged across the valley with the support of their tanks and IFVs. Artillery cover was continuous, keeping the Wolverines so busy defending their positions that they barely had time to launch into offensive mode.

The first hour of the battle was pure murder; the Russian infantry had no chance of getting close enough to the American positions to utilize their weapons before they were being systematically picked off. The HUD system in the Raptor suit, along with the M5 AIR, enabled the Americans to identify and kill the enemy at ranges as far as 600 meters; this was well beyond the range of the Russian infantry. It was not until the Russians began to blanket the area with so much artillery fire that even the Wolverines couldn't keep up with shooting down all the incoming rounds down that things began to change.

Within a couple of hours, several of Allen's Wolverines had been taken out by artillery or one of the many waves of anti-tank missiles. Steadily, the Russian artillery and anti-tank missile waves were finally starting to work their way through the Wolverine anti-missile screen and score a lot more direct hits against Allen's defensive positions. Several of his bunkers were destroyed; dozens of soldiers were starting to get wounded as artillery rounds continued to land amongst their positions. Unless they received some serious help soon, they would be forced to withdraw back to another defensive position, ceding to the Russians a key piece of ground leading into Fairbanks.

Just as the situation was starting to look dim for Lieutenant Allen's platoon, three Razorback helicopters swooped in low over the ridgeline to their left flank, and fired off a barrage of anti-personnel rockets and hellfire anti-tank missiles before ducking back below the ridgeline and moving off towards Ladd Army Airfield near Ft. Wainwright. This overwhelming barrage of missiles devastated the Russian advance, and forced them to retreat and regroup.

Lt. Allen seized on this opportunity to evacuate his wounded men and women from the front and reorganize their positions before the Russians came back. They needed to hold their position a little longer if possible.

Twenty-four hours after the first major attack against their lines, the rest of the Russian army began to arrive outside of Fairbanks. There was an increase in air activity, and a steady hammering of artillery against their positions. Allen knew this was going to be a tough battle ahead, and was determined to make the Russians pay for every inch of America they tried to take.

Through the display on his HUD, Allen received word that the engineers at the next position were almost done with their work. This meant that they could fall back soon and join the rest of the Marines in a fighting retreat out of the area to the next defensive position at Mt. McKinley. They just had to hold for two more days.

The Russians started their final assault against Lieutenant Allen's position shortly after dawn. A massive artillery barrage vibrated the very fabric of the sky as it rushed towards the Americans. Then, wave after wave of light drone tanks and infantry, many of them using their own exoskeleton suits, swarmed towards Allen's position. The infantrymen in the exo suits moved quickly, and needed to be the first ones taken out.

Allen used his HUD to alert his platoon sergeant. "Sergeant Jenkins, have the men focus on taking out the infantry in the exo suits. They are advancing fast!"

LT Allen began targeting an enemy soldier himself with his rifle. He spotted a Russian about 600 meters away, moving quickly and methodically; he was running from one area of cover to another, firing a few shots at Allen's line as he ran. Paul used his sights to hone in on him; he squeezed the trigger, sending a .25mm projectile towards the man at Mach 5 speeds. The Russian was hit in the chest and flew several feet backwards off of his feet; soon he was lying dead on the ground being trampled over as dozens of his comrades moved past his limp body.

Seeing that even more soldiers in exoskeleton suits were rushing his position than anticipated, Allen's heart began to race again. He used his HUD coms to call to the platoon TOC, "Requesting additional artillery support to our front positions. Have the Razorbacks on standby. We've got hundreds of exoskeletons headed our way, and I am starting to see waves of Russian tanks forming up."

Checking his platoon's status in his HUD, Paul could see that he had five soldiers injured and one soldier dead. The Russians were still getting closer, despite them picking off guys at maximum range.

As more artillery rounds began to land amongst their lines, the number of wounded and killed soldiers began to tick up. The Russians had now closed the distance to less than 200 meters away, and were still coming strong. Several of the light drone tanks began to speed ahead of the infantry, hoping to slash through Allen's lines and cause further problems for his fighters. As they drew within 75 meters of the American positions, several of Allen's soldiers lifted up their AT6s and fired off their anti-tank rockets. In seconds, four of the thirteen light drone tanks attacking their positions were destroyed, while the remainder continued to advance.

As the drones moved to within 25 meters of their position, several additional infantrymen produced more AT6s and fired another volley of rockets at them, destroying another five more of the nine drone tanks. The remaining four drones blew through his lines and made their way for targets further behind Allen's position. He quickly radioed in the threat to the company TOC and battalion, and returned his focus to the steady advance of the Russian infantry.

There were hundreds, if not a thousand infantrymen advancing on his position. They continued to pick them off with incredible accuracy, but they continued to progress, nonetheless. Like a relentless wave beating against the shore, they just kept coming. Soon they had advanced to within 25 meters of their position, and now both sides began throwing grenades at each other.

There was no room for doubt; the time to bug out and move to their second line of defense was right then, at that moment. LT Allen yelled over the HUD, "Everyone, fall back to the secondary positions and get ready to blow your claymores!" He hoped that they could all hear him over the growing cacophony of gun fire and explosions. As Allen got up to move to the next line, he was suddenly hit by half-a-dozen bullets and thrown on his back. Fortunately, the Raptor suit absorbed the hits, and they did not penetrate his armor, but the impact sure knocked the wind out of him. Time was of the essence though, and he had to move. He quickly injected himself with a shot of adrenaline from within the suit, and then moved swiftly to his fallback position.

Turning around to shoot at his pursuers, Allen jumped into his new foxhole and then immediately looked for the claymore mine clicker. He found three of them near the edge of the foxhole and grabbed them. In seconds, he was clicking through each detonator, setting off a chain of claymore anti-personnel mines in front of his position. Thousands of ball bearings were thrown like an iron wall against the attackers. He probably killed more than thirty enemy soldiers in that instant.

Seconds later, he was up shooting again at the attackers, assessing his surroundings. What he saw almost made his stomach turn. Blown apart bodies were strewn all over the place. The mines had torn the Russian soldiers apart as they advanced on him. There was no one left of the attacking force, at least for the moment. Ducking down in his foxhole again, he began to determine how many of his men were left and where they were. As he checked through his roster and blue force tracker, he could see only twelve of his soldiers had survived thus far; nearly a dozen lie wounded at their original defensive position, but there was no way they were going to be able to go back for them. Hundreds of additional Russian soldiers were advancing to fill the void of those that had recently been killed by the platoon's latest round of claymore mines.

"Everyone that can hear me, I want you all to fall back to my position. We are going to try and bugout back to rally point Charlie. Now, move like you want to live!" he barked over the HUD. In a matter of minutes, what was left of his platoon had rallied to his position and they began to move as a group to the next rally point. Hot on their heels was the next wave of Russian soldiers. This time they were moving a little more slowly and cautiously as they approached the now empty foxholes and trench lines.

When the engineers were building the foxholes and trenches, they knew that they might have to sacrifice those positions at some point, so they had placed enough C4 in each of them to kill or maim any enemy soldiers unfortunate enough to be close by. Allen kept waiting for the Russians to reach a predetermined point when this weapon would be most useful. Without batting an eye, Allen pressed the red button on the remote detonator one of the engineers had given him. A series of loud explosions could be heard behind them as they moved quickly now to the rally point.

As they closed in on rally point Charlie, which was nearly five kilometers from their position, they began to see other members from their battalion show up on their blue force trackers. At least they wouldn't be alone. Once there, they saw what was left of the battalion--not much, unfortunately. In total about one hundred and eighty-six soldiers had made it out. Their next orders were to move on into Fairbanks and join the rest of the division for their next defensive stand. This would be their last battle before they would fall back to the southeastern side of Fairbanks and catch their rides out of the area.

As they approached Fairbanks, they quickly saw the fortress the engineers had been building. This was going to be a house-to-house street fight through the city of Fairbanks. There was would be a total of 4,645 soldiers from the 32nd Infantry Division, who would have to try and hold the city for as long as possible. They had originally thought they would have closer to 6,000 soldiers, but casualties had been significantly higher than they anticipated. Two hours after arriving and getting set up in the buildings that Allen's group of twelve soldiers would defend, the advanced elements of the Russian infantry began to arrive.

At first, it was just a few soldiers taking shots at each other; then the artillery rounds began to land. Standing on top of one of the buildings looking towards the action, Allen and his platoon sergeant could spot dozens of Russian light drone tanks, supported by dozens of infantry fighting vehicles and a few of their venerable T14 Armatas.

They heard over the battalion net a call for whatever air support was left in the area and asked that they focus their effort on the T14s and then the light drone tanks. The infantry could handle the IFVs with their anti-tank rockets. Soon they saw five Razorbacks leave the area of Lad Army Airfield and begin their short trek to the edge of Fairbanks. Within minutes, they were on station and quickly decimated the Russian armor. They were laying a world of hurt on the Russian infantry. This would be their last support mission; they were going to rearm one more time and then begin their journey back to the Marine positions where they would rebase.

With the last bit of their air support gone, they were officially on their own. What was left of their self-propelled artillery was moving further down the line towards the Marine positions. Once they found a good firing position that could still support them, they would radio in. Allen had what was left of his company spread out across two low-rise buildings controlling the intersection of Airport Way and University Avenue. He had several soldiers positioned in the buildings and forest surrounding the area. Their goal was to establish a good crossfire to prevent the road from being used. Several other platoons were spread out ahead of them and to their flanks. Most of the defense of the city would be broken down by small units, platoon size elements spread throughout the city. The goal was to bleed the Russians as they moved in to the city.

A local Alaskan militia unit had also been raised; they had close to 1,500 volunteers who agreed to help the soldiers defend the town and turn it into a real meat grinder. There would be a soldier or militia man behind virtually every building, block and road in the city. Fairbanks and Anchorage were going to be a real test for the Alaskan militia. It would also be the first time a militia force had fought on American soil since the war of 1812. The Russians and Chinese were about to get their first experience at what it would be like trying to occupy an American city with a populace that is heavily armed.

As Lieutenant Allen sat in the Mt. McKinley Bank with his platoon sergeant, SFC Jenkins, waiting for the action to arrive, he hurriedly stuffed an MRE in his face and wondered how they had survived the past twenty-four hours. His Raptor suit was scarred from the shrapnel and bullets that had hit him. He was also filthy, covered in mud. All he wanted to do was take the suit off and get a hot shower. Unfortunately, the only thing he could take off right now was his helmet and let his head feel some freedom from the suit. "Sergeant Jenkins, what do you think our chances are of surviving another day?" asked Allen, in a way that was clearly joking at their misfortunes.

Jenkins chuckled in good humor. "Well, sir, you are our good luck charm. You survived the beach landing, the battle of Susitna and the last twenty-four hours. Not to mention the battle of Jerusalem and the Jordan Valley. I reckon you are at least indestructible. As for the rest of us…I think we are all up a creek without a paddle." Jenkins laughed at his own joke as he spoke.

Sighing and sitting back against the wall, Allen was deep in thought. He *had* survived a lot of battles that not a lot of others had. Maybe his luck was starting to run out. Maybe today would be his last day…or maybe he'd live to see another day. Only time would tell.

Off in the distance, they could hear the Russians inching closer to their position. The last report had the Russians at least a mile down the road. They were hitting heavy opposition as they entered the city. The house-to-house, block-by-block fight had started. Despite heavy losses, the Russians kept sending soldiers, IFVs and tanks into the meat grinder that was Fairbanks. They needed to capture the city, even if they had to destroy it in the process. The airport, the Army Airfield and the Air Force base down the road were going to be critical positions for their future operations.

As the fighting continued to move closer with each hour, Allen's men grew pensive as they waited for what felt like a death sentence, staying behind to defend the city like this. So far they had seen very few soldiers moving past their position or joining them. Several of the returning soldiers said their comrades had been completely overrun and did not have a chance to retreat. Others spoke of incredible bravery as one or two soldiers would stay behind and fight to the death while the rest of them retreated to fight another day. The hostilities were intense and brutal. Most of the combat was taking place less than twenty meters apart. Lots of hand grenades were being thrown in each direction. A number of soldiers had jerry-rigged claymore mines to the walls of some of the buildings overlooking the street, and when a number of Russians would rush the building or move through that area, they would detonate the explosives, wiping out entire squads of enemy soldiers before they even knew what had hit them.

Three hours had gone by and the Russians were still close to a mile away from LT Allen's position. Soon though, Paul started to see a trickle of American soldiers starting to fall back to his platoon's position. Nearly ninety soldiers joined his twelve men as they started to ready new defensive positions and re-arm. A truck had dropped off a couple of crates of claymore mines for them. Most had plenty of ammo, but they were starting to run low on grenades and claymores.

As nightfall loomed, the Russians had finally pushed their way to within half a mile of their position. As the Russians sensed victory, they rushed in several additional divisions of soldiers. Now they were attacking from three different points of the city, putting the squeeze on the defenders. By midnight, a call came across the Battle Net for everyone to fall back to the vehicles; the division was going to bug out. It took close to half an hour for his men to get ready to withdraw; they wired up a lot of booby-traps for the Russians, and also made sure to pass along as many claymores and grenades as they could to the surviving militia men who were going to stay behind.

The Russians knew the Americans were withdrawing, but did nothing to stop them or interfere with their efforts. After losing nearly 3,431 soldiers and three times that number wounded in a day, they were just happy the Americans were leaving. This was the first time they had gone up against an entire division using the Raptor suits. During the two days of combat, they had suffered some horrendous casualties just getting to the city, and then the house-to-house fighting was spectacularly brutal.

Russian soldiers had told each other stories of how they had shot an American in a Raptor suit and he just got back up and kept shooting like nothing happened. One Russian comrade said he fired nearly an entire thirty-round magazine into one soldier before he finally killed the American. If more American divisions started to field the Raptor suits, then this war was going to get a lot bloodier than it already had been.

The 32nd Infantry had earned the reputation as one of the most elite divisions in the Army after their battle in Fairbanks. They had faced off against nearly 240,000 Russian soldiers with just 12,000 men. They had suffered nearly sixty percent casualties, but had bought enough time for the engineers to seriously destroy the infrastructure in northern and central Alaska. Now it was time for them to withdraw with the Marines, get to safety, and await their next assignment.

Plans of Betrayal

November 2041

Japan

Prime Minister Yasuhiro Hata had spent the last couple of months vetting and replacing a number of senior military leaders, ensuring that each and every one was loyal to Japan and would do as their government directed. He had to ask for the resignation of some, and the reassignment of others to get his key people in place. The final preparations were being made to ready the fleet and the JDF. They had the sealift capability to move up to 35,000 soldiers and their equipment. Currently, these soldiers and the navy were being led to believe that they would be attacking the Chinese fleet at Pearl Harbor and conducting a landing to secure the island from the Chinese.

PM Hata had also coordinated with the PLA to have twelve thousand soldiers and equipment hidden inside of several roll-on, roll-off cargo containers. Instead of bringing thousands of Toyota, Nissan and Honda vehicles to the Port of Oakland and Port of Los Angeles, they would be offloading air defense systems, light drone tanks and infantry fighting vehicles. The soldier's orders were to secure the ports and then expand the perimeter as far out as they could until reinforcements began to arrive.

As part of the surprise attack, there would be nearly sixty commercial aircraft arriving in the US from Japan. They had all been timed so they would all be on the ground at the same time; once they pulled up to the terminal, they would then unload fully armed Special Forces who would do what they could to destroy as much of the airport as possible before they changed in to civilian clothes and faded into the American population. Each aircraft would carry a total of sixty Special Forces soldiers and plenty of explosives. Their secondary mission (after causing a lot of havoc at the airport) was to begin conducting sabotage operations across the American infrastructure. This included blowing up railroad bridges, highway overpasses and tunnels. This would dramatically hurt the Americans' logistical capabilities.

The key to making this operation succeed was complete and absolute secrecy. All of the Special Forces soldiers and JDF personnel who would be involved in the initial invasion were separated from the rest of the Japanese forces, and were conducting special training to keep them occupied and get them ready for the real deal. The JDF Task Force, which included their aircraft carriers, new battleships and 35,000 additional soldiers, would turn away from the

Chinese naval task force and head right for the West Coast of America once the assault at the airports begin. Their objective would be to secure Los Angeles, San Francisco and Oakland. Only Los Angeles had a military contingent near them, and they would be handled by the Chinese PLAN infantry, who would be launching a full-fledged beach assault against Camp Pendleton and the various naval bases in San Diego. If things went according to plan, they would control the ports and a large chunk of Southern California by the end of the New Year.

Thor and the Bodark

Mid-December 2041

White House Situation Room

President Stein was starting to get desperate in the war against Russia and China. The Russians and Chinese had officially captured the majority of Alaska and forced US Forces to withdraw to Slana, Alaska along Route 1. They had suffered some horrific losses...goodness only knew how they were going to replace them all. To add further insult to injury, the heavy snowfalls that Alaska is known for had finally started. The only good thing about the harsh winters of Alaska was that it would most likely halt any future operations until spring.

Despite these recent losses, there was good news in the world. NATO had defeated the Russians in central Germany, forcing them to retreat to the German/Polish border where they had established a new line of defense. NATO was in no shape to continue pushing the Russians out of Poland, so they hunkered down for the winter and continued to train more soldiers for a spring offensive.

Monty walked in to the Oval Office and interrupted the President's glassy-eyed gaze into a world of spinning thoughts. "Mr. President, the generals and the rest of the staff are ready in the Situation Room."

Looking up, Henry replied, "Thank you, Monty. Let's get going then." The President got up from his desk and followed Monty towards the Situation Room.

As they walked in to the room, they took their respective seats and the meeting began.

General Branson was the first to speak, "Mr. President, General Black has sent his final tally of their losses. It's pretty bad. We lost several tank divisions, and the 32nd infantry (which was our only infantry division equipped with the Raptor suits) suffered a sixty percent casualty rate during their defense of Fairbanks."

"Did the 32nd hold up as well as we thought they would?" asked the President, curious to know if the Raptor suits really made a big impact on the battlefield.

"They did, Mr. President. Their 12,500 soldiers withstood a Russian army of 230,000 soldiers for nearly forty-eight hours. They inflicted around 41,000 casualties on the enemy, compared to the seven or so thousand that they lost. If we could equip more divisions with the suits it would make a huge difference in the war in Alaska." General Branson spoke with pride in his voice; he was elated by the accomplishments of the 32nd.

Wanting to get a better grasp of the overall situation, the National Security Advisor spoke up and asked, "What was General Black's total casualty count?"

Branson's face fell into a disappointed wince as he replied, "General Black suffered 213,000 casualties during the last ten days. He assures me that his army is still combat effective, and will hold the Russians and Chinese at the next defensive line."

The President broke in to add, "Look, we knew he was going to take some heavy casualties; he's facing over two million enemy soldiers. As long as he can continue to hold them at the next defensive line, that is all that matters for the time-being. What I want to talk about is this Japanese Task Force that just left their home ports."

Admiral Juliano signaled that he would like to speak to this question. General Branson nodded towards him to continue. "Mr. President, the Japanese Task Force has officially left port and will be in striking range of the Chinese fleet and the Hawaiian Islands a few days before Christmas. We moved our SUDs into the area to support them when they begin their attack."

"Will their task force be enough to defeat the PLAN in the area?" asked the President, not totally confident in the Japanese's naval capability.

"When they prepare to attack the PLAN, we will have both flights of our F41s in the area to support them. We will also have four of our five SUDs there to engage the PLAN fleet as well. I am confident that our combined force can destroy the three PLAN supercarriers," said Juliano confidently.

"Where do we stand with the Third Army? When are they going to be ready, and where do we deploy them?" asked the President.

General Branson took this question, "The Third Army has reached 1,250,000 soldiers in strength. All of their tank divisions are equipped with the Pershings and the new Wolverine infantry fighting vehicles. Seventy percent of his soldiers have been equipped with the Raptor suits as well. They've been conducting a lot of training exercises, getting everyone up to speed and ready to face the Chinese and Russians. As to where we should deploy them, right now our plan is to move them to join General Black's First Army around March. This will hopefully give them a month to do the formal hand over of the area while Alaska is still buried under heavy snow. Once the snow thaws, then Third Army will begin their offensive and hopefully drive the invaders out of Alaska."

"So in the meantime, what are they doing now? And what are we doing with the new soldiers who are completing basic training each week now that they are at 100% manning?" asked the President.

The Secretary of Defense, Eric Clarke, spoke up to answer the President, "Right now Third Army is training. They will continue to prepare until it is time for them to deploy. As to the new soldiers, they are continuing to form new divisions. These divisions are then conducting a months' worth of training against one of the Third Army divisions and will be consolidated in Washington State. General Gardner established his Army headquarters at Nellis Air Force Base. He wants to position Washington State for First Army to form up, which makes sense. Right now, General Gardner has Third Marines training at Twenty-Nine Palms, California, and the bulk of his other divisions are training in Colorado, Utah and Nevada."

Continuing, the SecDef explained, "The Marines continue to crank out a new 20,000-man division every six weeks. We are holding two divisions on the West Coast right now to support the Japanese assault against the Hawaiian Islands. Once they drop their initial assault force, the ships will head to San Diego to load up the Marines and ferry them over."

The President smiled. He felt good about their chances in the war now that Japan was finally going to come to their aid. With the Japanese neutralizing the Chinese navy, it would then be a logistical war of attrition, which was one the Americans could win. They were, after all, fighting on home turf. "Excellent, Eric. I am glad we are finally starting to catch a few breaks. When Third Army takes over in Alaska, I want us to see what troops we will have available to send to Europe. Perhaps we can finish that fight off while we continue to battle the Chinese."

"Before everyone leaves, I want a brief update on Operation Pegasus. How are we going to protect the ship once it takes off, and more importantly, how are we going to protect the lunar base?" asked President Stein. He hadn't gotten firm answers to these important questions thus far, and he wanted something he could stand on before ending the meeting.

The new Director of Science and Technology, Dr. Peter Gorka, responded to this question in his deep baritone voice. "Mr. President. We have developed a series of nasty surprises for the Russians and the Chinese should they try to attack the HULK while it is in flight or at the lunar base. I will discuss the defenses on the HULK first; aside from the suite of electronic countermeasures, we have two laser batteries on the fore and aft section of the ship. These lasers can effectively engage targets in the atmosphere as far out as 150 miles. In space, they can hit targets as far as 350 miles away. They will more than be able to protect the HULK as it transitions from earth to space."

Bringing up some holographic images from his tablet, Dr. Gorka continued, "This is what we propose for the lunar base. Prior to landing on the Moon's surface, the HULK will deploy two satellites that will orbit opposite of each other around the Moon. This will provide complete coverage of the Moon for communications to earth and the lunar surface, but more importantly, will provide a defense for the base. The satellites are equipped with a pulse beam laser, which can engage any objects heading towards the lunar base or near any of our spacecraft within its range. We are working on building a couple dozen more of these satellites to place in ultra-high earth orbit. Our hope is to be able to use these satellites to help us gain control of the skies by sniping enemy aircraft from space."

"We are also working on developing another project called Thor, which is essentially placing special laser-guided projectile spears in space and then guiding them as they reenter earth's orbit to hit enemy positions anywhere on the globe," he said with a devilish grin.

The room sat in silence for moment as they sat there in awe of some of the weapons that were being developed, marveling at how far things had come in just the last few years.

The President was first to speak, "This is amazing, Dr. Gorka. Between you and Professor Rickenbacker, we have developed some of the most advanced weapons ever seen. We are going to need them if we are going to win this war, that is for sure. Thank you for the update, are there some other weapon systems you would like to bring us up to date on?" asked the President eager to see if his director of S&T had anything else up his sleeve.

Dr. Gorka nodded, and brought up an image that again silenced the room.

The Secretary of Defense spoke up first. "What the heck is that thing? A rock?" The picture at the moment did appear very much like a rock, but with a million tiny triangles all over it.

Dr. Gorka smiled that devilish grin of his. "What you are looking at is the dormant position of our newest fighters. This appearance allows us to catch the enemy completely off guard." Then he clicked a button to continue the presentation. The "rock" transformed into what appeared to be a weaponized werewolf, complete with fangs and glowing red eyes. Several of the advisors actually gasped—the psychological impact of the metamorphosis was truly fear-inspiring. "This…is the next generation in combat infantry. Like our flying drones, they do not require a pilot to be seated inside of the device, which allows us to reduce casualties. We have based this model off of the Russian werewolf legends, and are calling it the Bodark. It is made out of very strong alloys, and has been designed with claws and crushing mechanisms that can even cause damage to a tank at close range. For distance, the Bodark can use the lasers embedded in the eyes or the hands to attack. Should the battery begin to run low, it can return to the dormant rock shape to recharge with its micro solar energy cells."

National Security Advisor, Mike Rogers, whistled. "Holy…."

The President's eyes were wide. "Dr. Gorka, this is truly impressive. Back when I was fighting in the Second Iraq War in the 2000s, we used to dream about the day that we would have unmanned drones fighting, but we never thought of anything like this."

Mike Rogers had contained his shock, and asked the practical questions, "So, how soon until it is ready? And how many of them can we produce?"

"Normally, we would do a years' worth of testing and evaluation; however, we plan on skipping that and just field testing them in actual combat. Right now we have five prototypes. We plan to begin testing in Alaska in January. Once we make sure they work as they should, which we'll know within the first couple of outings, we can start to ramp up production. A lot of the manufacturing can be done using 3D printing, which will help immensely. We should be able to field the first 500 of them by the end of February and about 1,000 a month starting in March. It will take close to a couple of weeks of training with each operator before they will be ready."

The meeting continued on for another hour as they discussed more details. They eventually finished their briefing, and the President asked if everyone would like to join him and his wife for dinner--it was last minute, of course, but it was coming up on supper time and Henry thought to himself, *"Why not reward everyone with food and a social hour with the Commander in Chief? They've certainly earned it."*

The month of December was going to be a pivotal month for the Allies, one that might make or break the war. Tonight was a time to put all of that aside and just enjoy each other's company.

Sinking SUDs

Japanese Naval Task Force

300 miles away from Hawaii

Admiral Tomohisa Kawano was the Task Force Commander for the Japanese surprise attack that was heading towards the American West Coast. Two months ago, he had been a Vice Admiral and loyal supporter of the Prime Minister--after discovering the fleet admiral would not lead the navy to attack the Americans, he suddenly found himself in command of the fleet. The Prime Minister said the future of Japan was in his hands; they had to succeed or things with China might not turn out so well for Japan. Admiral Kawano was loyal to Japan and to the Prime Minister, but he had a bad feeling about attacking the Americans. He had trained for nearly two decades with the American navy, and had quite a few American friends. He had always enjoyed working with the Americans. He also feared the retaliation the Americans would unleash on Japan (especially after the nuclear holocaust they released on the Islamic Republic). That was truly barbaric what they had done.

He knew America might be down right now, but they certainly were not out of the war, despite what the Chinese may think or say. The Americans always seemed to find a way out of a tough situation and emerge stronger and meaner than ever. He just hoped that in delivering a devastating surprise attack, he might be able to help secure a quick victory and perhaps a ceasefire. Their objective was to sink the American SUDs as soon as they identified them and then turn the fleet towards Los Angeles and support the landing of the 30,000 troops he was escorting.

Because Japan was still an ally of the US, they had access to certain US Defense systems used specifically by the US Navy. Leveraging this access, Chinese and Japanese cyber experts were going to launch a new wave of cyber-attacks against the American Department of Defense. The first thing they were going to do was black out the American satellites and communications over the Pacific. They needed to blind the Americans and then trick their computers into believing that a great air battle had taken place over Hawaii and that the Japanese had lost. Then they would turn tail and rush towards the American shoreline and the "protection" of the American airpower.

The next wave of cyber-attacks would be against the communications system on the West Coast. They would shut down cell and internet service, hampering communications. This would be followed up with a fake mobilization order for the Marines at Camp Pendleton to deploy their forces to San Diego to repel a fake Chinese airborne assault. The few military computer systems that would be allowed to stay online would be tricked in to believing that somehow the Chinese had snuck in hundreds of transport aircraft and were dropping thousands upon thousands of paratroopers around the San Diego area. While the Marines would be in transit and moving away from their base, the Japanese battleships would launch a devastating cruise missile attack against them, catching most of them out in the open as they moved to engage the fake Chinese paratroopers.

The battleships would then launch a second barrage of cruise missiles at Camp Pendleton, with the aim of destroying the remaining soldiers in garrison there. The PLAN would have their amphibious assault force hit the beaches at Pendleton and move to destroy and then secure the last vestige of Marine power on the West Coast. The Japanese would land their ground force in Los Angeles and move to secure the major ports and airports before moving on to control the various valley entrances leading into the city. Their objective was to hold the area until the second wave of Chinese soldiers would be able to land. With full control of the airports, the goal for both China and Japan would be to transport thousands of soldiers quickly via commercial aircraft to bolster their force before the Americans could react.

It was believed that within three weeks they should have enough armored vehicles and infantry to push any American Forces in the area back and consolidate their gains. With an invasion force on the West Coast, the Americans would not be able to send any additional reinforcements to fight the Chinese and Russian army in Alaska. This would ultimately result in the collapse of the Alaskan front and open the entire top half of America to the invasion.

As Admiral Kawano's task force began to get closer to the Hawaiian Islands and the PLAN task force, they made contact with the American Navy, who was still oblivious to what was about to happen to them. They began to coordinate the positions of their SUDs with the Japanese so they could "best attack the PLAN task force."

As the SUDs began to move in to firing position against the PLAN fleet, Japanese anti-submarine helicopters (which had been following the SUDs from the air) dropped a series of torpedoes on the SUDs in an attempt to destroy them. They used Chinese torpedoes in order to mask that they had been dropped by the Japanese.

Two of the SUDs were completely destroyed, while the other two SUDs managed to evade the Chinese torpedoes. Chinese submarines, which had been lying in wait, also fired their own torpedoes at the surviving SUDs, quickly destroying them (but not before two of the Chinese submarines were destroyed by the SUDs). Unbeknownst to the Chinese and Japanese at the time, there had been a fifth SUD in the water, which had been lurking further behind the Japanese task force in hopes of identifying any Chinese submarines that might appear and try to attack the Japanese capital ships. Their surveillance caught the sheer betrayal on the part of the Japanese.

The SUD operator immediately signaled for one of his superiors to come to his station so he could report what he had just seen and recorded. As they were putting together information and reviewing it for the fourth time, the building they were operating out of in Bangor Trident Base, Washington State, was blown up before they could send their report to anyone.

As it turns out, the cleaning crew at this building (who had been cleaning the facility every night for years), were actually Chinese spies, who had been waiting patiently to carry out one specific mission. They had smuggled in a liquid explosive (not hard to do among all of the standard cleaning products) and assembled a device under the flooring panel in the center of the room, near one of the garbage cans they would frequently empty. A timer inside the device would remove the separation between the two active chemicals, creating a volatile mixture that was primed for explosion. A second timer would detonate the device. The Japanese had fed these Chinese spies all of the intelligence they would need about exactly when the attack on the SUDs would occur; their hope was to destroy the building and all of its personnel at the same time as the attack in Hawaii. The Chinese had already carried out a number of sabotage attacks in Washington State the previous week; this would help to belay any suspicion of Japanese involvement.

Once Admiral Kawano confirmed that the first wave of cyber-attacks and the sabotage against Bangor Naval Base had been completed, he immediately ordered his fleet to change course and head towards their intended targets at flank speed. All that mattered now was making sure they were in position at the right time to carry out the next phase of the attack.

He also had his operations center contact the Americans and send the following message, "May Day! May Day! We are breaking off our attack. The PLAN ambushed us and destroyed a large number of our aircraft. We are headed at full speed toward the American shore, so that you can provide friendly air support, if needed."

The US Navy sent their reply, "Acknowledged. We are ready to provide whatever support is needed."

Admiral Kawano smiled. He knew that it would not be long now before the American communications were taken down in the next wave of cyber-attacks. However, they were not out of the woods yet. At top speed, it was going to take them at least a day before they were in striking distance of US military installations, and closer to two days before they could begin to land their forces. He would try to position his ships as close as possible to the West Coast before revealing the true nature of their arrival.

Mirages

22 December 2041
Arlington, Virginia
Pentagon Situation Room

One of the majors monitoring a mirrored NORAD radar screen that was set up to watch the West Coast nearly jumped out of his seat, yelling for his superior to come quickly to his workstation. A Colonel walked over to his desk, annoyed that one of his young majors had made such a scene by freaking out over whatever he had seen.

"What the heck is the problem, Major?!" the Colonel barked, then looked down at the screen, and his eyes became wide as saucers.

"Get me the General, immediately! Major, have you confirmed this with NORAD yet?" he asked, clearly shaken by what he was seeing.

Several other officers and senior NCOs came over to the station, just as the Major brought his screen up to the wall projector for everyone in the room to see. What they saw was incredible. Somehow, the Chinese had managed to get an air armada of nearly three hundred transport craft and hundreds of fighters less than a hundred miles west of San Diego, and they were heading right for the coast.

The commanding general of the watch came out of his office and immediately took charge of the situation. "Get on the radio with our airbases on the West Coast, and scramble all available fighters to San Diego. Also, get on the F41s to head in that direction now."

Immediately, officers and NCOs in the room began calling various military installations in the area directly to warn them of the impending attack and to see what they could do to get ready.

A captain signaled to the general that he had the base commander at Pendleton on the phone. He grabbed the line. "This is General Sheldon, the watch commander at the Pentagon. We are watching a massive air armada of Chinese airborne troops heading towards San Diego from the west. You need to mobilize as many Marines as you can, as quickly as you can, to head to San Diego and engage those airborne troopers. We can't lose the naval facilities in San Diego, do you understand?" Despite being in complete shock at the situation, the general spoke with a firm controlled voice. This was no time for uncertainty.

The base commander paused for the briefest moment, processing what he had just heard before replying, "Yes, Sir. We will get everyone on the road within the hour. I'll be in touch." He hung up the phone.

General Branson walked in to the room with his aides and other staff. "General Sheldon, what in the tarnation is going on?"

"We are still compiling all the information, but from what we can tell, the Chinese somehow bypassed our detection so far, and they snuck a few hundred transports and fighters right past us and are flying them right for San Diego. They are on path to drop their airborne over the naval facilities, between Pendleton and the City. We are still trying to piece this together with the report we got from the Japanese task force and the loss of our SUDs," General Sheldon said, scratching his head.

Just as they were trying to piece everything together, the computer systems throughout the Pentagon and the rest of the Department of Defense went down. Then the communications systems went down, further adding to the confusion.

"What in the blazes just happened?" asked General Branson to anyone who could hear him above the chaos.

A Major, who was manning one of the communication workstations, was first to speak up. "Sir, it would appear that we are under a coordinated cyber-attack. I'm bringing up the backup system right now, and we will get a better picture in a moment," he explained as he pulled a secondary computer out of a case and plugged it into the system.

It took the major a few minutes to get his system up and running and start scanning the network. In the meantime, someone had gotten a hold of the NSA via one of the secured cell phones operating on a separate network for this very situation. The NSA was reporting a massive cyber-attack against the entire DoD communication system. The NSA Director told General Branson they should have the Pentagon and the rest of the DoD facilities back up and running within the hour, but it was going to take some time before they got things on the West Coast sorted.

General Branson signaled for everyone to quiet down so that he could speak to the room. "All right everyone, we should have our communications back up and running within the hour. What I want to know is--how are we going to get in touch with our forces on the West Coast right now? We need to alert them of what is heading their way.

A Colonel, who had just entered the room as General Branson began talking, spoke up. He was from the J6, which is the communications group within the Army, and so he had experience to draw from. "General, we had a similar problem last Christmas when the Chinese launched their surprise attack. After that happened, we had all of the military bases install some of their older ultra-high-frequency (UHF) radio systems as a backup. We have already made contact with General Gardner's headquarters and told him what we were seeing. He is issuing orders to the various Marine divisions in the area to move to engage the paratroopers now. He is also having one of his corps move from Colorado to California as we speak."

Turning towards the Colonel, General Branson replied, "Excellent work, Colonel. Make sure your guys are also in contact with the Situation Room at the White House and continue to keep them up-to-date. We need to figure out what the heck is going on and soon. General Sheldon, you are back in charge; I need to get to the White House and brief the President." With that crisis on auto-pilot, General Branson didn't stick around for the details. He turned and began to leave the room. He was on his way to the helicopter pad to take the short hop to the White House.

****

As General Branson exited the helicopter and walked towards the door leading to the entrance of the White House, he was greeted by Monty, the President's Chief of Staff. The two walked while Monty talked. "General, we heard from the NSA that the DoD communications system is under a cyber-attack right now. We also heard that the West Coast appears to be getting hit a lot worse than the rest of the DoD. The President is in the Situation Room waiting for you and some others to get here."

"I'm glad you guys are somewhat up to speed; I have more information being sent to the command post right now," Branson responded as they turned the corner and came to the entrance of the briefing room. Other senior officials were also arriving from around Washington D.C., either via motorcade, underground tunnels or helicopter.

Walking into the room, he could sense the energy, excitement and anxiety of everyone in the room. They had been through this before when the Chinese launched their surprise attack against the US last Christmas and destroyed the Pacific Fleet. Within a few minutes, most of the senior staff were present and the President ordered the room sealed so they could begin.

"All right, I know we are under a massive cyber-attack--who can tell me where it's coming from? How long is this going to last? What systems are being affected, and most importantly, what does this all mean?" spouted the President.

The Deputy Director of the NSA spoke first. "Mr. President, we have identified the attack as having come from Japan, though it appears their systems were breached by the

Chinese and then they used their access to gain entry into our systems and hit us. As of right now, we know the attack against the DoD communications system is separate from the second attack that is taking place across the DoD on the West Coast."

"The attack on the DoD communications system will be fixed within the hour. It was a simple attack, but will take a bit of time to purge the servers and bring everything back online. This attack was meant more to blind us for a short period of time. What the Chinese did not count on was our installment of UHF radios across our bases, specifically to handle a situation like this. The second attack, which is focused on the West Coast, is a bit more severe. That attack has issued hundreds of false deployment orders, FLASH messages and all sorts of other efforts designed to scatter our forces and cause a lot of confusion. We believe this is being done to support a large military operation that is currently underway. I believe General Branson can bring us up to speed on that better than I can," the Deputy Director said as he nodded towards the Chairman of the Joint Chiefs.

All eyes turned towards the senior military man in the room. "Mr. President, I will start with what I know from the beginning, leading up to the cyber-attack. The Japanese began their assault on the PLAN task force near Hawaii. We do not have all of the details from the attack as the first wave of cyber-attacks began to hit us at the start of the fight. Our SUDs reported being attacked by Chinese anti-submarine helicopters operating in the area. Four of the five SUDs were destroyed, and before we could find out what happened from the data on the fifth one, the control room at Banger Naval Base in Washington State was blown up by an explosive device from within. It's believed to have been a sabotage attack by PLA sleeper agents that the Trinity program must have missed. We received a message shortly afterwards from the Japanese task force commander saying they had been ambushed by a large number of submarines and enemy aircraft. He said they lost one of their carriers and a battleship and were abandoning the attack and heading for the safety of the West Coast. That was all we received before our entire communications grid went down," Branson said.

Before the President could ask a question, General Branson signaled for everyone to hold on as he had more information to deliver. "Just before the systems went out at the Pentagon, our satellites had detected a massive air armada off the West Coast, near San Diego. We have no idea how it got there, or where exactly it came from. We had counted around 300 military transport craft, along with nearly that many fighter escorts. It looks to be about a

345

12,000-man airborne division and they are headed towards our naval facilities in San Diego. We have to assume the PLAN infantry in Hawaii are on the way to San Diego and this is the initial force to hold the area until they can arrive."

Although no one groaned aloud, there was a palatable painful reaction to the general's news. Branson charged ahead, "We have used the UHF to alert General Gardner of the situation, and he is aware. We also alerted the commander at Pendleton, and he said he would have his Marines on the way to San Diego as soon as possible. General Gardner was sending orders to Third Marines to start heading to LA. They are currently fielding the Raptor suits along with the Wolverine IFVs. They are the most combat ready and hardened group we have on the West Coast. He also ordered one of his corps from Colorado to immediately begin to head to California. It'll be at least six days before their entire force arrives, but once they do, they will add about 350,000 soldiers."

The President spoke first, saying, "This is another colossal screw up General. How in God's green Earth were they able to fly that many aircraft this close to our shores without us even seeing it? Then we have the Japanese task force getting its butt kicked and heading towards the West Coast for safety. Can we at least get our F41s over there to start giving us some real-time intelligence and engage those transports?" The President's face was red with anger as he spoke.

"The F41s are being scrambled as we speak, and will be over the area within the next hour. We should have more intelligence then. In the meantime, we are moving our forces around to engage them," Branson said, trying to reassure his Commander-in-Chief that the military had the situation under control.

Patrick Rubio, the Director of the CIA, interjected, "Mr. President, this may be the invasion force our analyst had been warning about," he said.

Admiral Juliano still could not believe the PLAN could launch such an invasion. He did not believe they had the logistical capability to pull it off. Now he was starting to have some doubts. What worried him the most was the loss of the four SUDs and the destruction of the command center controlling them. They had no idea right now what the fifth SUD had seen or what was really going on…something else just did not seem right with the Japanese task force. They had more than enough firepower to destroy the PLAN in the area. Their new battleship alone packed a huge punch, and they had both of them present. He needed to get down to the bottom of this and soon.

The President turned towards Director Rubio and responded to his assertion. "You may be right, Pat. I honestly did not think they had the logistical capability to pull something like this off, but then again, who would have thought they could fly their transport craft completely under our nose like they have. Right now, I want answers people. Figure it out and let's meet back here again in the next two hours. I want an update then."

"Yes Sir," echoed the room.

The President got up and left the room; he needed to go for a walk to clear his head. He had to figure out what to do next, and that was going to require some alone time to think.

****

Nellis Air Force Base, Nevada
Third Army Headquarters

General Gardner walked in to the command center abruptly. In his usually booming voice, he bellowed, "Ok, people--what in the world is happening out there? How in the heck did the PLAAF manage sneak over 500 aircraft in to American airspace?"

A Colonel who was in charge of managing the airspace for Third Army spoke up. "Sir, the Chinese hit us with a major cyber-attack; they blinded us, and then when we did see something they were suddenly heading towards San Diego. We've sent a FLASH message to get the F41s airborne. They are scrambling them now as we speak."

Sighing before continuing on, General Gardner replied, "All right, here is what I want to have happen. I want General Smith's Sixth Corps to begin moving from Colorado to LA immediately. Tell him he has to be in LA with his entire Corps in five days. I don't care what he has to do, but he needs to have them there immediately. Next, I want Third Marines at to move immediately to a position between LA and Camp Pendleton. I want them standing by to support whatever happens next. I also want LTG Peeler on the phone as soon as possible. He's the on-scene commander in California, and I need him to take charge of the situation until I can get my headquarters moved. We are going to pack everything up and move to Twenty-Nine Palms immediately. I want the HQ up and running in twelve hours, understood people?!"

"Yes Sir!" responded the men and women in the room.

A Day to Live in Infamy

Japanese Naval Task Force
2,100 miles away from Los Angeles

Admiral Tomohisa Kawano's fleet was still a long way off from California, but the cyber-attacks had bought him some time. He had just received a message that the Americans had restored their DoD communications system across the country, with exception of the West Coast. The report also said the Americans had scrambled their F41 hyper sonic fighters to intercept the fake transports and fighters. Once they discovered it was fake, they would immediately report their findings, which meant he had precious little time until it was discovered that his task force was not retreating to the West Coast, but was rather the vanguard of a massive PLAN invasion force.

Their intelligence indicated that a large force of Marines had moved from Camp Pendleton to the initial drop zones and was awaiting the Chinese paratroopers, who would never show. His task force was now in range of their cruise missiles, and he was ordered to launch them at the Marine force, which was out in the open and completely unprepared to defend against such an attack. With a bit of uncertain reluctance, he gave the order to launch 150 cruise missiles at the Marine positions. He then gave the order to launch another 200 cruise missiles at Camp Pendleton, and 100 cruise missiles at the naval facilities in San Diego. If the Americans were able to get their radars operational within the next three hours, they would be able to identify and engage the incoming cruise missiles and would know they came from the Japanese task force. If not, then the likelihood is they would assume the missiles came from the PLAN task force.

While this was taking place, their surprise invasion against the Port of Los Angeles and the Port of Oakland had just started. In addition to the port attacks, thirty civilian Boeing 787s landed at thirty different major air hubs across the country at essentially the same time. As they taxied toward their positions within the terminal, they would unleash the greatest Trojan horse attack against America in their history. Today was truly going to go down as a day that would live in infamy as President Roosevelt had once said on December 7th, 1941, 99 years ago.

West Coast Landing

24 December 2041

Port of Los Angeles

While the DoD was experiencing a massive cyber-attack against their communications network, twelve Japanese freighters had arrived at the Port of Los Angeles over the past four days. Since December 24th was Christmas Eve and the Japanese did not celebrate that holiday, they used that day to launch the greatest sneak attack in American history. They started to unload their freighters, taking over control of several unloading shipping containers filled with military equipment and munitions, and connecting the roll-on, roll-off bridges to the ships. Within twenty minutes, they had unloaded nine infantry fighting vehicles and three tanks. Next came a dozen light drone tanks followed by nearly three thousand soldiers per ship. They quickly began to unpack their gear and vehicles, getting them ready for combat. A platoon's worth of troops and one IFV along with a mobile air-defense vehicle moved to each corner of the port to establish an initial air defense umbrella over their operations.

At first the sight of military vehicles driving around inside the port did not attract attention; the few workers slogging it out during the holiday had seen this before. What attracted attention was the markings on some of the vehicles and uniforms. Many of the vehicles and soldiers had Japanese flags identifying them, which made sense, since Japan was an ally. However, some of the vehicles had the Chinese flag on them, and America was at war with China. So why would Chinese vehicles be inside the port?

Some of the port security guards moved towards the soldiers to identify who they were and ask their intentions…they were quickly shot and killed. Once the first shots were fired, the on-scene Japanese Commander ordered his forces to move quickly to secure the rest of the port and prepare to move to their secondary objectives.

****

Port of Oakland

An Army officer who was assigned to the Port of Oakland to assist with the loading and offloading of military equipment was flagged down by some port security officials.

"Hey, are we expecting any Japanese soldiers and equipment to arrive?" they asked.

. Surprised and caught off guard, the Captain responded, "I was not made aware of any Japanese military forces heading to the U.S. We had better go check it out." He strapped on his side arm, got into the port security vehicle, and drove with them to the location where they had sighted the Japanese soldiers.

When he arrived, he was amazed at how *many* soldiers had landed, and how quickly they had established a perimeter. They had cut off a large portion of the port with concertina wire, stationed several light armored vehicles at various points, and had begun to set up a number of anti-air guns and missile systems. Not sure what was going on, he quickly tried to place a phone call to his superiors to report what he was seeing…only, his cell phone gave him nothing but, "Sorry, we are unable to complete your call at this time. Please try again later." The network was down.

As he approached one of the entry points, he saw the soldiers manning it quickly raise and point their weapons at him. The Captain quickly raised his hands up in a show of peace, hoping to not get shot. As he stood there, several Japanese soldiers advanced towards him quickly. One of them yelled at him, "Get on the ground with your hands on your head! Get down and don't move!"

In shock, he stood there for a moment, unsure what to make of the request. Japan was supposed to be an ally, not an enemy. The Japanese soldier shouted the order a second time. The Captain quickly complied with their request, and within seconds soldiers were on top of him, taking his weapon and zip-tying his hands together before they brought him to his feet and marched him off.

The Captain made several angry pleas, "Please, what is going on? Why are you doing this?" When he wouldn't be quiet, he was hit in the stomach with the butt of a rifle.

The Trojan Horse had arrived.

From the Authors

Miranda and I hope that you have enjoyed this book. We are currently working on the fourth book in the new Red Storm Series, *Battlefield Pacific*, which will be released June or July of 2018. We also just released an audio version of the first two books of the World War III series, *Prelude to World War III* and *Operation Red Dragon*.

The two biggest ways that you can help us to succeed as authors are:

1. Leave us a positive review on Amazon and Goodreads for each of our books you liked reading. These reviews really make a tremendous difference for other prospective readers, and we sincerely appreciate each person that takes the time to write one.
2. Sign up for our mailing list at http://www.author-james-rosone.com and receive updates when we have new books coming out or promotional pricing deals.

We have really appreciated connecting with our readers via social media. Sometimes we ask for help from our readers as we write future books—we love to draw upon all your different areas of expertise. We also have a group of beta readers who get to look at the books before they are officially published and help us fine-tune last minute adjustments. If you would like to be a part of this team, please go to our author website: http://www.author-james-rosone.com, and send us a message through the "Contact" tab. You can also follow us on Twitter: @jamesrosone and @AuthorMirandaW. We look forward to hearing from you.

You may also enjoy some of our other works. A full list can be found below:

Non-Fiction:

Iraq Memoir 2006–2007 Troop Surge
Interview with a Terrorist

Fiction:

World War III Series
Prelude to World War III: The Rise of the Islamic Republic and the Rebirth of America
Operation Red Dragon and the Unthinkable
Operation Red Dawn and the Invasion of America
Cyber Warfare and the New World Order

Michael Stone Series

Traitors Within

The Red Storm Series

    Battlefield Ukraine

    Battlefield Korea

    Battlefield Taiwan

    Battlefield Pacific (to be released June/July 2018)

    Battlefield Russia TBD

    Battlefield China TBD

Acronym Key

AAB	Air Assault Brigade
AFC	America First Corporation
AMRAAM	Advanced Medium-Range Air-to-Air Missile
AR	Armor Regiment
AWACS	Airborne Warning and Control System
BC	British Columbia
CENTCOM	Central Command
CMC	Central Military Commission
CNO	Chief of Naval Operations
CP	Command Post
CW4	Chief Warrant Officer 4
DARPA	Defense Advanced Research Projects Agency
DFAC	Dining Facility
DHS	Department of Homeland Security
DIA	Defense Intelligence Agency
DoD	Department of Defense
ECM	Electronic Countermeasures
EMDR	Eye Movement Desensitization and Reprocessing

EU	European Union
FDC	Fire Direction Control
FBI	Federal Bureau of Investigation
FIST	Fire Support Team
FTX	Field Training Exercise
HE	High Explosive
HQ	Headquarters
HUD	Heads Up Display
HUMINT	Human Intelligence
IC	Intelligence Community
ICE	Interrogation Control Element
ID	Infantry Division
IDF	Israeli Defense Force
IFV	Infantry Fighting Vehicle
IIR	Intelligence Information Report
IR	Islamic Republic
JCTF	Joint Counterterrorism Task Force
JDF	Japanese Defense Force
KIA	Killed in Action
LAV	Light Armored Vehicle
LDT	Light Drone Tanks
LNO	Liaison Officer

LT	Lieutenant
LTC	Lieutenant Colonel
LTG	Lieutenant General
MBT	Main Battle Tank
MEF	Marine Expeditionary Force
MI	Military Intelligence
MIT	Massachusetts Institute of Technology
MNF	Multi-National Force
MG	Major General
MRE	Meals Ready to Eat
NAD	New American Dollar
NATO	North Atlantic Treaty Organization
NCDC	National Control Defense Center (Russian Pentagon)
NCO	Non-commissioned Officer
NORTHCOM	Northern Command (covers North American operations and nuclear defense)
NSA	National Security Agency
NSC	National Security Council
OC	Operations Center
PAA	Pan Asian Alliance
PC	Platoon Commander

PFC	Private First Class
PLA	People's Liberation Army (Chinese Infantry)
PLAAF	People's Liberation Army Air Force (Chinese Air Force)
PLAN	People's Liberation Army Navy (Chinese Navy)
PM	Prime Minister
POW	Prisoner of War
PRC	People's Republic of China
PTSD	Post-Traumatic Stress Disorder
QRF	Quick Reaction Force
RPG	Rocket Propelled Grenade
RTR	Royal Tank Regiment
SACEUR	Supreme Allied Commander Europe
SAM	Surface to Air Missile
SAMF	South American Multinational Force
SDF	Self Defense Force
SFC	Sergeant First Class
SSG	Staff Sergeant
SUD	Swordfish Underwater Drone
TC	Tank Commander
TOC	Tactical Operations Center

UHF	Ultra-High-Frequency
USF	University of South Florida
VA	Department of Veterans Affairs
WP	white phosphorus
XO	Executive Officer
2AD	2nd Armored Division
12AD	12th Armored Division
66th AR	66th Armor Regiment Commander

Manufactured by Amazon.ca
Bolton, ON

23904969R00199